DEATH PERCEPTION

ALLAN LEVERONE

Special thanks to Elderlemon Design for the terrific cover art on Death
Perception and the other Jack Sheridan Pulp Thrillers, and to JD Smith
Design for the print edition formatting.

PART ONE:
TWO MONTHS AGO

1

It had been a long day for patrol officer Greg Daly. The A/C in his cruiser was being wonky, alternating blasts of arctic wind with long periods where he couldn't get the damned thing to work at all. Even though it was still only early June, the heat and humidity in Lawrence, Massachusetts had already approached midsummer levels for the last three days and wasn't forecasted to ease for at least another three.

On top of that, Greg had responded to three separate domestic disturbance calls since lunch, and even though department policy required backup for any officers answering that type of call, half the time there wasn't sufficient staffing to satisfy that requirement. It was dangerous and stressful as hell.

Overall, a long day.

But it was almost finished, and the A/C had been working normally for nearly forty-five minutes, and Greg could damned near taste the cold beer Michelle would have waiting for him when he got home. An hour to go.

He typically cruised some of the back roads on the western edge of Lawrence to end his shift, and today was no different. The area was wooded and as remote as it was possible to get inside a city of eighty thousand people, and Greg loved it out here.

He rounded a corner and in the distance saw a rust-brown late-model car angled off the side of the road, nosed in toward the underbrush as if it had exited the driving surface hurriedly. Greg thought it might be a Buick, although he was still too far away to be sure.

The car appeared abandoned, but as he approached Greg saw someone climb out of the back seat and walk along the side of the vehicle in the direction of the oncoming cruiser. It was a boy, and he looked too young to be the driver: maybe thirteen. He was skinny and angular, with the olive-toned skin of a Dominican or Hispanic.

He was alone.

The kid started waving his arms for Greg to stop, and as he eased behind the apparently disabled car at an angle designed to protect himself and the motorist, Greg flipped the switch to activate his blues. He didn't bother radioing dispatch, preferring to talk to the kid first and determine what the hell was going on.

The humidity enveloped Greg as he stepped out of the cruiser. It was like walking into a steaming hot shower while wearing a wool sweater. It was brutal.

As he approached the kid Greg said, "Are you alone? Where's the driver?"

The boy stopped in his tracks and didn't answer, and for a moment Greg thought maybe the kid hadn't heard him. *Hell, maybe he doesn't speak English.* Then the kid reached behind his back and that was when Greg stopped moving too, his cop senses telling him something was very wrong.

He reached toward the service weapon at his hip but chose to leave it holstered for the time being. He didn't want to scare the kid, didn't want to overreact to a situation that was weird but surely not dangerous.

Then the kid removed his hands from behind his back and Greg wished fervently he'd listened to his instincts and drawn his weapon when he had the chance.

Because the kid was holding a handgun, and he lifted it quickly until the business end was aimed straight at Greg. And now it was too goddamned late to pull his own gun, at least not without risking getting blown to kingdom come in the process.

Greg lifted his hands slowly, palms up and fingers spread. "Easy, buddy," he said. "Nobody has to get hurt here. Why don't you just put the gun down and we can—"

"Shut up!" the kid said, the words coming out high-pitched and terrified, and Greg's pulse began to race even faster than it already was, which was saying something because when he'd gotten sight of that damned pistol he'd thought his heart might just blast out of his chest. He'd never had a gun pointed at him before except in training, and he decided he didn't like it much.

What he liked even less was having a gun pointed at him by a frightened child. The kid could pull the trigger by accident and kill him without even meaning to.

In his peripheral vision Greg could see movement on both sides of the road. People were exiting the woods, and as the stand-off continued between him and the scared kid, nobody moving and nobody speaking, the new arrivals moved in their direction. Within seconds they'd surrounded Greg and the kid.

More or less.

They all knew better than to stand directly behind Greg, just in case the kid's damned gun went off.

All of them were all older than the kid with the gun, the youngest being maybe late teens, the oldest perhaps mid twenties. One of the older ones lifted the gun out of the kid's hands but continued to aim it squarely at Greg.

He'd been ambushed. Gang activity was a constant in Lawrence, with drugs and their attendant violence, but how the hell had these thugs known Greg would come along? Was his end-of-shift routine that predictable, or was he simply that unlucky?

And as bad as things were, they could worsen in the blink of an eye. Even though this area felt remote, they were still inside Lawrence city limits, and another vehicle could pass by at any moment. If that happened, things might turn deadly.

They might anyway.

The gang member who'd taken the gun away from the young boy moved slightly closer to Greg but was careful to remain out of arm's reach. "Take your gun out of its holster and toss it on the ground," he said. His English was heavily accented but understandable.

"You're making a mistake," Greg said. He was trying to remain calm and think but it was so damned hard.

"Shut up and do it."

The ambush was no spur-or-the-moment thing. It had been planned and meticulously rehearsed, because everyone who'd stepped out of the woods after the kid drew down on Greg was busy performing some felony-related task. Someone had already climbed into the cruiser and was even now sitting behind the wheel, ready to drive it away.

"Let's talk about this," Greg said. He was thinking about Michelle and wishing desperately he'd chosen to patrol somewhere else—anywhere else—during the last hour of his shift. "You know I can't give up my gun. It's against department policy." The words sounded stilted and stupid the moment they left his mouth and he regretted them but for the life of him couldn't think of any other goddamned thing to say.

"Drop the gun or die," the man said. "Doesn't make one fucking bit of difference to me either way. Decide now. I will not tell you again."

Greg believed him. He unsnapped his holster and lifted the weapon, moving slowly and deliberately, fully aware of the other man's tension. He held it to the side and then let it fall to the dusty pavement.

The kid who'd started this mess walked forward and picked it up, then scuttled away as if worried Greg might make a move for him. He examined the gun the way another kid his age might eyeball a pretty girl or a porn mag.

"Okay," Greg said. "What now?"

"Now you get in that car and sit quietly while I secure your hands and feet."

"You're making a big mistake here."

"Shut up."

"Dispatch knows where I am. If I don't check in soon they'll send backup and when that happens, a shitstorm is going to rain down on you. But you can still avoid all that. If you let me go right now and walk away, you—"

The man had begun sidling forward as Greg talked and now he slugged him, a roundhouse right that dropped Greg to his knees. "When I tell you to shut up, you will shut. The. Fuck. Up."

Blood filled Greg's mouth. It tasted coppery and hot. It tasted like fear.

The guy was telling him to get on his fucking feet and get into the fucking car, and Greg knew he had no choice but to do both things. He knew also that to do so probably meant he was signing his own death warrant. It wasn't clear what these guys wanted but letting him live didn't appear to be part of the plan, since not a one of them was wearing a mask, and no one seemed particularly bothered about him seeing their faces.

His lips were ballooning where he'd been hit and he could feel the beginnings of a monster migraine firing up in the back of his skull. Neither issue was his biggest worry.

He trudged toward the rust-brown car. He'd been right on target as to the make. It was a Buick.

He climbed into the back seat as instructed and wondered how long he had to live.

2

The man stepped out of his Jaguar, fedora tilted at a jaunty angle. Not many people wore hats anymore, particularly these types of hats, but he didn't care about that. He'd always felt a man of his social status should set fashion trends, not follow them.

Tonight, however, he wasn't making a fashion statement. He was using the headwear to help hide his identity, to shield his face in the unlikely event a passerby saw him or he walked within range of a security camera.

He had parked in one of the most dangerous neighborhoods in Lawrence. Maybe THE most dangerous. It was an area filled with drugs and crime and blight and hopelessness. He would seem a natural target in these surroundings, a fool with more money than brains, an overweight, middle-aged man living on borrowed time who would be jumped and relieved of his wallet and his expensive watch—and maybe also his life—at the first opportunity.

But the man wasn't worried.

This wasn't his first visit to the neighborhood.

Nor was it his first experience making the short walk from his car's unobtrusive parking space into what looked to the naked eye like an abandoned brick building. The structure was a crumbling relic of a bygone era, an ancient mill, invisible and ignored, awaiting the inevitable developer's wrecking ball.

But looks could be deceiving, especially in this area.

The building was far from abandoned.

The man in the fedora entered through a rear door that looked decrepit, dented and dinged, but was in fact heavily reinforced. A narrow slit cut into the door provided enough space for someone inside the building to observe anyone approaching. The slit was open to the elements but reinforced with heavy-gauge wire.

Just inside the doorway he was met by a muscular Hispanic man of indeterminate age wearing sunglasses and a skin-tight t-shirt, with an ugly black pistol strapped to his waist. Pistol-man frisked him quickly but thoroughly and then waved him on with the bored expression of someone who'd been doing his job for a very long time.

In no other circumstance would the man in the fedora put up with the rough treatment he received at the hands of the guard, but these were not typical circumstances. He received the same treatment every time he came here but never became upset or angry. He understood the need for caution and appreciated it.

He still didn't like it.

He climbed the stairs to a viewing area that had been con-structed just for him. It was Spartan and cramped, and consisted of a small round table, a couple of mismatched wooden chairs, a recliner that had probably been new about the time the man in the fedora graduated law school, and a small TV with a DVD player set up next to it. There was a minimally stocked bar and a tiny refrigerator like the kind a college kid might use inside his dorm room. Decades-old copies of Penthouse magazine were strewn randomly around the viewing area.

It was decidedly low-tech.

It was dirty and uncomfortable.

The man in the fedora loved it here. This was the one place in the entire world he could come and truly be himself.

* * *

The evening's entertainment was a little late getting started, so the man in the fedora passed the time watching DVDs of previ-ous shows. He mixed a strong drink and sat back in the recliner and rubbed himself languidly through his trousers as the action unfolded on the screen.

Then the sound of a door being shoved open downstairs signaled that the live performance was about to begin. The man in the fedora rose quickly and positioned himself in one of the mismatched wooden chairs, dragging it to the balcony railing for an unrestricted view.

Below, two men flanked a third, dragging/pushing/carrying him to a heavy wooden chair that had been set up precisely in the middle of the room. The victim wore a police officer's uniform and a blindfold, and he had been gagged. The two men—they were heavily muscled, like the guard at the doorway, and looked to be in their mid-twenties—dropped the cop roughly into the chair and in seconds had secured his ankles to the chair legs and his wrists to the chair's arms.

They strode to the door and exited the room, returning almost immediately with the supplies that would drive the show: a small metal trash can and a set of sturdy-looking gardening shears with long wooden handles and a heavy iron cutting jaw. They set the trash can next to the chair and aligned it with the right armrest.

The shears they placed on the floor next to the trash can, atop a section of grey concrete that had been stained rust brown.

Then the two men left the room once more.

When they returned again it was in the company of three nervous-looking males, all of whom looked young. Shockingly young. One of the kids was black, one was white and one appeared Hispanic.

The men in charge lined the three young boys up against the far wall. One stood with them while the other approached the police officer and removed his blindfold and then his gag.

The minute the gag came out the cop started talking, telling them they were making a mistake, that assaulting a police officer was a very bad idea but that they hadn't gone so far they couldn't still make things right, that it wasn't too late to let him go, and that if they did so the consequences to them would be minimal.

The man who'd removed the blindfold and gag shut the cop up by punching him in the face. The cop's head snapped back and a sickening *crack* signified a broken, probably shattered, nose, and blood spurted and began running down the cop's face and flowing onto his uniform shirt.

But he stopped talking.

The man who had punched the cop surveyed the three kids lined up against the wall like a junior high gym teacher picking out the next student to shimmy up the rope.

After a moment's thoughtful consideration he selected the white kid. Pointed at him and called him forward silently, rotating his hand until it was palm-up and then bending the fingers at the third knuckles in the universal "come here" gesture.

The kid looked liked he would rather be anywhere else in the world. But he stepped forward without hesitation. He clearly knew what was coming and he was shaking; the man in the fedora could see it from his viewing perch all the way across the room and up one level.

The man in the fedora was nearly shaking as well, but it was from arousal, not fear, and he could feel himself getting hard again in his trousers. Seeing the terror of the recruits was almost as exciting as watching the actual ceremony unfold, and that was about to take place.

"Do it," the older man said to the white kid, and then he stepped away, moving in the direction of the other two recruits and the second group leader. He stopped in between and waited impassively for what would come next, arms crossed.

The cop was moaning and bleeding heavily from the face, but now he started babbling again. His voice was thick from his ruined nose and all the blood he was swallowing, and any semblance of the authoritative manner he'd previously attempted to project was long gone.

He begged for mercy.

Begged for help.

Begged the kid to stop.

And for a moment the kid *did* stop. He had reached reluctantly for the shears and now he stood uncertainly, bony arms holding the gardening tool at his side as the cop continued to urge him to reconsider what he was about to do.

Finally the man in charge shook his head in disgust. He muttered something that the man in the fedora could not quite make out and then stepped forward. He jammed the gag back into the cop's mouth and secured it and the cop thrashed wildly in his seat, his ability to breathe through his rapidly swelling nose nearly nonexistent.

The group leader let him struggle for a moment and then yanked the gag back out. Before the cop could say anything the group leader rasped, "Not one more word, *cabron*. You say one word, just one, and the gag goes back in and stays in until we are finished, do you understand me?"

The cop panted, gulping wide mouthfuls of air, and for a moment the man in the fedora thought he hadn't heard the group leader. Then he nodded tiredly. With each downward motion of his head large droplets of blood splattered onto his shirt, which was now soaked and stained.

The kid with the shears looked like he might be about to cry, but the older man whispered something to him and he nodded.

The older man grabbed the cop's right hand and forced his fingers widely apart as the kid opened the jaws of the gardening shears and thrust them around the cop's pinkie finger. The kid was shaking badly and the man in the fedora could see the boy had already opened up a deep gash on the cop's knuckles.

But that would soon be the least of the cop's problems.

It already was.

The cop tried to struggle, but he had no leverage and the group leader was strong. His arms were massive and he'd performed this ritual many times and by now had it down to a science. The group leader held the cop's hand motionless between the jaws of the shears.

He looked up and nodded to the kid.

The man in the fedora watched, breathless, his hand in his pants as he waited for the show to continue.

And then it did.

PART TWO: PRESENT DAY

1

Jack Sheridan walked along through the rudimentary path in the woods. He had long ago left the clearing behind. He moved slowly, carefully.

High winds had accompanied a recent heavy downpour, and fallen branches of varying sizes and shapes littered the pathway. Stepping on one of the sticks would likely announce his approach to anyone paying attention, a scenario he wanted very much to avoid.

The sound of gunshots had drawn him here, and the gunfire continued slowly, one shot after the other, POP...POP...POP. They increased in volume as he drew near.

He rounded a corner and eased behind a tree, the shooter finally in sight. It was a woman, and she continued to blast away, unaware of his presence. Her concentration on the task at hand was obvious, and Jack suspected he could have tramped through the woods on the back of a circus elephant and the shooter still would not have heard him approach.

He stepped out from behind the tree, his own weapon still holstered, as the shooter fired another round. Sixty feet away, a

9mm slug thudded into the target: a life-sized silhouette of a man that had been nailed to a tree trunk.

"Nicely done," he said loudly. "But remember to exhale just before you squeeze the trigger, and then be sure not to take in your next breath until after you've fired. Do that, and your hands will stay steady. Instead of taking him in the shoulder, you'll hit center-mass. He'll go down and stay down."

Edie Tolliver turned to face him, her pretty face drawn in concentration. "A lot to remember," she said.

"It is, but you're doing great. You've made a lot of progress in a very short amount of time. Soon, all of this will be instinctive, no conscious thought required. That's the goal, to make the process second nature."

"I don't ever want my child—or me—to be a victim again."

"Hargus and Chilcott are gone," Jack said quietly, "and they're not coming back. Ever. I can personally testify to that."

"Doesn't matter. There's always another Hargus or Chilcott around the corner."

"True enough," Jack agreed. "But based on what I'm seeing here, they'd be well advised to leave you and Janie the hell alone and go bother someone else."

A brief smile lit up Edie's face and then disappeared. The half-second served as a bitter reminder to Jack of all that he'd had for the briefest of moments with this petite woman, and all that he'd lost.

He swallowed heavily and reached for Edie's weapon, a Sig-Sauer P-229. "Let's go inside and you can dazzle me with your gun-cleaning skills."

She handed the weapon over, grip-first, muzzle pointed away from them and toward the forest floor. "I never heard you coming," she said.

He smiled as they turned toward the path that would lead them away from the makeshift gun range Jack had hacked out of the miles of empty forest and back toward his secluded home. "I wanted to observe your technique without you knowing I was there."

"Mission accomplished. I would have sworn I was completely alone."

Jack didn't answer. Moving stealthily was a skill he'd mastered early in his career. It was a necessity for any operator, at least any one who wanted a chance at a reasonable life span.

They walked single-file along the narrow pathway, branches and underbrush clutching at them every step of the way.

"And?" Edie's tone remained civil. Not unfriendly, not exactly. But not filled with burgeoning love, either, as it had been in the days before her seven-year-old daughter had been kidnapped by a sociopathic politician determined to use the girl as leverage to force Jack into the assassination of a political rival.

Jack had rescued Janie and eliminated the threat, but not before revealing his true occupation to his new girlfriend and seeing their relationship break apart almost before it had begun. He wondered if the pieces could ever be put back together and knew it was probably too much to hope for.

"Going deaf, old man?" This time, Edie's voice carried a hint of the teasing tone she'd often used on him before Janie's kidnapping.

"I'm sorry," he said. "I was…somewhere else. What was the question?"

"You said you wanted to observe my technique discreetly. Well, what's the verdict?"

"I already told you. You're coming along well. I almost—but not quite—feel sorry for the misguided bastard who breaks into your house once you feel comfortable bringing this baby—" he held up the Sig—"home."

"Up until a few weeks ago, I would never have considered being anywhere near a gun, especially with a little girl running around. I had never given the prospect one second's consideration."

"Up until a few weeks ago you were an innocent," Jack said. "And once innocence is stolen, there's no getting it back." He cleared his throat heavily. "I'm…so sorry for stripping you of that."

No answer. Edie continued to work her way through the woods, Jack trailing a few feet behind. He loved watching her walk, whether outdoors or inside her restaurant, The Three Squares Diner. She moved with an economy of motion, feline and fluid, like a very sexy cat.

He wondered whether she'd heard his awkward apology and then realized it didn't much matter.

What kind of apology could ever make up for the hell she'd had to endure while her little girl was missing?

How many "I'm sorries" were sufficient to wipe away the emotional trauma of a young woman discovering her new boyfriend, the man she'd thought was some kind of corporate fixer, was actually a contract assassin? The fact that his work had removed some of the most despicable and dangerous people from the face of the earth didn't make much difference, either.

He was still a killer, and no amount of apologizing was ever going to change that. Neither was the fact that he'd quit The Organization following Janie's kidnapping. Expecting Edie to overlook all his baggage was simply a bridge too far.

Jack realized Edie had spoken again, and again he'd missed her words. *It's a good thing you did quit,* he thought. *You wouldn't last five minutes on a job, as scattered as you are now.*

"Uh, sorry," he said.

"Elsewhere again?" she said, the trace of a smile still in her voice.

"Something like that. Could you repeat the question?"

"It wasn't a question. It was a statement."

"Okay, could you repeat the statement?"

"I said thank you."

He stopped in his tracks. "*You're* thanking *me?* What on earth for?"

"For teaching me how to defend myself and keep Janie safe."

She'd never stopped walking, and now he hurried to catch up. "You don't ever have to thank me for that. Jesus, Edie, it's the least I can do. Thank you for giving me the opportunity.

"And you're a great student," he added after a moment, stopping short of what he wanted to say, which was that teaching her self defense techniques, and to shoot and handle a gun safely, offered him the opportunity to be close to her. And that even though their relationship was no longer a romantic one, he still treasured every last second spent in her company.

They broke through a clearing at the northeast corner of Jack's property, his small ranch home standing in the distance. The angle at which the house had been constructed allowed for an unobstructed view of the front door, and Jack stopped in surprise, reaching out and grabbing a fistful of Edie's sleeve.

"What is it?" she said, turning to face him with her eyebrows raised. "I thought you wanted to talk me through cleaning the gun."

He inclined his head, indicating the front steps, upon which stood a man. The man appeared elderly, although at this distance it was impossible to be certain, and his finger was pressed against Jack's doorbell button.

"Expecting company?" Edie said.

He snorted. "I think you know me better than that." Jack was a loner, an individual perfectly suited in temperament for the solitary life of a professional assassin. He'd only opened himself up to Edie and Janie after months of intense—and agonizing—introspection.

"You have to give him credit," she said as the man continued to press the bell, occasionally switching things up to bang on the closed front door. "He seems highly motivated."

"I can't remember the last time someone came to my door unannounced."

"Well, this place isn't exactly on the beaten path," she said.

"That's right," he agreed. "And that's just the way I wanted it."

"He doesn't seem in any hurry to leave, does he?"

"He will be when I get through with him," Jack said, slipping the Sig into the waistband of his jeans at the small of his back.

Then he moved past Edie and began crossing the yard. "Stay behind me."

2

"May I help you?" Jack snapped the words out, putting just enough aggression into them to ensure that the recipient of his question would understand he wasn't particularly interested in helping anyone with anything.

The man on the front steps had been so intent on ringing the bell and banging on the door that he hadn't seen Jack and Edie approach, and he started in surprise. Then he turned to face them and Jack realized his observation had been right on target. The man was elderly. If anything, he might be older than he'd appeared at first glance.

"I'm sorry to bother you," the stranger said. "I don't take coming here lightly, and am only doing so after serious consideration."

That's an odd thing to say.

Before Jack could respond, the man continued. "Could you spare a moment for an important conversation? I won't take up much of your time, and I wouldn't ask if the situation weren't dire. It's life or death, in fact."

Jack gazed at the visitor, taking measure of him. The man clearly wasn't here to sell anything, and it didn't seem he was standing at Jack's door to talk religion or push a political candidate.

When he answered, he'd softened his tone considerably. "If you're dealing with a life or death situation, sir, I'd suggest you either go straight to the emergency room or to the police, whichever is more appropriate."

"My name is Larry," the old man said. "Larry Daly." He descended the stairs and moved past Jack to shake Edie's hand before then turning and offering his hand to Jack. After a moment's hesitation, Jack took it. The grip was stronger than he would have expected.

"Jack Sheridan," Jack answered. "And this is my...friend, Edie Tolliver."

Daly offered a quick smile to Edie. "It's a pleasure to meet you, Ms. Tolliver."

Edie returned Daly's smile with a dazzling one of her own, even as the old man was turning to address Jack. "And I know who you are, Mr. Sheridan. I'm very familiar with your work, which is why I'm standing on your doorstep uninvited on a Wednesday afternoon. I know you're a man with a...unique...skill set. I find myself in desperate need of those skills."

Warning bells had begun going off in Jack's head as Daly spoke, and now they were clanging noisily. "You must be misinformed," he said, his face expressionless. "I don't know what you're talking about. I certainly have no particular skill set anyone would need, desperately or otherwise."

"I think you do."

"I already gave you my advice. Go to the police if you have a problem. Now if you'll excuse me, Ms. Tolliver and I have things to do." He reached for Edie's arm, using his own body as a barrier between her and the visitor. Then he went to move past the old man and climb his front steps.

"I know you work for The Organization," Daly said. "And I really must insist we talk."

*   *   *

They sat clustered around Jack's tiny kitchen table. It was the perfect size for one man eating alone, slightly cramped if a second place setting were added into the equation, uncomfortably tight for three people.

No one spoke for a moment, and then Jack said, "I still have no idea what you're talking about, Mr. Daly, but I've indulged you. How about you stop wasting our time and get down to business?"

Daly glanced from Jack to Edie and then back again, eyebrows raised. "Perhaps it would be best if Ms. Tolliver excused herself from the conversation?"

Edie pushed her chair back and began to rise. "Thanks for the help today," she said to Jack. "I'll see you again anoth—"

"No," he said sharply. The notion of sending Edie away had flashed through his mind the moment Daly mentioned The Organization, but Jack's secrecy about his past and refusal to share it with her had been a major reason—probably THE major reason, even more so than his actual career choice as an assassin—for the fact they were no longer together as a couple, and he wasn't about to make the same mistake twice.

Besides, Edie was now well aware of his past, and he'd quit The Organization to boot. What difference could it make now whether she left or stayed?

"Anything you have to say to me," he continued, "you can say in front of Edie."

Daly blinked, clearly surprised.

Edie hesitated, surprised as well, and then sat back down and folded her hands on the tabletop.

"Okay," Daly said slowly. He waited another moment, presumably giving Jack the opportunity to change his mind. When he didn't, Daly continued. What he said came out of left field. "I know about your employment by The Organization because I was once like you, and I've maintained a few connections over the years."

"Excuse me?"

"That's right. I wasn't always a broken-down old man. Once upon a time, I was an Organization member myself. I took on the types of jobs you do now. Like you, I shouldered the responsibility of ridding the world of stone-cold murdering sociopaths."

Jack sat back in his chair, stunned. He realized his jaw was hanging open and he closed it.

With extreme difficulty.

He supposed it made sense that there were elderly, retired Organization members living out their lives in anonymity, but he'd never once considered the possibility of what would happen if someone in his career field survived long enough to get old. He doubted it was a very common occurrence.

"How long ago…?"

"A long time. Decades ago." Daly smiled mischievously. "So long ago that Norbert Stanton was just a young buck, taking on assignments like the rest of us. That was long before he rose to his current prominence in The Organization."

"Norbert?"

Daly chuckled. "He never told you his first name? I suppose I wouldn't, either, if it were Norbert."

As Daly spoke, Jack had considered in the back of his mind that this might be some kind of elaborate scam. A setup. To what end, he had no idea, but suspicion and caution had kept him alive for years in one of the most dangerous occupations imaginable. The mention of Mr. Stanton, though—*Norbert?*—convinced him Larry Daly was exactly what he said he was, as difficult as that was to believe.

He realized silence had fallen over the table. Daly had been letting him work through his confusion, and Edie was just taking it all in, wide-eyed and confused but sharp as a tack and beautiful as ever.

Finally Jack spoke, still without acknowledging his Organization connection, although what difference denying it would make at this point he couldn't imagine. "Why are you here, Mr. Daly?"

"My son is missing."

Jack blinked. "You understand I'm not a private investigator, correct? If a family member is missing, you need to do what I said before and go to the police. File a missing persons report."

"The police are well aware of the situation. They won't help."

"I don't understand."

"Greg is a cop down in Lawrence. He's been missing for—"

"Oh my God," Edie said. "I saw it on the news. The missing police officer, that's your son?"

Daly nodded and Edie said, "I'm so sorry, Mr. Daly. But the reports I saw must have been…I don't know…several weeks ago. He's never been found?"

Jack rarely watched television, and he almost never turned on the news unless he was looking for information on a specific story. He hadn't heard anything about a missing cop.

"Two months ago, to be precise," Daly said. "Almost to the day."

"I still don't understand," Jack said. "If your son is a cop, everyone should be looking for him. Officers should be coming from all over New England to help in the search."

"You're right," Daly said. "They should be."

Jack sat back in his seat and shook his head. "One thing the police do above all else is to protect their own. It's hard to imagine they wouldn't blanket the northeast in an all-out search until they found…something."

Daly shook his head, his lips pressed together in a grim bloodless line.

"Are you sure he didn't just walk away, Mr. Daly? Disappear and start over somewhere else? I hate to be the one to suggest it, but it does happen."

Daly shook his head. "I know it does, but it's nothing like that in Greg's case. He had…has…a wife he loves and a little baby daughter he absolutely adores. His family has always been his number one priority, and he wanted to be a cop since he was a little boy. His life was perfect. He would never have abandoned everything and everyone now."

Jack sat back and stared at his visitor. "What am I missing?" he said softly. "What are you not telling me? There has to be something. Why are you so sure the police in Lawrence aren't doing their best to get to the bottom of your son's disappearance?"

The old man ran his hands through his thinning white hair and rubbed his eyes. He looked exhausted. "I'm sure you've heard about all the problems Lawrence is having with drugs and gangs."

"I've heard," Jack said.

"Well, it's even worse than most people know. Over the years the city has become a major distribution point for illegal drugs of all kinds, but heroin in particular. That includes Fentanyl and all the synthetic opiates, the stuff that is far more powerful, and far more dangerous, than even the similar drugs of just a few years ago."

"Okay."

"Well, as you might imagine, many people—including a large number of rank-and-file police officers, one of whom is Greg—find it impossible to believe the drug runners could have built the kind of operation they have going in Lawrence without involvement and cooperation to some degree from those at the highest levels of city government."

"Including in the department," Jack said.

"Including in the department," Daly agreed.

"At high levels."

"The highest."

Jack thought about it for a moment. The reasoning made sense in theory, but still…"So you're telling me the chief of police is involved?"

"Greg was convinced of it. And he was not alone in that assessment."

"It doesn't make sense," Jack said. "Even if that's all true, what possible motivation would the department head have to kidnap and possibly murder one of his own officers?"

The old man swallowed heavily and Jack said, "I'm sorry, Mr. Daly, but you must have considered the likelihood Greg is…gone."

He nodded. "Of course. It's just hard to accept, even now, months later. And to your point, I believe the most likely possibility is that the chief wasn't involved in Greg's disappearance and in fact probably had no idea it was coming. The gangs are fiercely independent and brutally violent and any alliance they have with city officials, especially those inside the police department, would be…tenuous."

"So you're saying Greg's disappearance came as a surprise to the gang's connection in the department—the chief or others at the upper levels—but once it happened, they had no choice but to sweep the investigation under the rug as a matter of self-preservation."

Daly had begun nodding halfway through Jack's statement and now he said, "That's exactly what I'm saying. The case was highly publicized in the beginning, which was undoubtedly when Ms. Tolliver saw it on the news. But despite the department's public promises of action and a swift response, the 'investigation' has ground to a halt. It's turned up nothing of significance in eight weeks. I can't get anyone inside the department to talk to me anymore. Even their media relations officer has stopped returning my calls."

"It's old news now."

Daly nodded. "They've moved on and Greg is gone and his wife and little girl are on their own."

"That's quite a story, Mr. Daly. It's sad and tragic and I'm so sorry for your loss."

"Thank you. So you'll help me?"

"No." Jack shook his head. "There's nothing I can do."

3

Larry Daly slumped. His shoulders dropped and he shrank inward. It was as though someone had let the air out of a six-foot-tall balloon.

Edie stood and crossed the kitchen to Jack's coffeemaker, where two-thirds of a carafe sat on the warmer. She reached into his cupboard and removed a mug, filled it with coffee and brought it back to the table.

She placed the coffee in front of the old man and then reached for his hands and clasped them in her own. "Would you excuse Mr. Sheridan and me for a moment? Have some coffee while we step outside, and we'll be right back, okay?"

Daly nodded and mumbled something Jack could not make out. He glanced from the old man to the young woman and she tilted her head in the direction of the deck built off Jack's back door. Her eyes were smoldering, her face set in a furious cast. Even angry she was the most breathtaking thing he'd ever seen.

She gave Daly's hands one final squeeze and then stalked off in the direction of the deck without waiting to see if Jack would follow.

After a moment he did. He stepped onto the deck and rolled the sliding glass door closed behind him and spread his hands in genuine confusion. "What gives? You're obviously pissed, and I don't have the first clue why."

"You don't know why I'd be mad? After sitting through that poor man's story and seeing how badly he's suffering, you turn down his request for help and you can't imagine why I'd be angry? What the hell is wrong with you?" Her face was red and furious, and despite her petite stature—she couldn't have been more than five foot two and a hundred-ten pounds soaking wet—she seemed somehow much more imposing, like a cat puffing out its fur when threatened.

This was the fiery woman he'd fallen in love with. This was the fiery woman he'd driven away with his deception, and his heart broke a little more. "Edie, I quit, remember? I retired. I don't work for The Organization anymore. My career got Janie kidnapped and nearly killed, and I couldn't live with myself if I put you or your little girl in danger again."

"That man's son has a wife and a little girl who are now alone. If Mr. Daly's story is even close to being true, they're alone because of a gang of amoral, bloodthirsty, drug-dealing thugs, and from where I stand, that is unacceptable."

"But I—"

"I know what that woman and child are going through, Jack. I've been there. I was left alone with a young girl to raise by myself, and even though it wasn't thanks to a situation like this one, I have a pretty good idea how Greg Daly's wife is feeling." Her eyes had filled with tears and she sobbed, and Jack moved to put his arms around her.

She pushed him away. "Janie and I will be fine. We *are* fine. But that man sitting at your kitchen table needs help, and his daughter-in-law needs help, and it's the kind of help that only you can give."

"That's no true. He can go elsewhere, Edie."

"Like where, exactly? Who's going to help him?"

"The FBI, for one. He can take his story to them."

"Come on, Jack, you know better. He doesn't have any proof. All he has is a theory, and with a two-month-old case and much higher priorities for an outfit like the FBI, how much will they really do? They're going to assume Greg Daly is dead, and—"

"Of course he's dead."

"Exactly. And the FBI may well launch an investigation into the drug connections inside the Lawrence Police Department. They may even root out the bad guys and hold them accountable.

Maybe. Eventually. But you know as well as I do *none* of that will ease that man's suffering, not to mention the suffering of his daughter-in-law and his granddaughter."

"Let me get this straight," Jack said. "My career drove us apart. It took away the woman and the little girl I love more than anything else in the world, and now you're telling me you want me to go back to work? You want me to continue in the career field that destroyed us, and thus ensure we'll never have a chance to be together? Is that what you're telling me, Edie? Because I really don't understand."

She swallowed heavily and turned away. Leaned on the deck's railing and looked out over Jack's back yard. Remained silent for a long moment.

When she spoke her voice was thick with emotion. "I don't know what the future holds for us, Jack. Things have always been black and white in my world. Right and wrong. Good and evil. Clear. Simple. That's all changed in the last few months. Everything's changed, and it's thrown me for a loop. I won't deny that."

She fell silent again, and Jack waited patiently. It was obvious she wasn't finished speaking.

Eventually she continued. "But there's one thing I know for certain. If you have the capability of helping that poor man—and I know you do, my little Janie is alive right now because of your unique abilities—you cannot justify ignoring his request, slapping him down like he's nothing more than an annoyance. Not on my account, not on Janie's account. Not for any reason."

He crossed the deck and placed his hands lightly on her shoulders. Her back was still turned and her shoulders were shaking and she was crying quietly. She seemed upset far beyond what the situation demanded, and he realized her tears were only partially for the tragedy that had befallen Larry Daly's family.

They were also for herself and her own little family. For having fallen in love with a man who was far different than she'd imagined. For having woken up one morning to discover everything she thought she understood about the world and the way it worked had been blown up and replaced with a completely different world, a world that was foreign to her, and bleak and dangerous and terrifying.

He squeezed her upper arms and expected to be brushed off like he had been before, but to his surprise she turned and allowed him to envelop her in a hug.

"You have to help that man, Jack." The words came out muffled, with her face buried in his chest, but he understood them perfectly. "You have to."

"Let's go back inside," he said quietly. "It's rude to leave a guest alone for too long."

*   *   *

Daly had rallied slightly by the time Jack and Edie reentered the house. He was sitting and sipping his coffee, hands wrapped around the mug like a drowning man clutching a life preserver, his expression heartbroken but resigned.

"Tell me everything," Jack said.

"Are you saying you'll help me? Because I don't see any reason to go through the whole awful story only to walk out of here in the same situation I was when I knocked on your door."

"I don't know if I *can* help you, Mr. Daly. But I'll see what I can do."

Daly nodded and turned to Edie. "Thank you," he said, and she offered him one of the dazzling smiles that had rocked Jack's world from the moment he met her.

The old man returned his attention to Jack. "I'm not sure what else you need to know beyond what I've already told you. Hit me with any questions you may have and I'll answer them to the best of my ability."

Jack thought for a moment and then said, "Did Greg ever mention if there was one dominant gang that the patrol officers felt had sunk their hooks into the department? Along those lines, could his disappearance be somehow related to a power struggle between competing factions?"

"In the early days," Daly said, "when the drug trade was just getting a foothold in the city, there were multiple gangs all vying for control. As you might imagine, the violence during that period was extensive. But over time, one outfit drove the others out, or at least into irrelevance."

"Do you happen to know the gang's name?"

"It would be impossible to live in Lawrence without knowing their name. They call themselves the Eighth Street Dragons, or the Dragons for short. They're vicious and bloodthirsty and unpredictable. Greg told me once that if anything ever happened to him, to look at the Dragons first. Even though a lot of the cops felt the Dragons had established a foothold in the upper echelons of the department, the rank and file gang members hate the police and the cops have long suspected they were responsible for more than one officer's death over the last few years."

"But nothing could be proven."

"Exactly. No one was ever arrested in any of the officers' deaths, much less convicted. Greg said there was always just enough successful law enforcement interception of the drug trade to convince the citizens that something was being done to eradicate it. But it was always street dealers going away, never any of the high-level gang members that would make a real dent in the criminal activity."

"So you believe the Dragons would be the logical place to start."

"There's no question about it. I even have a name for you."

"A *person's* name?"

"That's right," Daly said. "Greg had been on the job long enough to develop relationships with a number of confidential informants."

"Street snitches."

"Yes. And one of them told him to watch out for a guy named Hector de la Cruz. Said de la Cruz is a psychotic son of a bitch. Those were his exact words, 'psychotic son of a bitch.' The snitch told Greg this de la Cruz character had a thing for forced mutilation and torture, and that the guys he killed did not die easily."

Daly's eyes had welled up while he was speaking and his hands had begun shaking, but to his credit his voice remained steady and he held Jack's gaze.

"I assume you told the police all this regarding the Dragons and de la Cruz when they investigated Greg's disappearance."

"Of course!" Daly snorted, his disdain clear. "They wrote down the information like it was a hot lead and promised to follow it up.

Like everything else, it fell into some kind of investigative black hole."

"You understand the police may have followed up and discovered there was no connection between the Dragons and Greg's disappearance, or even between Hector de la Cruz and the Dragons, for that matter."

"Sure. Just like there's no connection between smoke and fire."

"I'm just saying, it's not outside the realm of possibility."

"Fine," Daly said. "I agree, it's possible. But if that were the case, why wouldn't they take five minutes to call me and fill me in? After all, I was the one who gave them the information and it's my son who's missing."

Jack nodded and thrummed his fingers on the table. For a moment he gazed over Larry Daly's shoulder, staring at nothing, deep in thought. Then he said, "What's your daughter-in-law's name? Greg may have mentioned something to her that he didn't tell you."

Daly was shaking his head, and he raised his hands to stop Jack. "Greg tried to protect Michelle. He didn't want her worrying about him twenty-four hours a day, so he told me once that he never shared anything about the job with her. She doesn't have any information. Trust me. This situation has been hard enough on her, and unless it's absolutely necessary, I'd like to leave her out of it."

Jack sat back and considered the old man's words. He understood Greg Daly's desire to protect his wife from the ugliness of his world. It was exactly what Jack had tried to do with Edie.

"Okay," he said. "For now. I can't promise it won't become necessary to talk to her, but I'll hold off, at least initially."

They stared at each other across the table and Jack said, "Is there anything else you can think of that I might need to know?"

"Only that I want these sons-of-bitches to suffer. I want it more than I've ever wanted anything else in my life. I understand Greg is gone, and I accept it. But I don't want his death to have been in vain. And I don't want the animals responsible for his death to foul this earth with their presence one second longer than is absolutely necessary."

He paused. The defeated old man was gone. In his place was someone strong and angry and committed, and suddenly Jack had little difficulty believing Larry Daly had once been an operator like himself.

Daly opened his mouth to speak and Jack knew exactly what he was going to say before he spoke.

"I want someone to pay."

4

"I'm sorry," Edie said.

They'd just walked Daly out of the house and watched him drive away, and Jack had expected her to climb into her own car and follow the old man down the road. Instead she'd joined him back at the kitchen table after pouring coffee for both of them.

He shrugged. "What do you have to be sorry about?"

"You left The Organization because of me, and just a few months later I've brow-beaten you into going back."

"It's a lot more complicated than that, Edie. But even if it weren't, you have nothing to apologize for. My first instinct was to help Larry Daly. The only reason I turned him down initially was because salvaging what little I can out of the wreckage of our relationship means far more to me than just about anything else in the world, including my career."

"Thank you," she whispered, and not for the first time Jack marveled at the monumental stupidity of her ex-husband, who had simply walked away from Edie and their daughter and disappeared.

On the other hand, who was he to pass judgment? His actions had been different, but arguably just as bad.

She cleared her throat and said, "So where are you going to start? How can you possibly take on a whole drug gang all by yourself, when an entire police department is either unable or unwilling to do so?"

"That's a legitimate question, but the reality of the situation is even worse," Jack said.

"How so?"

"The police can't be the only ones involved. Remember early in the conversation, when Daly mentioned the cops' suspicion that the Dragons had infiltrated not just the police, but other facets of the municipal government?"

"Sure."

"I think he's right on target. I think the Dragons have established a foothold not just in the police department, but in the District Attorney's office as well."

"What makes you say that?"

"Think about it. A police officer disappears while on duty, inside a city that has already suffered more than its share of violent gang activity. Even if the police chief is compromised—hell, even if the entire command structure of the department is compromised—the investigators are damned well going to do their best to bring the perpetrators to justice."

"Unless they're compromised as well."

He shook his head. "You're on the right track, but think about it in terms of logistics. Even the biggest gang's resources are finite. They can buy off or blackmail some people, yes, but not everyone. It's just not possible. So to be successful, their efforts have to be concentrated at the top of the food chain."

"They don't have the capability of controlling what happens at the investigative level."

"Exactly. And even if they were able to co-opt an investigator, that man or woman would be under enormous pressure from the rank-and-file to do their job. They would have to follow leads and work the case, at least to a degree where they didn't risk exposing the fact they were compromised. But let's continue this line of reasoning just a little farther. What has to happen before anyone goes to court or gets charged with anything?"

She stared into her coffee cup, her eyebrows knitted in concentration. Jack thought he'd never seen anything so beautiful. When she raised her gaze to meet his, her eyes were troubled. "The District Attorney has to file charges."

"That's right. If the DA's office doesn't believe there's sufficient evidence to convict, nothing happens, no matter how hard the investigators have worked."

"And in that scenario, there's nothing anyone can do about it. The investigators are helpless."

"At least in the short term."

"Jesus, Jack, how deep does this thing go?"

"I guess we'll find out."

She rubbed her eyes and sighed deeply. "I hope I didn't get you killed by convincing you to take on this job."

He grinned. "I already told you, my instinct was to take it on. No matter what happens, it's not on you."

"That doesn't make me feel any better."

"I'll be fine," he said. "This is what I do."

Edie fell silent. Her eyes were large and frightened and beautiful. Then she said, "But this brings us back to my first question. Where do you even start?"

"I'll admit this is a little different than a typical Organization assignment. With those, there is little to no investigating required. I receive an intel packet on the target, decide how to proceed, and then complete the mission."

"That doesn't answer my question."

"I've got to start with some old-fashioned research and see where that takes me," he said.

"Tell me what I can do."

"Oh no. No, no, no. You're not helping me. No way. You're going to stay as far away from this as you can. You've got a restaurant to run and a little girl to raise. All I need from you is the assurance you'll still talk to me when this is over and done."

"I love you, Jack. I've come to the realization I'll always love you. You don't have to worry about that."

He smiled and took her hand. "Likewise. Now, unless my clock is wrong, you need to hit the road. Janie's day at summer camp ends in about fifteen minutes."

"Your clock isn't wrong."

"Then get moving. The apple didn't fall far from the tree with Janie, which means you'll catch holy hell from one feisty seven-year-old if you're late."

Edie smiled and nodded and finished her coffee. Then she stood and they walked in companionable silence out to her car.

She opened her door and said, "Promise me you'll be careful."

"I'm always careful."

"Humor me. Say it."

"I promise I'll be careful."

"Thank you."

Jack thought she would climb into the car, but instead she wrapped her arms around him and hugged tightly. It was like being squeezed by a particularly enthusiastic boa constrictor. She lifted onto her tiptoes and kissed him on the cheek and whispered, "I love you" into his ear.

Then she slipped behind the wheel. She slammed the door and fired up the engine.

She backed out of the driveway and was gone.

5

Jack almost didn't even bother trying the most obvious form of research first. It was impossible to imagine that in a city with a substantial Hispanic and Dominican population, there wouldn't be dozens of men with the name of Hector de la Cruz.

But he was glad he kept it simple, because against all odds, he struck gold with his Internet name search. There were two Hector de la Cruz's listed as residents of Lawrence, Massachusetts. One was an eighty-seven year old nursing home resident, the other a twenty-two year old unemployed high school dropout.

"I guess it's safe to say eighty-seven year old Hector isn't sneaking past the nurses and orderlies to kidnap and torture cops," he muttered. He jotted the information he needed onto a notepad and powered down his computer less than fifteen minutes after going online.

* * *

Two hours later he was sitting inside a rental car half a block from the address he'd written down as belonging to Hector de La Cruz. The twenty-two year old likely gangbanger, not the octogenarian nursing home resident.

His early research success notwithstanding, Jack knew he might be in for some difficulty identifying de la Cruz. The man's home address was a dilapidated wood-framed triple-decker that had either been built in the waning days of the nineteenth century or the very early portion of the twentieth. It was showing its age, with sagging windows, peeling paint and drooping porch railings.

More to the point, the building was clearly either filled with small apartments or maybe even single rooms for rent. It was entirely possible anywhere from a handful to more than two dozen people called the place home, and the odds were good that the majority of them were men whose ages were within shouting distance of de la Cruz's twenty-two years.

Jack screwed the cap off a water bottle and took a sip, settling in for the long haul. The area was downtrodden but busy, with vehicular traffic as well as plenty of pedestrian activity. He had little concern about being made by de la Cruz. Having parked on the side of a busy street, the rental was flanked in front and behind by cars in parking spaces as far as the eye could see.

He would watch his target's building from this location for awhile, and then take up surveillance somewhere else if it seemed anyone was getting too curious about the guy sitting alone in his car. He doubted it would become necessary to move.

There was no way to know how long he would need to watch the building, of course, or even if surveillance would yield results. Ideally, he wanted to get a feel for the comings and goings of the building's residents and, if possible, narrow down the list of potentials to those fitting the profile of a violent gang member in his early twenties.

He had an alternative course of action in mind for identifying de la Cruz should it become necessary, but he fervently hoped it would not. Jack guessed The Organization would be familiar with the Eighth Street Dragons, and probably even Hector de la Cruz, if the man was as big a sociopath as Larry Daly had described. But he had no desire to go crawling back to Mr. Stanton for help just two months after severing all ties with his employer firmly and in no uncertain terms.

As midday melted into late afternoon and then early evening, Jack began to suspect his surveillance might bear fruit faster than he'd anticipated. Foot traffic into and out of the triple-decker was steady, so much so that Jack wondered whether perhaps the de la

Cruz or some other resident might be running a cash and carry business of the chemical persuasion out of the structure.

In any event, after just a few hours he'd identified an early favorite in the scumbag derby.

A young man had come in and out of the house on three separate occasions, each time hanging on the front porch chatting with a much older man who'd been seated in a wicker rocking chair since Jack's arrival. The older guy hadn't taken so much as a pee break, and Jack felt a mild stirring of jealousy. Though only in his mid thirties—Edie would have defined his age as late thirties, but he hadn't yet come around to her way of thinking—he'd found himself getting out of bed to take a leak at least once in the middle of most nights.

But the younger man was the one who drew the bulk of Jack's attention for a number of reasons, not the least of which was the elaborate dragon tattoo adorning his shaved head. The dragon's tail curved gracefully around the man's left ear, and a scaly body covered most of his cranium. Open jaws spewed angry flames from the top of the man's skull down onto his forehead, the tips of the yellow-red flames just licking his eyebrows and the area between.

The entire effect was chilling. Intimidating. And it was high quality work; Jack could see that even from a distance. This was no clumsy prison tat. Dragon Man had spent a lot of money—and suffered through a fair amount of pain, if the design's detail and location on his body was any indication—to create a striking image.

Dragon Man.

The Eighth Street Dragons.

Coincidence? Jack supposed it was technically possible, but nearly two decades worth of experience in his line of work had taught him that coincidences were exceedingly rare. Yes, they did sometimes happen, but an apparent connection was typically an actual connection. Occam's Razor: when two or more explanations exist for an event, the answer is usually the one that requires the fewest assumptions.

It didn't take many assumptions to tie a young man with a striking dragon tattoo on his head to the Eighth Street Dragons.

Jack dragged his gaze away from the tattoo and took in the

rest of the man as he leaned on the rickety porch railing smoking a cigarette. The age looked right. He was definitely no longer a teenager but didn't yet appear deep into his twenties.

His face looked hard. Cruel, even, although Jack allowed for the possibility he was projecting his own perceptions of the type of sociopath Larry Daly had described onto this guy. Maybe the man simply suffered from Resting Asshole Face.

A chiseled upper body stretched the limits of a stained t-shirt, with a barrel chest and bodybuilder arms. The entire package suggested either a man who spent hours every day in the gym, or a serial steroid abuser who spent hours every day in the gym.

After a few minutes spent talking with the old guy, Dragon Man finished his butt and flicked it off the porch. He mock-punched the other man in the upper arm and stalked back into the apartment/rooming house.

Jack had sat up straight behind the wheel at the appearance of Dragon Man and had unconsciously been squinting in concentration. Now he eased back against the seat, thinking. None of the passersby for the last several hours had paid the slightest attention to him, so he'd risked using his mini-binoculars to get the best possible look at Dragon Man, and the more he saw the more confident he became that this was his target, subject to a few very important *ifs:*

If the information Larry Daly had gotten from his now-missing son about a Lawrence street gang with a vendetta against the cops was accurate.

If the name of the gang really was the Eighth Street Dragons.

If the sociopathic gang member with a thirst for blood was actually involved in Greg Daly's disappearance, and *if* his name was actually Hector de la Cruz.

Jack had no reason to doubt any of it, but no particular reason to credit it, either. All of it was either second or third-hand information, and all more than two months old. And it had been given to him by a man shattered by grief and desperate for someone to do something about a situation nobody in officialdom seemed to give a damn about.

That said, it felt right. Intuition meant a lot for an operator, and Jack's was telling him Dragon Man was, in fact, Hector de la Cruz, and Hector de la Cruz was, in fact, the Eighth Street Dragons leader with a thirst for blood and dismemberment and a burning hatred for the cops.

Plenty of other people had entered and exited the ancient apartment/rooming house, but none had raised Jack's hackles the way Dragon Man did. Even the other young men who matched the age profile of Hector de la Cruz seemed somehow different. They exhibited varying degrees of attitude, something Jack supposed was to be expected in this hardscrabble section of a hardscrabble city. But none of them affected the aura of hardened cruelty and looming psychopathy that Dragon Man had.

It was always possible Jack was wrong.

But he didn't think so. One thing he knew for sure was that Dragon Man warranted much closer inspection.

6

Lowell Stevenson strode into Sylvia's Steak House like a man on a mission, which, in a way, he was. He would be dining tonight with Lawrence Police Chief Tim McKenna in what had become a semi-regular meeting, scheduled for the sole purpose of talking the excitable McKenna off panic's ledge.

The hostess met him at the door and took his overcoat and hat. Then she led him to his usual table in a quiet corner. "Your guest has not yet arrived, Judge Stevenson," she said. "Would you care for a drink while you wait?"

"Of course." Lowell waved her away imperiously. "The usual."

The girl smiled uncomfortably and then hurried off without another word.

Lowell Stevenson had been a Massachusetts circuit court judge for decades and by now was well used to accepting the deference of those below him on the social strata. Gaining a judgeship had been his life's goal for practically as long as he could remember. It had been the driving force for his performance in grade school, junior high and high school, and then on through higher education.

The law degree he'd eventually earned had been achieved not so he could aid the downtrodden or use legal avenues to help forge a better world. It hadn't even been so he could chase ambulances and make fistfuls of money, although Lowell Stevenson had no quarrel with the concept of making money and had, in fact, chased plenty of ambulances early in his career.

He'd done it all because he had always wanted to be a judge.

Period. The notion of adjudicating disputes from on high held the utmost appeal to Lowell. Dictating terms, wielding a totality of power unmatched in modern American society, including by politicians at any level, was the fuel that drove him. The rush he experienced from issuing rulings was almost sexual in nature.

In fact, to Lowell it was *better* than sex; at least the way normal people did sex. That had ceased to be satisfying for Lowell—assuming it ever had been—sometime around the middle of his undergrad days at Yale, and he literally could not recall the last time he'd had missionary intercourse.

Power was what got Lowell off. Domination. Intimidation. The kind of intimidation he projected from the bench, translated to the bedroom, was his only route to climax. Handcuffs and spreader bars, floggers and gags, these were the implements of sexual satisfaction for Lowell Stevenson.

But Lowell's fantasies had grown steadily darker over the years. His desire to wield unrestrained power had eventually driven him to underground sex clubs and into dalliances with prostitutes to whom little if any behavior was off-limits, short of ending their lives during sex.

And his fantasies of restraining and whipping men and women alike—the sex of his victim was irrelevant to Lowell, although he would never have abided anyone calling him gay—had over time morphed into bloody dreams of victims' fingers being chopped up like carrots.

Of throats being sliced at the carotid and fountains of blood arcing gracefully across large rooms.

Of hands wrapped around delicate hooker throats, and the hands squeezing with such impeccable timing his victim expired at the exact moment he climaxed inside them.

Of things so twisted and bizarre he refused to utter them aloud, ever, not to anyone.

But they were always there, capering in the back of Lowell Stevenson's mind, demanding his attention even as he sat behind the bench in his black robe, raised above the common men and women, administering justice and adjudicating disputes.

He supposed, given his…unusual…proclivities, it was inevitable he would eventually take action to realize some of his fantasies.

And he'd finally gotten his chance when was approached by the leader of Lawrence's most notorious street gang with an offer of quid pro quo.

The co-opting of Lowell Stevenson had been a gradual process, of course. In the beginning, Lowell's association with the Eighth Street Dragons involved nothing more than the traditional American judicial practice of accepting under-the-table cash donations in exchange for the issuance of favorable rulings in certain circumstances: acquitting an important gang member accused of a violent crime, or, if guilt was impossible to overlook, offering the lightest possible sentence.

Over time, as Lowell and the Dragons became more comfortable with one another, he'd begun to take occasional advantage of other opportunities. Drugs, for example, or prostitutes.

Oh, the prostitutes.

Professional girls were every bit as welcome in Lowell's world as money, particularly those young women willing to allow him to explore his unusual tastes in the bedroom. One girl in particular struck Lowell's fancy. She was busty and beautiful, hardened, of course, as were most prostitutes, but perfectly willing to be restrained and struck, choked and beaten.

The frequency of their sessions gradually increased until becoming a weekly occurrence, and after one particularly intense evening, as they lay side-by-side in bed, the girl bruised and bloody, Lowell had confessed some of his more exotic—and brutal—fantasies to her. She'd left a little while later and he'd thought nothing more of it.

Until the following week.

That was when a menacing tattooed thug named Hector de la Cruz had shown up uninvited at Lowell's home with an unusual offer. The Dragons would be initiating a few new members the following week in a ceremony that—perhaps coincidentally, perhaps not—would include a few of the practices Lowell had confessed to his "girlfriend" of fantasizing about. Would Lowell like to attend and view the ceremony?

He'd hesitated, but only for a moment. The possibility of a trap occurred to him, that perhaps the Dragons were luring him to the specified location for nefarious purposes, but he'd discounted that thought almost immediately. The relationship between Lowell and the Eighth Street Dragons was by then well established, and it was of mutual benefit to both parties. There would be no reason for the Dragons to upset that apple cart.

Besides, if the evening's schedule included anything close to what Lowell's visitor described, it would have taken an act of will stronger than Lowell possessed to decline their offer.

So he had accepted. Of course he had.

And on the night in question, Lowell Stevenson's eyes had been opened to a world he'd never known existed outside his imagination. His fevered fantasies became reality, and although he had not been the one wielding the implements of torture, the show he'd seen unfold over several hours had been one he would never forget.

He'd thought that night would remain forever unsurpassed in his experience, but he'd been invited to observe the next Dragons initiation, and the one after that, until his inclusion in the semi-regular ceremony became expected and routine.

Lowell wasn't stupid; he knew he now belonged to the Dragons lock, stock and barrel. But he didn't care. He was raking in exorbitant amounts of cash and seeing his most twisted fantasies played out below his perch on the second floor of the Dragons home base several times a year.

The experience was definitely worth the minimal risk involved.

Lowell realized he'd finished his drink quickly and was well into his second, and that pussy Chief McKenna still hadn't showed. He checked his watch, sipped his drink, and vowed to give the panicky little bastard five more minutes. Then he would down his drink and walk right the hell—

Here he comes. McKenna had slunk into the steak house through the front door and was even now crossing the busy dining room.

Lowell swallowed his whiskey and arranged his facial features into some semblance of a welcoming smile. It was once again time to tamp down on the ugliness in his soul, to lock it away behind closed doors for the time being.

Because even though Police Chief Tim McKenna was involved with the Dragons, too, his participation in gang activities was mostly reluctant and peripheral. If he had any notion of the things

Lowell had seen and done, he would probably pull out his service weapon and shoot Lowell right between the eyes.

Lowell stood as McKenna approached and offered his hand.

"Tim," he said warmly. "So good to see you again."

"Lowell." McKenna took his hand and shook it, but the act was perfunctory and half-hearted, as though the chief's mind was miles away.

"You're running late," Lowell said. "Busy downtown?"

"Always."

The stilted conversation died away until the waitress had hurried to the table and taken their drink and meal orders. Lowell knew exactly what the subject of discussion would be when she walked away, if not the precise words that would come out of the chief's mouth.

He was right, of course. McKenna stared at the table for a few seconds and when he lifted his gaze to meet Lowell's, his eyes were troubled and his voice hushed. "I hate this," he said.

Lowell felt a rush of scorn. The chief was weak. Lowell had known McKenna for over thirty years, so he'd been well aware of the man's lack of intestinal fortitude long before Tim McKenna rose to the top spot in the Lawrence Police Department, long before he'd begun his association with the Eighth Street Dragons.

But the constant handwringing and mealy-mouthed expressions of regret were getting old. Lowell wanted to scream at the man, to knock some sense into him, to take the fucking steak knife currently resting atop his folded linen napkin and plunge it into the man's chest, to stab him and carve him up until he was nothing more than a lump of bloody, inanimate tissue.

He did none of those things.

He spoke gently, calmingly. "The pressure must be easing up some," he said, choosing his words carefully. "It's been over two months now. The newspapers and TV stations have long since moved on to other stories. And it's not unusual for disappearances to go unsolved, even if the guy who vanished was a cop."

"Not just a cop," McKenna said. "An on-duty cop, working inside the city limits. That's a bad look."

"Still," Lowell said. "These things happen. You're staying strong and not talking to the officer's father any longer, I hope."

"I'm not talking to him. But good God, that poor man is suffering something awful."

Lowell wanted to roll his eyes. He doubted he'd ever seen such a spaghetti-spined individual in a position of power in his entire life. McKenna most definitely did not deserve the chief's job, and once things quieted down fully, say in another couple of months, Lowell decided he would bully the mayor's office into getting McKenna shitcanned and replaced by someone more suitable ASAP.

"I know," he answered, keeping his tone gentle and his voice low. "But maintaining a dialogue with Larry Daly will do nothing for either of you. You came to me for advice, I expect you to follow it."

"I am, I am."

"Good."

"But when am I going to feel better? When I agreed to an association with the Dragons, I had no idea they would kidnap and murder one of my own cops. I didn't sign up for that. Gun running and drugs and prostitution are bad enough, but murder? Of my own officer?" He shook his head miserably.

Lowell sat back and considered a range of possible responses. God, he wanted to slap some sense into the man. But of course he couldn't. It occurred to him that after orchestrating McKenna's removal from the chief's job in a few months, perhaps he could suggest the man to the Dragons as a subject for one of their initiation rituals.

He smiled at the thought. It was delicious.

He realized McKenna was staring at him expectantly. The thought of seeing this weak-willed jellyfish restrained in a chair inside the Dragons home base, his fingers plopping to the concrete floor one by one as young boys wielded the hedge trimmers, had been so pleasing he'd allowed his attention to wander.

"I'm sorry," Lowell said. "I've got a bit of a headache and I missed that. What did you say?"

"I said we need to take action to ensure something like this never happens again with the Dragons. They're far too unstable and I can't live with the thought that another officer might disappear."

"Of course," Lowell said. "That's a wonderful idea. I'm sure the Dragons leadership will be receptive to such a suggestion."

Good God, he thought. *If I approach the Dragons with that kind of silly restriction on their operation, I'll find* myself *strapped to a chair. The sooner we remove this buffoon from a position of responsibility, the better.*

7

Jack felt the progress he'd made thus far was solid. But he knew if his surveillance was to yield anything of value beyond what it already had, it wouldn't come by watching Dragon Man hang around his home shooting the breeze with a retiree in the middle of the day.

It would come at night, which was when most criminal activity of the gang-related persuasion tended to take place.

So after watching de la Cruz saunter inside the apartment/rooming house for the third time, he eased his rental car away from the curb and drove off in search of a reasonably-priced restaurant that wouldn't saddle him with heartburn for the rest of what was shaping up to be a very long night.

He was starving.

*　*　*

When Jack returned two hours later, he was driving a different vehicle.

He tried never to use his own Dodge Ram when he was working, for obvious reasons, and the Chevy Caprice he'd rented for use during his initial surveillance had been sitting in Dragon Man's neighborhood for the better part of the day.

He didn't think anyone had noticed it but wasn't willing to

take the chance of being wrong. Plus, there were no guarantees the Eight Street Dragons' operation was contained within the Lawrence city limits, and he didn't want to have to break off surveillance just when things were getting interesting because he hadn't had the foresight to rent a four-wheel-drive vehicle.

So he'd returned the Caprice after dinner and then rented a Toyota pickup at a different location. His first stop after leaving the rental agency had been a car wash, where he soaked the truck's exterior. Then he drove it straight to an off-road trail he'd located just outside Lawrence.

By the time he pulled to the curb in a spot close to where he'd parked earlier in the day, the vehicle was dusty and dirty and looked as though it hadn't seen the inside of a car wash in six months, if ever. It was perfect. It shouldn't be the least bit noteworthy among the hordes of late-model vehicles in the area.

Jack sipped a coffee and eyeballed the tenement house. There was no way of knowing how late he'd be working. No way of knowing whether de la Cruz would leave his home, or if he did, whether he might slip out a rear door to do so.

Jack wasn't particularly concerned about that possibility. Dragon Man didn't strike him as someone who would skulk around, certainly not in his own neighborhood, where maintaining street cred would be important. He guessed if de la Cruz did leave his home tonight, he would strut right out the front door.

That was Jack's theory, anyway, and he had to start somewhere. If it got late and de la Cruz hadn't yet made an appearance, Jack would take some time to conduct a visual inspection of the boarding house on foot. He would check for other entrances and maybe even strike up a conversation with one of the residents if possible, see if he could get some idea of the location within the building of Dragon Man's room or apartment.

The plan was extremely fluid, in other words.

Jack sipped his coffee and watched the building and waited to see what would happen next, if anything. There was less activity in the surrounding area than there had been in the middle of the afternoon, but it was still a busy section of the city, with a fair amount of pedestrian as well as vehicular traffic. That would undoubtedly change as the evening progressed.

* * *

Dragon Man left the building around 8:30. Unlike his earlier appearances, when he'd sauntered onto the porch to shoot the breeze with the old guy in the wicker rocking chair, this time he moved with a purpose. He still sauntered—Jack guessed de la Cruz wouldn't know how to take more than a dozen steps without putting on a show for anyone watching—but he crossed the now-empty porch without slowing and descended the stairs to the sidewalk two at a time.

Jack sat up in his seat and tracked de la Cruz's every step. Dragon Man was walking directly toward Jack's dirty pickup and for a moment he thought he'd been made, as unlikely as that seemed. About thirty feet before reaching Jack's location, Dragon Man stepped off the sidewalk and pulled a set of keys from his pocket. He unlocked an old blue Monte Carlo and slid behind the wheel and Jack smiled. Maybe things were about to get interesting.

Tailing Dragon Man was easy at first. De la Cruz's Monte Carlo was a distinctive-looking car, and it was still early enough in the evening that there was plenty of traffic, so leaving a gap behind the target to be filled by other vehicles was no problem.

Initially.

But as the subject moved from one neighborhood into an even sketchier one, traffic began to thin out. Jack wasn't willing to take the chance of revealing himself to de la Cruz, so he fell back. Then he fell back again. Eventually he reached a point where he was only able to catch an occasional glimpse of the Monte Carlo.

Still, he wasn't concerned. It was obvious de la Cruz wasn't going far. He was heading deeper into the bowels of the city, meaning he should arrive at his destination soon.

The surroundings grew steadily bleaker, abandoned buildings the rule rather than the exception. The few pedestrians out and about in this area were street people, vagrants and the occasional hooker, and when Jack had gone two minutes since he'd last had eyes on de la Cruz, he decided the man must have pulled off the road.

He swung a one-eighty on the nearly deserted city street and backtracked for a block before turning left at the first intersection.

Lawrence had once been a thriving mill town, and abandoned brick and concrete structures filled this area, some of them massive and all in various states of decay.

Not far away, urban redevelopers had reclaimed some of the old mills, repurposing them into restaurants and shops, bars and apartments. But it might as well have been a million miles from here rather than a few blocks. Here, the buildings stood empty, looming in the night, forlorn reminders of a city that had once thrived but was now struggling to reinvent itself.

Jack cruised slowly, paying close attention to the crumbling parking lots outside the abandoned mills. It was always possible de la Cruz had turned in to a garage or parked out of sight of the street, and if that was the case, Jack was obviously wasting his time. If he were unable to locate de la Cruz tonight, he would have to try again tomorrow and risk following the man more closely.

He doubted that would be necessary. These mammoth structures had been built long before underground or covered parking garages were a priority. He would simply zigzag south, covering the blocks immediately east and west of the street on which he'd last seen de la Cruz, and he felt confident eventually the blue Monte Carlo would turn up.

And he was right. Ten minutes after turning around, Jack spotted the target's car among a cluster of a half-dozen vehicles, all pulled nose-in to an old factory building that looked exactly the same as countless other structures he'd passed. De la Cruz was nowhere to be seen.

Jack continued past the factory, maintaining a steady speed. If de la Cruz or anyone else happened to look out a window they would see only a dirty truck of indeterminate age driving down the street away from the building.

Once out of sight of the old mill, Jack pulled to the curb and stopped the truck. He stepped out and locked it and began moving on foot back toward the Monte Carlo parked outside the big brick building. As he got close, he melted into the shadows and continued.

This section of the city was deserted, empty even of the vagrants and street people he'd seen earlier. It might mean nothing. Or it might mean even the denizens of the night knew a vicious street gang was headquartered here and they were smart or savvy enough to give these couple of blocks a wide berth.

Jack eased along the side of a concrete structure located directly across the street from the abandoned factory he assumed housed the Eighth Street Dragons. This building was much smaller, but still it loomed over Jack, large and silent and ghostly. He slipped into a decrepit brick-and-concrete entryway, confident it would provide adequate cover, and then he made himself comfortable— relatively speaking—and focused his attention on the other side of the street.

*   *   *

Nothing happened for a several hours.

By the time people started exiting the abandoned mill building it was well past two a.m. Jack had kept warm and alert—more or less—by moving around inside the sheltered entryway, doing occasional deep knee bends or running in place. But he'd wanted to maintain uninterrupted surveillance on the target, so for the most part he'd sat quietly, watching…nothing in particular.

The first thing that grabbed Jack's attention when people began piling out of the old mill, aside from the fact they were all male and all around the same age as Dragon Man, was the front door. Its exterior was dented and worn, entirely consistent with the overall condition of the building.

But when the door swung open Jack could see it was heavily reinforced, designed for maximum security. It looked as though it would prevent access to anything short of a rocket launcher. The obvious question was, why? Why would an abandoned building require a door suited more to a maximum-security prison than a clandestine meeting place?

Maybe because the Dragons use the interior for more than just planning drug shipments and running guns and hookers. Maybe because they use it as a clearinghouse for those items. Maybe they even use it to torture and murder innocent victims.

He forced his attention away from the door and onto the young men leaving the mill. To a man, they exhibited the swagger and exaggerated confidence Hector de la Cruz had shown during Jack's surveillance of his home, and as they dispersed toward their cars he counted three visible handguns, one being displayed in plain sight and the other two poorly concealed in shoulder holsters under light, unbuttoned jackets.

The men were making little effort at maintaining stealth. They spoke loudly, teasing each other and talking over one another in Spanish. If these were the Eighth Street Dragons they seemed secure in the knowledge they were safe from interference by the local police.

As the men walked to their cars, roughhousing and grab-assing, the reinforced front door swung slowly closed. Its steel panels were illuminated from the inside by what appeared to be some kind of security lamp, and Jack caught a glimpse of something stenciled in blood-red paint on the door.

It was a single word.

It was written in Spanish.

It said, "Dragones."

8

The last of the cars roared off into the darkness and Jack was alone.

He sat across the street from what he now was convinced was the Dragons' headquarters and considered his options. There weren't many that would advance his mission. In fact, there only seemed to be one.

He needed to check out the building.

And there was no better time to do it than now. He couldn't be sure it was empty—it was possible the Dragons stationed one or more sentries on-site twenty-four-seven—but if that were the case, tomorrow would be no better than now, and neither would next week or next month. And given the time, it was unlikely in the extreme that the men he'd just seen leave would be back tonight.

Jack could spend every evening crouched in the darkness, watching from across the street, and maybe over time learn most of the Dragons' secrets.

Maybe.

But he didn't believe in taking a passive approach when an active one was available. A much faster way to make progress would be to break into the building and conduct a little up-close and personal reconnaissance. A couple of hours spent inside might give him enough information to decide how to proceed with his mission: avenging Greg Daly.

He waited twenty minutes, more than enough time to allow any Dragon who might have forgotten something to come back and retrieve it. When no one had returned within twenty minutes, he figured no one was likely to.

He placed his binoculars into his backpack and zipped it closed, then shrugged it onto his shoulder and broke cover. Kept to the shadows and circled the Dragons' headquarters, approaching the building from the rear.

When he arrived behind the building he lurked in the trash-littered alley, alert for any sign of activity. There was none. After satisfying himself that the Dragons hadn't left a sentry patrolling the exterior—an unlikely occurrence but not an impossible one—he turned his attention to the old factory's roof, as well as the roofs of the surrounding buildings.

He was searching for security cameras. The best location on which to place CCTV surveillance would be up high and focused down on the area immediately surrounding the building. Jack doubted there were any cameras present, since security lighting was nonexistent around the exterior. But the skies were clear and the moon was full, and there was plenty of ambient lighting. It made a lot more sense to exercise caution than to take unnecessary chances.

He took his time, searching thoroughly, and could find nothing. No telltale domes protecting cameras from extreme weather conditions, no rectangular metal brackets housing eyes in the sky.

Once he felt as confident as possible he hadn't missed anything, Jack worked his gaze down the sides of the buildings. He studied each floor, one at a time, paying close attention to window frames and ledges, anywhere a camera or other surveillance device might be secured.

Still nothing.

By the time he'd studied the roof plus the two upper floors, Jack became convinced he wasn't seeing any surveillance cameras because there weren't any surveillance cameras. The Eighth Street Dragons were so secure in the knowledge they were untouchable by the Lawrence Police Department they didn't feel the need for video surveillance. And they'd long ago broken the will of local rival gangs. It was clear they felt they had nothing to fear from anyone.

Still, Jack took his time and continued his methodical search, moving floor by floor until he'd checked every level of the Dragons' building and all of the surrounding structures as thoroughly as he could in the dark and with the naked eye. It was possible he'd missed something, of course, but he didn't think so.

Finally it was time to proceed.

He crossed to the Dragons headquarters building, keeping to the shadows as much as possible but eventually having to cross an open expanse of parking lot. He moved quickly and quietly and then pressed himself against the cool brick wall next to what had at one time been a rear service entrance.

Up close it was clear this door had been custom fitted to the building, exactly as the front entrance had been. As was the case in front, the exterior was dented and dusty, but that was just for show. The door was top-of-the-line, expensive, designed to prevent unauthorized entry. It was about as far from original equipment on this old factory as it was possible to get.

A small slit had been cut into the middle of the door at eye height and covered with a heavy wire screen, also exactly as was the case in front. There was a doorknob that Jack knew would be locked but one he decided to try anyway. Stranger things had happened than a gangbanger forgetting to secure the rear entry to what should be a secure facility, and he would feel pretty silly scaling a sheer wall or breaking in through a window if he could simply have entered through an unlocked door.

He grasped the knob and turned and nothing happened. Not a wiggle. It was as if the door was part of the wall and wasn't meant to open at all.

Calling it "secure" would be an understatement.

Jack fished out his lock-picking tools and got to work. The lock was a high-end model, designed to resist efforts like Jack's. It took what felt like forever to gain access, and once he'd broken the lock, he turned the knob and was entirely unsurprised at the result: still nothing. The door had been dead-bolted from the inside, with no exterior lock available to pick.

Jack shrugged and moved to the closest window. The mill was ancient, easily more than a century old, and at the time of its construction there had been no building codes in existence covering the number of windows required, because they were few and far between.

Of the ones he could see, all had been boarded up with plywood.

The wood fully covered every window on every floor and had obviously been placed with dual intent: to keep unwanted visitors out and prevent passersby from seeing within.

He unzipped his pack and rummaged around until finding and removing a claw-handled hammer. Prying one of the plywood sheets away from a window would not have been his first choice—it would be noisier than he preferred and would also provide the Dragons evidence that someone had been snooping around—but he couldn't see any reasonable alternative if he wanted to gain access to the building tonight.

So he would do what he had to do.

He examined the sides of the window, where the plywood had been secured to the frame, looking for screws and finding none. The wood slabs had been fastened from the inside, which only made sense from a security perspective. It would have been nice to unscrew the plywood and then replace it when he had finished, but he'd known all along that possibility was a long shot, which was why he'd pulled a hammer from his pack rather than a screwdriver.

He felt around until locating a small area where the edge of the wood had warped a bit. It was slightly spongy and bowed outward. Not much, but enough for Jack to slip the claw of the hammer into the narrow gap between the plywood and the frame.

He seated the hammer and paused. Took a deep breath. Held it for a moment and then blew it out. Then he jammed the hammer's handle against the brick wall.

The plywood splintered with a *crack* that sounded about as loud as a gunshot in the three a.m. stillness. *Guess I'm about to find out if anyone's here.*

Jack drew his weapon and retreated into the shadows. He left the hammer and backpack under the window. If the building were empty the tools wouldn't matter. If a sentry came to investigate the noise, Jack would use his supplies as a lure to draw the Dragon into the open.

He waited two minutes. Three. The silence was uninterrupted.

He continued to wait. *Patience is a virtue.*

When ten minutes had passed and no one had opened the door or looked through the slotted opening or come prowling around the corner of the building or done anything at all, Jack crossed the parking lot one more time to the window he'd started jimmying. He kept his gun in his hand although he was by now convinced no one else was here.

When no one had challenged him by the time he arrived at the window, he slipped his weapon back into its holster and picked his hammer up off the pavement. He pried more of the plywood off the frame, and when enough had been stripped, the extent of the Dragons' security measures became clear: they had installed heavy iron bars running from the top of the window to the bottom.

The boarded-up windows were just for show. The iron bars provided the actual security. Obviously the Dragons hadn't wanted to advertise the fact that they'd gone to the trouble and expense of securing what appeared to be a crumbling, abandoned husk of a building. They wanted it to look no different than all the other empty shells.

That's interesting, Jack thought. It had become apparent he wasn't going to access the Dragons' lair tonight. He'd brought nothing with which to cut through the thick iron bars on the window, and it would have made no sense for the Dragons to secure one window this heavily if they weren't going to do the same with the others.

Jack's plan had been to climb to the roof if unable to access the building through a door or window, and now even that felt like a waste of time. Why would the gang take such stringent measures to protect their headquarters at ground level unless they were willing to do the same thing everywhere?

But he was already here, and he still had a couple of hours before sunrise. Once the Dragons realized someone had been sniffing around, they *would* station sentries to protect their turf, and Jack would never get another opportunity to recon the area undisturbed.

So he would make good use of his time.

He circled the structure until locating an old cast-iron fire escape. It was inaccessible from ground level, but that wouldn't be a problem. Jack lifted a length of coiled nylon rope out of his pack: he carried thirty feet, and that would more than suffice.

He tossed one end over the lowest rung of the ancient ladder, letting it fall to the ground at his feet. Then he picked it up and twisted the ends together and began climbing hand over hand, praying the iron hadn't rusted through so badly it would snap and drop him flat on his back onto the pavement.

It took maybe twenty seconds to reach the lowest level of the fire escape, and the good news was that the structure held. The bad news was that his shoulders and arms were burning and he was breathing heavily after a relatively minor physical exertion. Ten years ago he could have climbed the damned rope five times as high as he had tonight and felt twice as good as he did right now when he'd finished.

Getting old sucks, he thought. He took a moment to gather himself before finishing the climb to the roof of the four-story building. When he vaulted over the retaining wall he moved directly to the only access door, knowing it would be locked and shrugging at the confirmation. This door seemed every bit as sturdy as the other two Jack had seen.

He checked the knob but didn't waste his time picking the lock. There was zero chance this door wouldn't be dead-bolted from the inside, exactly as the first floor entrance had been.

The only remaining possibility to gain access to the building's interior was through a vent shaft. A mill building this old would probably have vents plenty large enough for a grown man to crawl through, but the Dragons had been so thorough in securing the structure it seemed beyond unlikely they would have ignored or forgotten about the ductwork.

They hadn't. There was a pair of oversized covered vent shafts on top of the roof, one on each side. Both had been secured using iron bars, exactly like those on the windows.

Jack sighed and returned to the fire escape. He clambered over the side and down the three stories to the lowest rung. Then he slithered down the rope to the ground.

It had been a long night and he was exhausted, and although disappointed he hadn't been able to access the building, the night hadn't been a total loss. The "Dragones" written on the interior of the front entrance confirmed for him that this was, in fact, the home of the Eighth Street Dragons.

And the lengths to which these men had gone to fortify their little clubhouse told him something important, too. Only an outfit that had a lot to hide—like torturing and murdering innocent victims—would bother with the kind of defensive measures present in this old mill building. Not even a regional heroin clearinghouse would justify this kind of extreme security.

Before leaving for home, Jack picked out two more boarded-up windows to attack with his claw hammer. Even the most careless of gangs would notice the damage he'd done to the window nearest the rear door, and the Dragons didn't strike him as careless. Dangerous and psychotic, maybe, but not careless. Since there was no way to hide the fact he'd been here, he wanted to emphasize it instead.

Maybe there was a way to use it to his advantage.

It took less than five minutes of vigorous work for Jack to inflict the damage to the building he wanted, and then he packed away his rope and his hammer and hiked back to his rented truck. He had some thinking to do in the morning.

Right now, though, all he wanted was sleep.

9

Mr. Stanton's choice of locations for their rendezvous surprised Jack. During his more than eight-year career working for The Organization, every meeting Jack had had with Mr. Stanton—*Norbert,* Jack thought, and smiled—took place in the city of Boston or one of its immediate suburbs.

And there had been a lot of meetings.

Discussions regarding the particulars of the dozens of contracts he'd fulfilled were always accomplished face-to-face, never via email or telephone. Those methods of communication could be hacked or intercepted, whereas it would be nearly impossible for authorities to conduct surveillance of a meeting in a public location that had been set up with virtually no advance notice.

Jack had long suspected the United States government was not particularly interested in interfering with The Organization's work, anyway. The shadowy group was responsible for taking some extremely problematic and dangerous sociopaths off the board, and there was plenty of incentive for authorities to look the other way.

That said, there was also no reason to take unnecessary chances. Thus the constantly changing Boston rendezvous locations.

This time, though, Mr. Stanton had suggested they meet at the Roger Williams Park and Zoo, located outside Providence, Rhode Island. It was nearly an hour south of Boston, far from Mr. Stanton's usual haunts. But Jack wasn't in any position to argue, and whether he drove an hour from southern New Hampshire down to Boston or continued for an extra hour to Providence didn't make a damned bit of difference as far as he was concerned.

He would have driven to Florida if necessary, to get what he needed. He'd been reluctant to contact his former handler but knew his chances of decimating the Eighth Street Dragons without help, based on what he'd learned last night, were just about nonexistent.

So he'd swallowed his pride and set up a meeting.

He parked outside the zoo and bought a ticket at the entrance. Mr. Stanton would reveal himself at his leisure, and in the meantime Jack began walking along one of the gravel pathways. He made it several hundred feet along a wooded trail, then turned a corner and there was his contact.

Mr. Stanton was dressed as always in a long overcoat and expensive gray suit, a thin black tie on his chest and fedora perched on his head, looking like he'd just stepped out of a 1940s noir film. Jack had always thought the man's look was so retro he should appear in black and white.

The older man smiled thinly and fell into step next to Jack and the two of them strolled companionably, saying nothing at first, as was their habit.

"So," Mr. Stanton said after a fashion.

"So," Jack agreed.

"Nice day," Mr. Stanton said, and Jack didn't bother answering. It really was a beautiful morning. "The sun is shining and the birds are chirping."

"This is a zoo," Jack reminded him. "There are so many birds here I imagine the apocalypse could happen and it wouldn't eliminate the chirping."

"Probably true."

"This is an unusual choice of meeting places," Jack offered.

Mr. Stanton stopped and smiled again. "I like to expand my horizons whenever possible." They resumed walking and the older man said, "Retirement not holding the allure you anticipated?"

"It's okay," Jack said. "Why do you ask?"

"Well, as pleasant as it is to see you—and I do enjoy seeing you, Jack, you've always been one of my favorites—I assume you're not here to pass the time idly or to swap lies about our better days."

"You know why I'm here."

"Excuse me?"

"You heard me."

Mr. Stanton chuckled. "I'm not sure how powerful you think The Organization is, Jack, but contrary to what you seem to believe, we don't have the ability to read minds. Not yet, at least."

"You sent him to me, didn't you?"

"I sent who to you, son?"

"Larry Daly. Maybe you remember him? Former operator. Son's a cop in Lawrence. That son is currently missing and almost certainly dead."

"Ah," Mr. Stanton said. He rubbed his chin and nodded. "Yes, well, Mr. Daly needs help, and the sort of help he requires would seem to be right up your alley, wouldn't you agree?"

"Sure. Except for one small detail."

"That being?"

"I'm retired."

"And yet here you stand."

"You could have sent that poor man to an active Organization member. Instead you sent him to me. You knew his story would move me, and you knew I'd agree to help him. And you also knew that to help him I would need to come to you."

"The Eighth Street Dragons do seem quite the formidable opponent."

"You're trying to pull me back into The Organization."

"As I said, you've always been one of my favorites, Jack."

"I'm also getting old. This kind of work is for kids in their twenties. Hell, when I started doing it in the military I was a teenager. I'm now closer to forty than thirty."

"You're not giving yourself sufficient credit, Jack. Talent is talent, regardless of age. But perhaps a conversation vis-a-vis your future with The Organization would be better suited—"

"I'm retired," Jack interrupted.

"For later," Mr. Stanton finished. "You already mentioned you agreed to take on Mr. Daly's case and you need my help."

"That's right," Jack agreed grudgingly.

"Tell me what I can do for you."

Jack outlined the basics of his plan and when he'd finished, Mr.

Stanton remained silent for a long time. The only sound was the crunching of their shoes on the gravel pathway and, of course, the ever-present chirping of hundreds of species of birds.

When he finally spoke, he sounded strangely subdued, even for a man to whom displays of exuberance were anathema. "Sounds risky," he said.

"They're all risky."

"True enough," Mr. Stanton agreed. "But this seems especially so."

"The Dragons' headquarters is impenetrable. I know, because I tried to penetrate it last night."

"No location is impenetrable."

"Maybe not, but unless you want to send me an M1 Assault Vehicle and maybe a shoulder-fired rocket launcher or two, this is the best plan I can come up with. Assuming, of course, The Organization's emphasis on maintaining stealth at all times and operating in the shadows hasn't changed in the two months I've been gone."

Mr. Stanton smiled. "I could, of course, get you those items."

"But."

"But your point is well taken. Our emphasis has not changed."

"So you'll get what I asked for?"

"There is a bit of a problem."

"Of course there is. And what would that problem be?"

"The problem, Jack, is that we're not in the habit of assisting vigilantes. You claim to have retired from The Organization, and yet here you are, requesting our help. It's nothing personal, but it is still a problem. I'm sure you understand."

"I understand you engineered this whole situation to put me in the middle. Come back to work and get the assistance I need to help a grieving old man, or stay retired and either die at the hands of a violent street gang or return to Mr. Daly and tell him there's nothing I can do for him."

Mr. Stanton remained silent. Jack knew he should be angry at the man's blatant manipulation, but he couldn't quite manage it. He'd known Mr. Stanton for a long time, and while he would have liked to consider them friends, he knew that was not entirely accurate. Mr. Stanton ran The Organization with a ruthless efficiency, and while he undoubtedly was telling the truth when he said he was fond of Jack, he would do whatever was necessary to maintain its peak performance. If manipulating his former operator helped accomplish that, it was what he would do, no more and no less.

And if he was being honest with himself, Jack could not deny he missed the rush that had until recently filled his day-to-day existence: the thrill of the chase, the jolt of adrenaline that fueled a mission, the sense of satisfaction that came with completing a dangerous assignment successfully. He'd quit in part because of his age, but mostly in hopes of salvaging some kind of relationship with Edie Tolliver, even if only one of friendship.

But Edie was the one who'd insisted he *take on* this freelance job. Whether that meant she was now fine with his status as an Organization assassin remained unclear, but she had obviously come to grips with the fact he'd spent his entire professional career operating inside one massive gray area.

Jack realized he'd stopped walking. He was leaning against a wooden podium upon which a placard had been fastened outlining the mating habits of the Red-Crowned Crane. Mr. Stanton stood next to him. He still hadn't spoken.

"If you acquire what I need to complete the Daly job," Jack said, choosing his words carefully, "I'll consider coming back to work, possibly on a limited basis. I'll *consider* it," he repeated for emphasis.

Mr. Stanton lifted his fedora off his head and swiped a hand through his hair. Then he replaced the hat and said, "Ms. Tolliver is beginning to see your vocation a little more clearly after the situation with her daughter, isn't she?"

Jack's initial reaction was to snap at Mr. Stanton, to tell him to leave Edie, and especially Janie, out of the conversation. But he bit his tongue. He needed The Organization's help and wasn't the least bit surprised by Mr. Stanton's knowledge of his personal situation. Maybe The Organization didn't yet possess the ability to read minds, but it seemed they might be a damned sight closer than most would believe possible.

"Yes," he answered. "She is."

"I'll see what I can do about your request," Mr. Stanton said. "Do you still have your encrypted email account?"

"You know I do."

"Good. Check it regularly and I'll notify you when I have what you need."

"Thank you."

"No problem. I look forward to resuming our professional relationship."

"I told you I'd consider coming back," Jack said, "not that I definitely will. It's not a commitment. It's not a promise. It's not anything."

But it was too late. He was wasting his breath. Mr. Stanton had spun on his heel and was already walking away. Jack shook his head and chuckled, gazing out at the birds.

10

When the phone buzzed on Big Tony Mercadante's desk, he fixed it with an angry glare. It was a look that would have turned the insides of almost every member of his crew to jelly had it been focused on them.

Jesus Christ. He'd told fucking Janousz out in the fucking reception area he didn't want to be fucking disturbed.

Less than five fucking minutes ago.

And now the fucking phone was buzzing.

Tony stabbed at the button with one fat finger and almost buried it inside the phone's plastic console. "What part of 'Don't fucking bother me' do you not understand?" he spat into the phone. Literally spat.

The boss of Vegas's biggest organized crime family weighed well north of three hundred pounds, with fleshy jowls and three chins, and when he got angry—which happened a lot—Big Tony's salivary glands tended to shift into overdrive, flooding the immediate area like a partially plugged fire hose. Gang members who'd been around awhile were savvy enough to take a discreet step or two back from the desk just before delivering bad news.

Tony wiped the phone's handset on his shirt while he waited for an answer. He'd recruited Janousz Bejko into his organization a few months ago, and English proficiency was not one of Janousz's primary skills.

Killing was Janousz's primary skill.

He'd been one of Eastern Europe's most lethal assassins for

more than a decade before flying to the states to join Big Tony's crew, and while his language skills were improving daily, it still often took Janousz a little time to translate what he was hearing into Polish or Ukrainian or whatever the fuck language he spoke in his head and then formulate a response in English.

"I understand all of it," Janousz finally responded. The words were heavily accented, of course, and it took Tony a moment to decipher them.

When it became obvious no further explanation was forth-coming, he spat—literally again, unfortunately—"Then why the fuck am I talking to you right now?"

"The caller says he is someone you will want to talk to." With Janousz's accent, the statement came out, "Zee coaler says hee ees sahmone yoo weel wahnt to toke to."

Jesus Christ, Tony thought. *Janousz might be one of the best, but damned if he doesn't try my fucking patience.* "Well, who the fuck is it on the phone?"

"He says his name is Stanton."

Stanton. Why does that name sound familiar? The information was right there, slithering around in his brain, but he couldn't quite access it even though he had a sneaking suspicion it was important. "What's his first name?"

"Mister."

Tony would have thought Janousz was fucking with him, but the man didn't have a wiseass bone in his body. He was straight-forward and direct, no screwing around. It was one of the things Tony appreciated about him because it was a rarity in the Vegas organized crime world, where everyone thought he was fucking Kevin Hart. Besides, Janousz didn't know the language well enough yet to discern shades of meaning.

"Mister Stanton?" he said. "Who the fuck is—"

And then it came to him. The Organization's head man was a guy named Stanton. Not Tony's organization, not another of Vegas's crime families, or any other outfit. Stanton represented *The Organization,* the shadowy group of paid killers who had made it their mission to rid the world of the worst of the worst. The Organization eliminated terrorists and psychopaths, evil men and women from whom even other killers and criminals cowered if they had any goddamned sense.

The Organization had sent an operative to Vegas not long ago to deal with just such a man inside Big Tony's family who'd caused immense problems before being put down.

Without another word to Janousz, Tony stabbed at the flashing white button to activate the line and talk to the person on the other end. He had no idea what Mr. Stanton could possibly want, but keeping him waiting one second longer than absolutely necessary struck Tony as an exceedingly bad idea. Not to mention a dangerous one.

The connection went through and Tony said, "Mr. Stanton, what a pleasant surprise. How are you doing on this fine morning?"

"I'm well, Mr. Mercadante. I assume your days are passing a little more smoothly now with Mr. Standiford out of the way?"

"Much smoother, thanks for asking. I've given that situation a lot of thought and I still can't figure out how your guy pulled off the whole 'home invasion gone wrong' scenario using some psycho from New York City."

When Stanton answered, Tony could hear the smile in his voice. "We sent one of our best. I'm glad to hear you're satisfied with the result."

Big Tony Mercadante wasn't accustomed to currying favor with anyone; it was the sort of thing people typically did with him. But keeping Stanton happy seemed like a wise move. "Extremely satisfied," he said. "But I have to admit I'm surprised to hear from you. I was under the impression we'd never speak again."

"In most situations that would be true," Mr. Stanton said. "However, something's come up with one of my operatives. It's the man who worked on your case, in fact."

"Okay. I still don't follow. What does that have to do with me?"

"My man has taken on a freelance assignment, and to complete it he's going to need professional assistance. Now, I could provide one of my other operatives, but I happen to know you've recently acquired a hitter from Poland. I'm familiar with his work and believe your new addition would be perfectly suited to the task of assisting my operative."

"Janousz Bejko," Tony answered, speaking slowly. "How the hell did you know...?"

"It's my business to keep abreast of these situations," Stanton replied. "I hope you don't think I'm boasting when I say I probably know more about Mr. Bejko's professional history than you do."

Tony blinked. This conversation was getting stranger and stranger. "Nah," he finally said. "I don't think you're boastin'. But what are you asking me?"

"I'd like to borrow Mr. Bejko for a very short-term operation. Or, to be more precise, I would like to rent him."

"Rent him?"

"Yes. The Organization would fly your man to the Boston area where he would assist my operative. At the conclusion of the operation we would fly him back to Las Vegas. We will put him up in five-star accommodations while he is here and will pay all his expenses as well as a significant stipend. We will also, of course, pay you a handsome rental fee as a token of our appreciation."

"Define handsome."

"Say, five thousand dollars for Mr. Bejko, and an additional twenty-five for you. It shouldn't take longer than a week and, in fact, may require much less time than that, perhaps as little as a day or two. But regardless of length, you and your man would keep the full amounts."

Big Tony had negotiated literally thousands of deals over the course of his criminal career and he couldn't recall one single time when he'd accepted anyone's initial offer, regardless of what was being negotiated. There was a first time for everything, however, and he couldn't quite bring himself to counter.

Maybe he could wring an extra five grand out of Stanton if he really worked at it. Maybe. But getting twenty-five large for sending Janousz on a job was a fucking windfall, particularly since the hitter would be thrilled to get his five. It would get Janousz off Tony's ass about doing some real work, and the hitter could sharpen his skills on a job that wouldn't affect Tony in the least.

More importantly, Tony's stomach had been doing flip-flops ever since he'd figured out who was on the other end of the line. Something in Stanton's manner suggested barely contained violence, in spite of the fact the man came across like a trust fund pussy, with his east coast accent and crisp Ivy League diction.

Tony just wanted to get him off the line.

"That sounds fair," he said. "When do you need Janousz?"

"As soon as possible. Tomorrow works, today would be better."

"He can fly out in two hours."

"Perfect. A first-class ticket will be waiting for Mr. Bejko at the National Airlines desk at McCarron, say for Flight 316 to Boston at two-twenty?"

Tony checked his watch. It was eleven-thirty in the morning. "That doesn't give you much time to buy the ticket. What if the flight's full?"

The note of amusement returned to Stanton's voice. "Not to worry. That won't be an issue. The ticket will be available upon Mr. Bejko's arrival at the airport, and the rental fee will be in your liquid assets account within the hour."

"Excellent. Let me get you the account number."

"No need," Stanton said. There was that damned smile in his voice again. "I have it."

Tony blinked again in surprise. For a guy who'd risen through the ranks to the top spot in Vegas's premier criminal enterprise— and someone who considered himself as crafty and manipulative as they came—he felt off-balance and confused. He bit his tongue before asking the obvious question of *how in hell* The Organization would have that information, deciding it might be better if he didn't know.

"Sounds good," he said weakly.

"Thank you so much for sharing a man as talented as Mr. Bejko with The Organization," Stanton said, pretending not to notice Tony's weakness. "I won't forget your generosity."

"It's my pleasure."

The line went dead and Tony sat back in his chair and took a deep breath. He realized the armpits of his shirt were soaked through, even more so than usual.

He took a moment to compose himself and then buzzed the front desk. When Janousz answered, he said, "Get in here. We need to talk."

11

As far as Judge Lowell Stevenson was concerned, Caller ID technology rivaled the development of the remote car starter as among the finest inventions of his lifetime. Because the moment his cell started ringing, he knew who was on the other end of the line. That knowledge gave him the opportunity to prepare a suitable mindset for the conversation that would follow.

If the caller were, say, someone from the DA's office, he would get ready to answer in one way. If the caller were a defense attorney, he would be ready for a slightly different kind of conversation. If Hector de la Cruz were on the line, Lowell's mindset would again be completely different.

And if the caller was Lawrence Police Chief Tim McKenna, Lowell knew he would be in for a bumpy ride.

He glanced at his phone's screen and sighed deeply. Rubbed a hand across his face. Pressed the green button to answer the call. "Hello, Tim. How are you doing today?"

"Lousy. Really lousy."

Jesus Christ, I am sick and goddamned tired of listening to this little pussy piss and moan. "I'm truly sorry to hear that. What's bothering you?"

"You know what."

"Tim, listen to me. You need to find a way to deal with the pressure and whatever guilt you're mistakenly feeling. Everything's fine."

"If you say so."

"I do."

Silence.

McKenna was becoming a problem. He was cracking under the strain of the Greg Daly situation. Even though that whole mess was now more than two months in the rear view mirror, McKenna couldn't seem to let it go.

The chief's depression was visibly worsening; that fact was obvious to Lowell, who spoke to the chief almost every day and visited with him at least once a week. While Lowell couldn't bring himself to give a damn about the feelings of one oversensitive little bitch, what he *could* do, and quite easily, was worry about how the feelings of one oversensitive little bitch affected Lowell Stevenson.

And those feelings could potentially affect him in the most negative way possible. McKenna wasn't as connected with the Dragons as Lowell was, not even close. But he knew enough about the inner workings of the gang, particularly in regard to Greg Daly's murder, to upset the entire apple cart if he decided to crack and spill his guts to the FBI or the DEA or DHS.

Any one of the alphabet soup federal agencies could bring everything crashing down in Lawrence, and if everything came crashing down, many of those bricks would fall directly onto Lowell. He would be sent to prison for decades, a sentence that would be rendered moot by the fact he wouldn't last six months trapped on the inside, sharing space with many of the killers, rapists and other sociopaths he had incarcerated over the years.

His power would be gone, his reputation destroyed, and he would die in prison, just another anonymous con shivved in the shower, bleeding out while inmates stepped over and around his body.

That outcome was unacceptable, obviously. Lowell wasn't about to go down thanks to the crumbling psyche of one supposedly tough-as-nails police administrator who couldn't stand the heat but couldn't find his way out of the kitchen.

All of this flashed through Lowell's brain in less than a second. After all, this wasn't the first time he'd considered the situation, and every time he did he reached the same conclusion.

Meanwhile, the silence on the telephone stretched out like a deserted highway.

Lowell cleared his throat and said, "I'm going to figure out a way to help you deal with the stress, Tim. How does that sound?"

"It sounds impossible. What's done is done, and unless you can turn back time I'm afraid you'll be spinning your wheels no matter what you do."

"You let me worry about that. I have a couple of ideas about how to deal with the issue. I just need to work through them and determine our best course of action."

"Fine. If you say so."

Lowell clamped down on his burgeoning anger and tried to put a smile into his tone. "I do say so. You just hang in there and be strong, my friend. I'll talk to you soon."

"Fine."

He disconnected the call and tossed his phone down on the desk. Sat for a long time, staring across the room at nothing in particular and thinking hard.

Then he picked up his phone again and made a call.

12

Hector de la Cruz didn't even get inside the front door of Dragons headquarters before being met by a grim-faced Omar Garcia, who headed him off on the crumbling sidewalk and said, "We have a problem."

"Tell me."

"Someone tried to get into the building last night."

"How do you know?"

"Follow me," Omar said, and led the way around the side of the structure.

They had no sooner turned the rear corner and begun approaching the access door when Hector spotted the damaged plywood. It was impossible to miss. The wood had been pried away from every first floor rear window and hung in tattered ruins. Splintered strips of plywood lay on the ground beneath each window like victims of a Dragons beating, while the rest had been pulled partially away from the openings.

"Did they get inside the building?" Hector asked quietly as he approached the damage for a better look.

"I don't think so," Omar said. "Nothing is missing or damaged inside, and the bars covering the windows don't appear to have been touched."

"What about the roof?"

"Same thing. The bars look undisturbed."

Hector glared at the offending plywood, squinting as if staring directly into the sun. He was no longer examining the damage as much as he was trying to determine who might have been ballsy enough—or foolhardy enough—to attempt such a straightforward assault on his building.

"Death Squad?" he muttered. The Death Squad crew had at one time been locked in a bitter war with the Dragons for control of the drug trade north of Boston. The Dragons had decimated their rivals through a series of very public and very bloody assassinations of Death Squad leadership, reducing the gang to irrelevance. Or so Hector had assumed.

"That was my first thought," Omar said. "But I've seen no indication Death Squad has even tried to regroup in any meaningful way, much less have the *cojones* to come at us so directly."

Hector nodded. "And Death Squad was well aware of our security measures. They would have known about the bars on our windows and brought along something they could use to cut through them. Whoever did this," he spit in the direction of the plywood littering the pavement, "was caught by surprise."

"What do you want to do about it?" Omar said.

"Good question. We obviously cannot respond until we know who or what we are dealing with. Until we can make that determination, I want at least one Dragon here twenty-four/seven. Develop a sentry schedule and implement it beginning tonight."

Omar nodded. "Maybe it was a one-time thing. Some stupid kid playing around."

"Maybe," Hector said. "But that would have to be one *very* stupid kid. Either way, I want to be prepared. We are the Eighth Street Dragons. We play offense, not defense. We take the fight to the enemy, always."

He'd just turned toward the rear entrance when his phone rang. He spit a curse and lifted it from his pocket, glaring at it like he'd glared at the damaged plywood a moment ago.

"Jesus Christ," he said, and punched the button to answer.

13

"What is it?" Hector de la Cruz always sounded like he was in the middle of committing violent murder when he answered his phone. Lowell had called him dozens of times over the years and his Eighth Street Dragons contact had always answered with exactly the same words, spit out in exactly the same manner.

"Hello, Hector, it's Judge Stevenson."

"I know who it is."

"We need to talk."

"No shit. I figured that the second my phone rang. I'm listening."

"Not over the phone. In person."

Lowell could hear de la Cruz mumbling under his breath and for a moment he thought the kid would refuse to see him. Then he said, "Alright. Give me twenty minutes. We will meet in the usual place."

De la Cruz hung up without waiting for an answer.

* * *

Rodriguez Salvage Yard was located on a sprawling lot just over the Lawrence/North Andover line. The place was isolated, the surrounding area heavily wooded, and a visitor to the yard would get the impression he was the only human being for a thousand miles in any direction as he bumped along the extended dirt driveway.

The place was a front for Dragons operations. It served as a legitimate salvage yard, with the rusting hulks of wrecked cars, trucks and buses littering its many acres, but its main purpose was to serve as a secluded meeting place for the Dragons and the home away from home of their criminal enterprise.

Lowell felt the familiar flutter of nervousness as he turned from the road into the Rodriguez yard. His stomach rolled and he wondered—as he did every time he came here—how many bodies were buried among the Chevys and the Fords and the Toyotas in this creepy automotive graveyard.

He rolled to a stop in front of a low-slung concrete block building and stepped out of his car. Walking toward the office he could feel the weight of multiple eyeballs tracking him, even though as far as he could tell he was alone.

Hector de la Cruz was waiting for him as he stepped through the door. The man nodded wordlessly toward the rear of the building and then turned in that direction. He didn't wait to see whether Lowell followed. They threaded their way through the shop, dodging partially rebuilt engines, transmission parts and other auto-related items awaiting pickup by customers. Lowell couldn't identify most of the parts and didn't care.

They exited a rear door and began a walk around the junk-car graveyard along a pathway with which Lowell was by now thoroughly familiar. The trail was formed of equal parts dying grass, weeds and loose dirt, and Lowell knew that by the time he'd finished speaking with Hector his black dress shoes would become a dirty dull brown and the cuffs of his trousers would be the same, requiring immediate dry cleaning.

He didn't care about that, either.

They moved far into the acres of cars and still Hector remained silent. He didn't walk as much as he stalked, like a beast of prey preparing to pounce on its next meal, and the sensation of violence radiating off the man was palpable.

Not to mention terrifying.

When he finally spoke, it was with a paucity of words. "You wanted to talk to me. Here I am. Talk."

Lowell had been rehearsing what he wanted to ask de la Cruz on the drive from the courthouse to the salvage yard, but it still took a moment to corral his nerves and speak. The Dragons' leader was that intimidating. "When do you expect to hold your next initiation ceremony?"

De la Cruz stopped and fixed Lowell with a glare. "What did you say?"

Lowell cleared his throat and attempted to put a little firmness into his voice. He was a circuit court judge, for chrissakes. De la Cruz wasn't the only one who could project an air of authority. "I said I want to know if you've set a date for your next initiation ceremony."

"That's why you called me? That's why we're meeting out here in the middle of the day when we could both be doing other things? Because you can't wait to observe your next torture session?"

Lowell glared at the man despite his nervousness. "No, I called you for something critically important. We have a problem, and that problem is getting worse. And I think the best time and place to deal with it might be at the next Dragons initiation."

"What are you talking about?" De la Cruz had started walking again, and Lowell considered how odd they must look to anyone watching; not that anyone was: the heavily muscled olive-skinned man with the dragon tattooed across his skull and the overweight white middle-aged man sweating through his dress shirt.

He said, "I'm talking about a potential threat to all of us. Chief McKenna knows far too much about what happened to that cop you used as the subject of your last initiation, and he's crumbling. I'm afraid he's going to talk soon, and to the wrong people."

De la Cruz smirked. "So? Let him talk. He wasn't there. Any information he has is secondhand and cannot be proven. Without a body—and the dead cop will never be found, believe me on this—he cannot hurt me, or any of the Dragons."

"But he can hurt *me*," Lowell said, raising his finger and jabbing it at de la Cruz.

The Dragons leader flashed a look at Lowell, and Lowell immediately dropped his finger but continued speaking. "He certainly has enough to send me to jail, or at the very least destroy my career and my life."

"Not my problem." De la Cruz affected a look of disinterest.

"Of course it's your problem," Lowell countered.

De la Cruz stopped short, his mouth turning down into a frown and his eyes darkening. "I hope you are not threatening me, Mr. Big-Time Judge. Rolling on me or any of the Dragons would be very unhealthy for you."

"No, no, that's not what I'm saying," Lowell answered quickly, his heart hammering in his chest. "I just mean if I go away, you lose access to the judiciary. Your men disappear into maximum-security prisons for decades instead of receiving short sentences or even probation in many cases. Unless you want to start developing a relationship with another judge—which might take years and may not even be possible—we need to deal with this issue as a team. We all want the same thing."

De la Cruz had not stopped staring directly into Lowell's eyes, and now he fixed Lowell with a look he could not quite decipher. The short soliloquy was probably the greatest number of words he'd ever spoken to the Dragons' leader at one time, and he began to worry he'd overstepped his bounds and might end up joining Officer Daly and the other Dragons victims buried under these rusting old automotive hulks.

But when de la Cruz answered, his voice was soft, measured. "So what do you propose to do about it? Tell me why I should not simply send a couple of men to wait outside the chief's home with AR-15s and cut him in half one evening when he comes home from work."

"You have the right idea," Lowell said. "I think we've reached the point where we must, unfortunately, eliminate the chief. He is a danger to everyone and putting him in the ground is the only feasible solution."

"*We?*" de la Cruz said wryly. "You are not a Dragon, my friend, you are merely an occasional observer of one of our rituals. So *we* must not do anything."

"Point taken," Lowell said. "But since Chief McKenna's situation affects me every bit as much as the Dragons—more so, really—we are at the very least riding in the same boat for the time being."

"Fine," de la Cruz answered. "I will ask again. If you do not like my plan for taking out the chief, what is your proposal?"

"I already said I agree the chief must be disposed of. I just believe taking him out in such a...public way would bring far more attention than either of us needs. It might just be the final straw and draw the federal authorities to Lawrence, which in turn might bring everything crashing down on us."

De la Cruz made a circular *hurry up* gesture with his hand. "Your plan, Judge. What is it? Maybe you have so much free time you can afford to hang around a fucking junkyard all day, but I do not."

"My plan is simple. We lure Chief McKenna to the next Dragons initiation and use him as the centerpiece."

De la Cruz raised an eyebrow and the corners of his mouth curled up in amusement. "By 'lure' you mean kidnap."

Lowell shrugged. "Whatever it takes."

"And explain to me what the difference is between killing him outside his home and killing him inside our headquarters. Are you telling me if we chop off his fingers and torture him to death we *won't* face the kind of scrutiny from the feds you just described?"

"That's exactly what I'm telling you, provided the situation is handled properly. In your scenario McKenna bleeds out on his front lawn, another victim of escalating gang violence. In my scenario the chief simply disappears. No one knows for sure he's dead. Maybe he skipped town because he had a mistress, or because he owed a lot of money to his bookie. Maybe anything."

"May I remind you Officer Daly simply disappeared, too."

"Sure, he disappeared, but too many people know what really happened to him. We have to make sure we don't make the same mistake with McKenna."

The amused look on de la Cruz's face had disappeared, replaced by one of attentive consideration. "You have given this a lot of though, haven't you?"

"Of course I have. It directly affects me and my future: specifically, whether or not I have one."

"So, fill me in. How do we avoid making the same mistake with McKenna we made with Daly?"

"The focus of your upcoming initiation ritual stays just between you and me. We make sure no one else knows Chief McKenna will be sitting in the victim's chair."

"They'll know when my men kidnap him."

"Your men aren't going to kidnap him."

"You've lost me."

"All I need to know is the date and time of the next initiation. Leave McKenna to me. I'll get him there."

De la Cruz grinned. It transformed his expression from latent evil and violence to joy. For just a moment the leader of one of the most dangerous criminal organizations on the East Coast looked almost innocent.

Except for his eyes. His eyes remained hooded and dark, unreadable.

When he spoke, his words took Lowell by surprise. "Perhaps I spoke too soon about you not being a member of the Eighth Street Dragons. Perhaps you should not just observe the next initiation, my conniving friend. Perhaps you should participate."

Lowell's heart began hammering in his chest, thudding like a freight train pounding down the tracks on a long straightaway. He felt a stirring in his trousers as he began to get hard just thinking about slamming the long handles of the gardening shears together, and seeing/hearing Tim McKenna's fingers plink onto the blood-stained concrete floors as the man who'd become a massive thorn in his side screamed for mercy that was never going to come.

He should reject de la Cruz's suggestion immediately. Becoming an Eighth Street Dragon could not possibly end well. He was too high profile, too established in the community. It would be a mistake, a stupidity of a magnitude he could probably not even imagine.

He cocked his head. "We'll see."

14

Jack Sheridan was intimately familiar with Boston's Logan International Airport. He'd flown into and out of the facility dozens of times traveling to and from assignments, and had met Mr. Stanton here to discuss missions more than once as well.

But cooling his heels waiting to meet an arriving passenger was a new experience.

Fifteen minutes in he'd already decided it was an experience he could do without. People were everywhere, milling about as they, like Jack, awaited an arrival or rushed to find their departure gate or just did…whatever. Jack was a solitary individual, uncomfortable in crowds when not stalking a target, and the constant commotion of a big-city airport was every bit as annoying to him as a mosquito buzzing around his head while trying to fall asleep.

He couldn't wait to meet his contact and get the hell out of Dodge.

The man's name was Janousz Bejko, and he would be arriving on National Airlines Flight 316 from Las Vegas, due to land at any moment. Mr. Stanton had said Bejko was one of the best, and Jack believed it without reservation. The Organization's policy was to spare no expense in support of their people, and while Jack preferred to operate alone, he had never failed to be impressed with the quality of the contractor on those occasions when one had been required.

It was even possible Bejko was an Organization member himself. Jack doubted that was the case, because Mr. Stanton had told him that prior to coming to the States Bejko had been one of the most accomplished hitters in what used to be known as the Communist-bloc states. So unless The Organization maintained a Eurasian branch—always a possibility—it seemed likely Bejko had been a freelancer in his old career.

Jack would never know for sure, because Mr. Stanton would never tell him. Rule Number One in The Organization was to maintain strict operational secrecy at all times. Each Organization operator had one contact—Jack's was Mr. Stanton—and was never provided direct knowledge of other Organization members unless absolutely necessary.

The benefits of this arrangement to The Organization were obvious: should an operator be apprehended during the course of an assignment, he or she could not possibly implicate anyone besides his or her handler. And the operator's knowledge of any details regarding that handler was extremely limited as well. Mr. Stanton's name was almost certainly not "Norbert Stanton," and whether he lived in Boston or Providence or Salem, New Hampshire or anywhere else on the eastern seaboard Jack had no idea, nor did he have a clue where The Organization's base of operations was situated.

To an observer, the benefits of this arrangement at first glance might have seemed one-sided, with all of the risk being assumed by the operator. And as far as it went, that was true.

But the risk to the operator was made palatable by The Organization's first-rate support system: anything he or she might need to complete an assignment was provided, with little apparent regard for cost. Weapons, clothing, credit cards, multiple false identifications, whatever. Jack had never had a reasonable request turned down.

And another benefit was significant, as well. Jack had heard rumors of operators being apprehended by law enforcement while on assignment, and those operators being provided—free of charge—the finest legal representation available. They were just rumors, of course, and Jack had no desire ever to learn whether or not they were true.

But he believed them.

So without even meeting Janousz Bejko, Jack knew the man

would be solid and reliable, as well as lethal when the time came. But that knowledge did little to make him feel better as he waited among crowds of sniffling children and short-tempered travelers.

Finally, passengers from the arriving National Airlines flight began straggling through the jetway tunnel into the terminal building. Mr. Stanton had texted Jack a snapshot of Bejko, but the picture was decidedly low quality: grainy and slightly blurry, like the person taking the picture had done so surreptitiously.

Janousz Bejko had been told his contact would be wearing a San Francisco 49'ers baseball cap, and Jack adjusted it on his head as the passengers began entering the main terminal building. He wondered whether a guy from Eastern Europe would have any clue what the hell a "San Francisco 49'er" even was, but he supposed that knowledge was irrelevant. Bejko had undoubtedly memorized the logo and color scheme, and that was all that mattered.

Jack assumed the man would be among the first people to leave the plane, for the simple reason that The Organization would have flown him here first-class. And he was right. He recognized the assassin the moment the hitter turned the corner from the tunnel.

Bejko was an unassuming-looking little man, probably no taller than five-seven and maybe one hundred forty pounds after eating a big meal. Clearly younger than Jack, he was also prematurely balding, and perched on his nose were a pair of ridiculous-looking black horn-rimmed glasses.

Elvis Costello, Jack thought.

He walked forward to meet the hitter, sizing the man up as he went. Bejko appeared harmless and overmatched as he peered around the terminal. He looked like the kind of guy who would struggle to beat up a ten-year-old even if the kid spotted him the first punch.

In other words, he was perfect. The last thing a professional assassin wanted was to stand out in a crowd. Being memorable meant...well...*being memorable* to witnesses. Obviously that was something to be avoided if an operator expected to have a long career.

Jack himself had been as successful as he had for as long as he had for the very reason that he—like Janousz Bejko—was entirely unmemorable. Good-looking without being remarkably handsome, not too tall or short, average weight. A man in whom no second glance would be warranted when he passed people on the street.

Jack approached with a smile. "Mr. Bejko," he said as he offered his hand. "I'm Jack Sheridan."

"Call me Janousz, please," the man said. He took Jack's hand and shook it firmly, and they turned without another word and began walking toward the Central Parking lot. Jack had a healthy respect for operators as closed-mouthed as he, and Bejko seemed to fill the bill.

Once inside Jack's truck they could chat. There would be plenty of time to do so on the way to New Hampshire after meeting up with Mr. Stanton.

* * *

Today's rendezvous took place at a small Italian bakery in the North End. Jack had requested an item from The Organization that he thought might come in handy during the Dragons operation, and of course Janousz needed weaponry. He certainly couldn't carry a gun on a cross-country airline flight.

Everything was to be delivered by The Organization's head man himself.

Mr. Stanton was waiting inside a nondescript gray minivan parked in a narrow alley next to the bakery upon their arrival. Jack had never rendezvoused here before, but he got the distinct impression the location was a regular delivery point for Organization materials. The alley was quiet and secluded and private—not a single window from any of the surrounding buildings opened onto the location as far as he could tell.

Inside of ninety seconds the transfer of the requested items was complete and the items stashed away under a blanket in the back seat of Jack's truck.

Then the three men strolled out of the alley and around the corner into the bakery. The proprietor was an elderly Italian man who was so small he made Janousz Bejko look like Andre the Giant. The shopkeeper greeted Mr. Stanton warmly and Mr. Stanton responded by wrapping his arms around the man in a gentle bear hug.

The action was so out of character for the reserved Organization boss that Jack stopped in his tracks, eyebrows raised. When Mr. Stanton clapped the old man on the shoulder and pulled away, Jack waited for an explanation or some form of introduction, but none was forthcoming. The proprietor retreated behind his counter and Mr. Stanton waved Jack and Janousz over to a table. Jack looked a question at his contact and Mr. Stanton simply winked.

The scene was among the most unexpected Jack had ever witnessed, and he made a mental note to ask Mr. Stanton about it at some point in the future. It was obvious he would be seeing a lot more of his former and once again current contact, regardless of the fact he'd only said he would "think about" coming back to The Organization.

It was becoming ever clearer that retirement would have to wait.

Mr. Stanton selected a box of cannoli for Jack and Janousz, for which the old Italian guy refused to accept payment. He waved off the proffered cash with cheerful insistence and it occurred to Jack that at some point The Organization had done something significant for the shopkeeper.

The three men took a seat at a small table and each enjoyed a cannoli along with a cup of some of the strongest coffee Jack had ever tasted.

He loved both.

Twenty minutes later, Mr. Stanton had departed for…wherever Mr. Stanton went when he wasn't meeting Jack.

And the assassin from the United States and the assassin from Eastern Europe were motoring up I-93 for New Hampshire, tools of their deadly trade stashed in the rear of the club cab and a box filled with cannoli on the console between them.

15

Lowell Stevenson wasn't convinced Hector de la Cruz was taking his concerns about Chief Tim McKenna with the seriousness they deserved.

McKenna was cracking like a Christmas pecan, his mental state deteriorating rapidly, and at the end of Lowell's meeting yesterday with de la Cruz inside the Rodriguez salvage yard, he hadn't gotten the impression the Dragons' leader was planning to move as quickly as Lowell believed necessary to implement the plan of attack that would save their asses.

Or at least Lowell's ass, which was really the only one he cared about.

So when Lowell's cell phone rang—the secret one, the phone nobody in Lowell's legitimate world knew existed—he was moderately surprised to see Hector's number on the call screen.

Lowell called Hector every now and then, and although he knew de la Cruz hated hearing from him he didn't let that stop him if he had business to discuss. But it was a rarity for a call to come from the other direction. Virtually the only time Lowell ever heard from Hector was when the Dragons were setting up an initiation. He would call, pass along the date and time to Lowell, and be off the line almost before Lowell could respond.

Lowell rose from behind his desk. He padded to the office door and closed it firmly.

Then he locked it.

Then he punched the green button on his phone and answered. "Yes?"

"You said you were worried about a security leak."

"You're damned right I'm worried."

"You mentioned a possible solution to our little problem. Were you serious about implementing that solution?"

"I wouldn't have wasted my time meeting with you if I weren't serious."

"Then I believe we should proceed. I've considered your plan and I like it. We have a few prospective new members, so instead of waiting, I am ready to move forward with their entry into my organization. We will move quickly."

"How quickly?"

"How soon can you get your hands on our security problem?"

"Tell me when. I'll make it work."

"Tomorrow night."

"The usual time?"

"Yes. The usual time."

"Consider it done." Lowell pressed the button to disconnect the call and felt a rush of adrenaline pounding through his body that was unlike anything he'd ever experienced. Even the feeling he'd had while observing his very first Dragons initiation a couple of years ago paled in comparison to this.

He had risked everything the moment he first set foot inside the Eighth Street Dragons headquarters, but if he went through with what he had proposed to Hector de la Cruz—and he *was* going to go through with it—he would graduate from mere observer of beautiful atrocities to active participant. There would be no going back.

He was breathing heavily.

He was hard as a rock.

He couldn't wait.

16

Almost no one knew Jack's cell number. Mr. Stanton had it, of course, and so did Edie. That was it. The phone was reserved solely for his work as an Organization contractor, making it critical he maintain its secure status. The device—and the number—were changed regularly, at the Organization's expense.

So when it began trilling in his pocket, he didn't hesitate to answer despite the fact he did not recognize the incoming number. "Hello."

"Hello, Mr. Sheridan?"

"Who's asking?"

"This is Larry Daly." The moment the man said his name Jack kicked himself for not immediately knowing who was on the other end of the call. He should have remembered giving Daly his number and should have recognized the voice as well.

It was a minor, mostly harmless mistake, but Jack knew it wouldn't have happened ten years ago.

"Mr. Daly, good morning. It's a little soon if you're looking for an update. I don't have anything new to tell you, and even if I did we wouldn't have the conversation over the phone. Please know I'm working hard on your case, and as soon as I know anything, I'll—"

"I have some information you might want."

Jack glanced at his watch. He had a lot to do and not much time to do it. Holding Daly's hand couldn't be part of his itinerary, however badly he felt for the old man. Still, giving the guy another ninety seconds of his time wouldn't kill him.

He said, "Did you remember something you might have forgotten to tell me when we met?"

"No, this is new information."

"Where would you have gotten new information?"

"Over the years I got to know some of Greg's cop buddies pretty well. I used to host cookouts for the guys and gals he worked closely with. A lot of those cops were just as broken up about Greg as I was, or close, anyway. We keep in touch and one of them called me a few minutes ago."

"Is it something concrete? Something I can use?"

"I think so, yes. You need to hear this."

"Are you familiar with Wagner Park in Manchester?"

"I know where it is, yes."

"Can you meet me in thirty minutes?"

"I can be there in twenty."

"I'll be near the Greek style temple at the northern edge of the park."

* * *

Jack didn't believe there was any way Larry Daly could make it to Manchester from Lawrence in twenty minutes, but he was there waiting just in case, and sure enough, nineteen minutes after they hung up the old man climbed out of his car. Maybe he'd been in the area when he called. He crossed the park's sun-splashed open field at a brisk pace but looked pale and drawn as he offered Jack his hand.

"Thank you for meeting with me," Daly said.

"Of course." Jack answered. "I hope you don't mind me saying you look tired. I doubt Greg would want you putting yourself in the grave over this."

"I am tired. Nothing I can do about it. I fall asleep and the nightmares start. I wake up screaming and can't get to sleep again for hours." He shook his head and smiled weakly. "It's kind of ironic."

"How so?"

"You remember I told you I was once an Organization operator like you?"

"Of course."

"All the things I did and saw while working for the Organization, all the nasty shit I took part in, I always slept like a baby. Never had a single bad dream. Now, after what happened to Greg, I doubt I'll ever get a good night's sleep again."

Jack wanted to offer a word of encouragement but had no idea what to say. He understood perfectly, because he'd always slept just fine, too, until the last few months. Now it was a rare night he didn't wake up in a cold sweat picturing little Janie Tolliver trussed up in an out-of-the-way cabin on Lake Winnipesaukee, her future depending solely on Jack's ability to find her and save her.

"You have information for me?" he finally said.

Daly nodded. "As I told you on the phone, one of Greg's cop buddies called me. Edgar was just as convinced as Greg that the Eighth Street Dragons had compromised the Lawrence Police Department's command structure."

"And?"

"And Edgar grew up in the city, in one of Lawrence's roughest areas. He's maintained a close relationship with some of the guys from his neighborhood, including a couple of friends who went a different direction than Edgar."

"They joined the Dragons."

"Yes."

"And one of them became a CI."

Daly half-shrugged. "He's not officially a confidential informant, not exactly. But he does pass along the occasional bit of intel."

"Is he reliable?"

"Edgar seems to think he is, and so did Greg. I don't have any first-hand knowledge on the subject, of course, but I wouldn't have called you if I didn't feel it was solid."

"Okay. What did Edgar tell you?"

"Something big is happening tomorrow night."

"Big how?"

"Edgar's contact didn't say. But what he did say was that the top rung of Dragons management is going to gather at their headquarters tomorrow night to, and I quote, 'rectify a situation.'"

"He didn't say what that situation was?"

"No. But he did say that the rank-and-file Dragons members are not invited."

Jack ran a hand through his hair and stared into the distance. Across the park a young mother was watching her three kids closely as they cavorted on the open lawn. "Did Edgar's man have anything else to say?"

"No, that was it."

"So the upper level of Dragons management is all going to be together tomorrow night. Alone. Rectifying some unknown situation."

"I thought you would want to know."

"You thought right. I'm sure de la Cruz and his men will bring along a couple of goons to act a s security, but they'll never expect to be hit right on their own turf. It sounds like quite the opportunity."

"That was my impression, and why I called you as soon as I hung up with Edgar. I wish I was younger, I would handle this situation myself."

"I know," Jack said. "But I'll take care of it exactly as you would. You have my word on that."

Larry Daly didn't answer. Jack noticed he was watching the woman herding her kids across the field, a wistful smile on his face. "I've got to run, Mr. Daly," he said. "I have a lot of work to do."

Daly nodded, tears in his eyes. He was still watching the kids play as Jack drove away.

17

Janousz Bejko took a bite of cannoli and shook his head. He met Jack's eyes with a look of confusion. "My knowledge of your language is improving, but I am afraid I must have misunderstood you."

The two men were seated at Jack's tiny kitchen table, discussing the upcoming operation and Janousz's role in it. They had eaten grilled steaks and baked potato, and were now drinking coffee and working their way through the remainder of the North End desserts Mr. Stanton had provided.

Jack smiled. "I think you probably understood my words correctly."

"Then I do not understand your reasoning."

Mr. Stanton had told Jack that in addition to being highly skilled and ruthless in the execution of those skills, Janousz Bejko was smart as a whip and extremely intuitive. He was proving it now.

Jack took a sip of coffee and said, "Walk me through it. Tell me what you're having a problem with."

"I understand there is a group of murderers you need to eliminate."

"Correct."

"And that group of murderers is using as their headquarters a building that is difficult to access."

"Very difficult."

"Alright then. I do not understand why your plan does not

consist of the two of us making a simultaneous assault on the front and the rear of the building. I do not understand why you would allow yourself to be captured by this group of criminals, and why I must wait twenty minutes after your capture to then make an assault on the building. It seems to me that this plan increases the risk to both of us, but most especially to you."

Bejko shook his head and took another bite of cannoli. He was clearly mystified. "It seems to me this plan increases the risk by a lot. Why would you do that?"

Jack took a moment before answering. Janousz's question was a good one. It was one he had asked himself multiple times, going back to before he'd even contacted Mr. Stanton for help.

"I took on this job," he said, speaking slowly, "as a favor to an old man who is suffering. The man's son disappeared months ago. He was kidnapped by this gang of thugs and there has not been a trace of him seen since."

"He is dead," Bejko said simply.

"Yes. He is most certainly dead."

"You still have not answered my question."

"I don't want to simply avenge the death of the old man's son. I want to know what happened to him."

"Why?"

It was a one-word question.

One syllable.

Three letters.

There were few simpler words in the English language, and few more complicated ones.

"I'm not sure," Jack admitted. "At first I told myself it's because I want to be able to provide the old man with details, but if what was done to his son is as brutal as I fear, I could never share the information. It would probably kill him."

"So again, why?" Bejko spread his hands in confusion.

"I just need to know," Jack said. "For myself. I need to know."

Janousz cocked his head to the side. "I have worked with many assassins over the course of my career. I have only been working inside the United States for a few months and so have little experience here."

"You come very highly recommended," Jack said.

Bejko nodded. "Thank you. But I wanted to make a point."

"And that is?"

"Many of the men and women I have worked with in the past were the equal of anyone you could find operating inside the United States at any price. They were highly skilled and deadly. And out of all those people, I have never worked with anyone who looked at the world the way you seem to."

Jack grinned. "Thanks. I think."

"Knowing what happened to the man we are working to avenge does nothing for you, and yet you are willing to put yourself at significant risk in order to gather that information."

"That's where you're wrong," Jack said. "It does do something for me."

"What could it possibly do for you?"

"It helps me understand. I need to understand."

The two men fell silent and Jack assumed the subject was now closed. They ate their cannoli and sipped their coffee in companionable silence.

When Janousz spoke, his words surprised Jack. "You come very highly recommended to me as well."

"Thank you," Jack said. "But where would you possibly have gotten any information on me?"

The hitter smiled. "You might be surprised. Secrecy is critical in our profession, but information is sometimes available if you know where to look. I know where to look."

Jack raised his eyebrows. He'd lived his entire adult life inside a shroud of secrecy—or so he thought—and it was more than a little unsettling to discover this man, whom he'd never met or even heard of until just a couple of days ago, had been able to gather intel on him. It was always possible Bejko was blowing smoke, but Jack couldn't imagine what he would have to gain by doing so.

Across the table, Bejko grinned. It was an impish look, and it radically transformed the face of a man Jack had already discovered was typically drawn and quiet. "I apologize if my words have disturbed you," he said. "That was not my intention."

"I just prefer people know less about me than more."

"As do I, my friend."

The kitchen fell silent again, and after a moment Jack's curiosity got the best of him. "What was your intention?"

"Excuse me?"

"You said your intention was not to disturb me with what you said. What was your intention?"

The smile returned to Janousz Bejko's face. "I merely wished to make an observation, and that was the prelude to my observation."

"Okay. And what might your observation be?"

"That you do not strike me as a man who possesses the personality typical of a professional assassin."

"Is that so?"

"Yes. I long ago learned not to feel."

"Not to feel what?"

"Anything. I learned not to feel or to question. An assignment to me is exactly that: an assignment. Nothing less but certainly nothing more. I put everything I have into completing that assignment successfully and then move on to the next one. But you…"

"Yes?"

"I believe that you feel too much. It is dangerous to feel too much in our profession, Mr. Sheridan."

Jack didn't know how to respond. It was a good point. It was one he'd considered at length over the past several years.

It was also one he couldn't bring himself to dispute.

18

Lowell's initial instinct was to contact Tim McKenna immediately to set up their meeting. He was anxious to get the show on the road, so to speak, and the fact of the matter was that McKenna presented a real and serious threat to him, a threat that was becoming more dangerous with every passing day.

But a quick review of the situation convinced him to exercise a modicum of patience, as difficult as that would be. McKenna had recently been calling him nearly every day, sometimes multiple times daily, as his mental state deteriorated and his panic took hold, and Lowell assumed today would be no different.

If he waited just a little while McKenna would be in touch. And if the chief contacted him, rather than the other way around, that should minimize the likelihood of McKenna's suspicions becoming aroused.

At least until it was too late.

And Lowell's assessment, as usual, was right on target. He didn't have long to wait, either. Less than an hour after taking the call from Hector de la Cruz, Chief McKenna's number was buzzing on Lowell's cell. *This is almost going to be too easy,* he thought as he stabbed at the button to answer the phone.

Before he could even say, "Hello," the chief was talking into his ear. "I don't think I can take this any longer," the man said. "I've got to come clean. I can't eat, I can't sleep, I'm screaming at my wife from the moment I get home from work until the moment I go to bed, I can't—"

"Slow down," Lowell said soothingly. He was so incredibly sick of this merry-go-round, of listening to the same old crap from the spineless pussy day after day. Ordinarily at this point in the call, he would be gnashing his teeth in frustration, itching to tell McKenna to just do the world a favor and eat his service revolver.

Today, though, it was different. Today Lowell was as serene as Mahatma Gandhi. The whole untenable situation would be over after tomorrow night and he would never have to listen to McKenna bleat again.

The chief ignored Lowell's words—of course—and instead of slowing down, he plowed right on ahead with his whiny, self-pitying blathering.

Lowell raised his voice and tried again, this time putting an edge into his words. "Tim," he said sharply. "Stop talking for a second and listen to me."

"What is it?" McKenna said miserably. "What can you possibly say that will change anything?"

"I've been giving your situation a lot of thought," Lowell said, shifting back into soothing mode. "And I've come up with a solution that I believe is going to work well."

"Solution? What solution could there possibly be besides me telling the DA's office everything?"

"You can confess if you truly feel you need to."

"Are you serious? I have to be honest, Lowell, that was not the sort of reaction I expected from you."

"Tim, we've known each other a long time, wouldn't you say?"

"Of course. You're among my oldest friends."

"Exactly. And as your friend, I can see how badly you're suffering. I don't want you to torture yourself." *I want to do it, instead,* Lowell thought, and grinned wickedly, grateful this was a phone call and not a video chat.

"It's a relief to hear you say that. Because I literally do not believe I can carry this weight any longer."

"It's no problem, Tim. All I ask is that you do me one favor before making the appointment to speak with the DA."

"A favor? What is it?"

"I'd like you to see someone, to speak to a man of my choosing."

"See someone?" McKenna's confusion was plain. "You mean, like a counselor?"

"That's right," Lowell said. "That's exactly right. A counselor of sorts. It's someone I've used myself on occasion, and for quite some time. Almost since this whole Eighth Street Dragons business started, in fact."

"You've been receiving counseling?"

"Not on a regular basis. But yes. Of sorts."

"I just don't see what good counseling would do in my case. I'm certain I'm not going to feel better until I can make amends for all the damage I've caused with my Dragons association."

"I understand. That's why I only ask that you do me this one favor. I'm so convinced this is what you need that I've already made the appointment for tomorrow night. If, afterward, you're still determined to confess to DA Andrews, I will fully support your decision. In fact, I'll accompany you. We can do it the following day."

Silence.

Then, "Are you serious, Lowell? Because this sounds completely unlike everything you've been telling me for weeks."

For the first time since answering the call, Lowell felt a tiny tug of concern. He'd been having fun, playing with McKenna, and it seemed he might have laid it on a bit too thick and perhaps begun to make the chief suspicious. Even in the depths of his depression and all-consuming guilt, he was still a career law-enforcement officer, after all.

Deep breath. Answer in a tone filled with gravitas and concern for his friend's wellbeing. "I am serious, Tim. One hundred percent so. And don't misunderstand what I'm saying. It's not going to be easy for you to morrow night. It may well be painful. Agonizing, even. But, as I said, I've given this plenty of thought, and I believe it's exactly what you need."

"But...tomorrow night? What kind of counselor works at night?"

"This is not typical counseling, Tim. It's a little more... unorthodox."

"I-I guess...wait a minute. I can't do it tomorrow night. I'm scheduled to speak to the school board about security concerns in the Lawrence school system. It's the last thing I want to do, God knows, I can hardly keep my mind on work when all I can think about is this Dragons mess, but I *am* scheduled."

"You need to do something for yourself, Tim. You're digging yourself into an early grave." *Earlier than you realize, in fact.*

"That is so true."

"You're obviously not thinking clearly, so here's what I want you to do," Lowell said. "Have your administrative assistant cancel for tomorrow night with the school board. Don't say anything to anyone about counseling, though. Your personal issues do not need to become part of their or anyone else's agenda. All anyone needs to know is you've fallen ill. You can reschedule the school board meeting for sometime next week."

"I'll be in jail by sometime next week."

"Not necessarily. Keep an open mind, Tim, and give my idea a chance."

McKenna sighed, the sound whistling through Lowell's earpiece like a hurricane. God, Lowell couldn't wait for this unnecessary drama to be over. "Fine," the chief said, his voice almost a whisper.

"Good man," Lowell said heartily. "You're doing the right thing." *For one of us, anyway.*

"We'll see about that. What's the therapist's address?"

"It's a little hard to get to, so why don't we meet for dinner first and then I'll drive you to the appointment?"

"That's not necessary, Lowell. I've been a police officer in this city for thirty years. I'm sure I can find the office, wherever it is."

"I insist. I have nothing else on my schedule for tomorrow night, and I truly do want to accompany you. We're in this together. So stay home from work tomorrow and then meet me at Marconi's at, say, seven in the evening. How does that sound?"

Another sigh, this one more forlorn than the first. "Very well."

"I'll park at the rear of the lot so my car will be easy to find. Look for me there."

"Will do. And Lowell?"

"Yes, Tim?"

"Thank you for trying so hard for me. I know I haven't been an easy man to be around lately."

"Not a problem."

"Honestly, I don't think I ever realized what a true friend you are."

"Not at all," Lowell answered truthfully. "Not at all."

19

Lowell had tried to make McKenna believe he chose Marconi's to meet for dinner on the spur of the moment, but the truth was he had given the subject a lot of thought.

First of all, there would be no dinner. There was no way on God's green earth Lowell would allow himself to be seen dining in public with a man who was going to disappear off the face of the earth in a matter of hours.

Even meeting McKenna in the Marconi's parking lot was a risk, but there was no way around it if Lowell wanted to be finished with the man by tomorrow. They had to join up somewhere, and it couldn't very well be at the Dragons' headquarters. The chief of police knew that particular street address every bit as well as did Lowell, even if McKenna had never been there in person. The minute he heard it, the game would be up.

So after a good deal of risk/reward analysis, Lowell had settled on Marconi's as their meeting place. The restaurant had a well-deserved reputation for offering quality food, but served a more middle-class clientele than did most of the dining establishments Lowell chose to frequent. This lowered the likelihood he would be recognized while loitering in the parking lot waiting for McKenna.

There was one other advantage to Marconi's, and it was critical: the lot was dark. Really dark. The restaurant was nearly as legendary for their poor exterior lighting as for their outstanding cuisine. Lowell felt confident he could get in there, pick up McKenna, and get out while minimizing his exposure, particularly if he confined himself to the outer fringes of the lot.

Things seemed to be progressing nicely. Lowell had had butter-flies in his belly since convincing McKenna to go for "counseling" on the phone yesterday, and the butterflies were getting more active the closer it came to tonight's main event.

He figured a little nervousness was understandable. His partic-ipation in tonight's activities would be equal parts foolhardy and exhilarating.

He couldn't wait.

20

Jack felt uncomfortable and off his game as he finalized preparations for tonight's assault on the Eighth Street Dragons.

This entire mission felt markedly different from the type of assignment he'd excelled in over the course of his career, and had from the very beginning. He was a hunter, an aggressor, a man to whom facing danger was a given, but who typically received an assignment and then executed it. The concept of passive victimhood was utterly foreign to him, and yet tonight he would voluntarily offer himself up as a victim to one of the most ruthless street gangs on the eastern seaboard.

It was not a comfortable feeling.

Plus, he preferred working alone, but tonight he would take a major leap of faith, putting his trust—not to mention his life, in all probability—in the hands of another operator. And Janousz was not just another operator, he was a virtual stranger, a man unknown to Jack barely twenty-four hours ago.

If Janousz Bejko turned tail and ran at the wrong moment, Jack would almost certainly die tonight.

If Janousz stood and fought but did so tentatively or used poor judgment when things went sideways, Jack would almost certainly die tonight.

And there was another possibility as well. Jack and Janousz could fight well, using solid tactics and outthinking their enemy, and they could still both die tonight. They would be outnumbered by what was likely to be a substantial margin and their only tactical advantage would be surprise. If they did not make the best use of that advantage, they would both end up bleeding out on a dirty, ancient floor.

And for what? Jack wasn't getting paid. No money had exchanged hands—at least not his hands—and even if he was successful in ending the Dragons' reign of terror tonight, none ever would. Larry Daly was an old man living out his years in anonymity; a long-ago operator who had probably socked away enough cash on which to survive his "golden years," but who was obviously not rich.

And even though Mr. Stanton had referred Daly to Jack, and even though the Organization had provided weapons and support, this was not technically an Organization assignment, so no pay would be forthcoming from that corner, either. In fact, Jack knew the opposite was true. Mr. Stanton had spent a lot of money in support of Jack's freelance mission, and he would expect something in return, assuming Jack survived.

Something like Jack's renewed association with The Organization.

With all of that as a background, Jack's acceptance of this mission made little sense. Yet he felt more strongly committed to tonight's mission than he had to any Organization assignment in a very long time.

Maybe that was due to Larry Daly's status as a former Organization contractor. Maybe in Daly Jack saw himself forty years down the line, a man itching to right a wrong but physically no longer able to do so.

He suspected also that this operation struck a chord with him because of the intense emotional bond he'd formed with Edie Tolliver and little Janie. The grief and fear and sense of helplessness he'd experienced when Janie was kidnapped less than three months ago had been nearly overwhelming. It was easy to imagine Larry Daly's anguish in knowing how much his son had likely suffered.

Only for Daly, the pain would be much worse, because Janie had been recovered basically unharmed, while Larry Daly's son was gone forever.

All this was going through Jack's head when a knock came

at his front door. He glanced across the room, eyebrows raised, mystified as to the possible identity of his visitor. Janousz was relaxing at his hotel in Manchester, and would remain there until Jack picked him up later this afternoon.

Larry Daly had been here a few days ago, but there would be no reason for him to return.

For a man who treasured his privacy and rarely received guests, Jack's home had recently begun to feel a little too much like Grand Central Station.

He padded into his living room.

Pulled the curtain away from the picture window as a second knock sounded.

Blinked in surprise.

Edie's Tolliver's car was parked in his driveway.

Jack hurried to the front door and pulled it open to find Edie standing on the small landing. "Edie? Is everything alr—"

She launched herself into his arms and as he wrapped them around her he realized she was saying something. He was squeezing too hard, though, pressing her face into his chest and making her muffled words impossible to understand.

He released his grip on her and she stepped back. "—so sorry," she was saying.

"You're sorry?" he said. "For what? What's the matter, Edie?"

She breathed deeply and ran a hand through her shaggy blonde hair. "May I come in?"

"Of course," Jack ushered her down the hallway to the kitchen and said, "You're always welcome here, I would hope you know that by now. And you never need to knock, either. Just turn the knob and come in, and if the door's locked, use your key. You still have your key, don't you?"

"I do," she said. "But it didn't seem right just walking into your house considering…you know…our situation."

Jack busied himself making coffee as Edie slipped into the chair Janousz had occupied yesterday. "Our situation," he said, "as I understand it, is that we're friends. Whether or not we ever advance beyond that—as we did before—is irrelevant to the current topic of conversation. As my friend you are always welcome in this house, at any time and under any circumstances."

"Thank you, Jack. You're so…thank you."

"No worries. Now, what's going on? Why did you show up here unannounced—not that I don't love seeing you—and tossing out apologies for no particular reason?"

"It's not for no reason. It's for a very good reason."

"Well, fill me in then. Because for the life of me, I can't think of a single thing you have to apologize for."

Jack poured two coffees and joined Edie at the table. He placed one in front of her and took a sip from the other.

Edie blew delicately on her coffee and said, "What's happening with the Larry Daly situation?"

"I'm making progress," Jack said evenly. "Why do you ask? And what does that have to do with this feeling you seem to have that you owe me an apology?"

"It has everything to do with it. Jack, you're putting yourself in harm's way for Mr. Daly because of me. I was the one who guilted you into retiring when I found out what you did for a living. And then, once you did that, I guilted you into getting right back in the saddle. And now, if you get hurt—or God forbid, killed—trying to help Larry Daly, it will be all my fault, and I'm so, so sorry."

Jack reached out and placed his finger gently on her lips. They were soft and moist and warm from coffee. "It's true that I value your opinion," he said. "But you didn't browbeat me into giving up my career after Janie got kidnapped, and you didn't guilt me into resuming it, either. We all have to answer to ourselves, Edie. And while I will always give serious consideration to anything you have to say, on any situation, I also take full responsibility for the decisions I make. That was true before we ever met, it's every bit as true today, and it will continue to be the case in the future, no matter our relationship."

"But these Eighth Street Dragons people sound so…awful."

"They are awful. That's a pretty good reason why they should be shut down, don't you think?"

"Sure. But I hate that you have to be the one to do it."

Jack shrugged. "You said it yourself. Who else will? The Dragons have the locals in their pockets."

"I've been giving a lot of thought to this question, and I think the federal authorities would be the best bet."

Jack smiled at Edie. Her hair was wind-blown and she looked upset, but she was still the most beautiful thing he'd ever seen. "You want to know what I think?" he said.

"Of course. That's why I'm here."

"I think you're letting your concern for my well-being cloud your judgment. And while I appreciate that concern more than you know, I think you recognize that involving the FBI or another federal agency would be a mistake. It's possible they would take action. Eventually. But what's the one thing the federal government is known for?"

Edie answered instantly. "Bureaucracy. Red tape. Inefficiency. Ass-covering. Shall I go on?"

Jack couldn't hide a grin. "No, you've made my point for me. So the question is, how many more innocent people will die while the feds conduct an investigation and line up enough ducks in a row to make them feel comfortable prosecuting, if ever?"

Edie was silent. She stared at Jack over the rim of her coffee cup with eyes that were large and frightened and beautiful.

"Scenarios like this are exactly why The Organization was formed in the first place," Jack said firmly. "If ever there was a situation that demanded an Organization-type response, this is it."

"I don't want you to die," she said, her voice a papery whisper.

"I'm not going to die. I'm not going to end up in the hospital. I'm not going anywhere," he said softly. "You're not getting rid of me that easily, I promise."

He hoped he wasn't lying.

21

Jack picked Janousz up from his hotel nice and early. The sun had just started its steady slide toward the western horizon and wouldn't fully set for well over an hour, and both men were already seated inside Jack's rental car as it moved south on I-93 toward the Massachusetts line.

The entire mission would take place in the dark, but Jack wanted to take advantage of the waning daylight to familiarize Janousz as much as possible with the neighborhood surrounding the Dragons' lair. They would keep their distance, of course, but he felt confident they would be invisible to any gang presence as they cruised the area in a several-years-old Ford Focus.

This was the ultimate seat-of-the-pants mission. Larry Daly had said tonight's meeting would include only high-level Dragon membership, but neither Janousz nor Jack had any idea how many men that entailed, nor how heavily armed they would be.

Likewise, they had no familiarity with the layout of the old mill's interior. Perhaps only part of one floor was being used by the Dragons; perhaps the gang had retrofitted the entire building.

So, given all the uncertainty they would face inside the Dragons' headquarters, Jack knew it might be critical they at least have a working knowledge of the blighted block surrounding their target.

It seemed they were facing long odds, but Jack told himself he and Janousz held the upper hand in at least a couple of areas. Their biggest advantage would be surprise, obviously. Even though the Dragons would by now realize someone had attempted to access their facility, they would never expect a full-on assault, especially not an assault conducted by just two men.

Additionally, both Jack and Janousz had received elite military training in assault tactics and close-quarters urban combat techniques. Both men had honed their skills over years in the field, and then transferred those militarily developed skills to the civilian arena. Even if any of the Dragons had military backgrounds—and that was a distinct possibility—there was virtually zero chance the men's training and practical experience would be anything close to that of Jack and Janousz.

It was no small advantage, because for all the Dragons' ruthless lethality—and there was no doubt the gang was brutal—each individual member may have killed one or two people in his lifetime, maybe three. And many of those kills had undoubtedly been with their victim secured and helpless, as had likely been the case with Officer Greg Daly.

What Jack had planned for the Dragons tonight would be something far different, and he was counting on using his and Janousz's experience and training to plant a seed of doubt into the minds of men who envisioned themselves as tough and battle-hardened.

He would then exploit that doubt and prove to the Eighth Street Dragons they didn't know as much as they thought they knew.

Janousz was quiet and focused as he tossed his gear into the back seat of the rental and buckled in for the ride. Jack had already learned the man was not much of a talker. His philosophy seemed to be, *Why waste my time and my breath on multiple sentences when one word will do?*

It was not that far removed from Jack's philosophy.

Today, though, Janousz seemed even more withdrawn than he'd been yesterday. Jack interpreted that as a good sign. The man didn't come across as fearful, or even particularly worried, about what would go down tonight. As professional athletes would say, he had his game face on. He was focused and absorbed in what he needed to do to achieve a positive outcome.

The drive from Janousz's hotel in Manchester down to Lawrence was not a long one. If necessary, Jack could have made it in less than forty minutes without even having to drive at a speed that would draw attention from law enforcement. Today, though, he took his time, maintaining the speed limit on the highway, discussing the plan of attack for tonight and stressing that Janousz should be prepared to freelance as necessary if things started mushrooming out of control.

"I still do not understand why you want me to wait," he said.

"I know you don't," Jack answered. "And I don't think I can explain my reasoning any more effectively today than I did last night. But there's a concrete advantage to doing it this way as well."

"And that is?"

"If we attack the facility with one of us in front and the other in the rear, the Dragons can easily adjust as soon as they figure out what's happening. If they send a man to the roof, which they undoubtedly would, it might take more time to breach their defenses than we can afford. Remember, this is an urban location, densely packed with civilians, and even though the immediate area is deserted, all we need is one passerby to hear the gunfire and the authorities would be on their way, much too soon."

"And we would be trapped between the Dragons and the police."

"Exactly. But with me getting inside before you show up, I can pick off some of these guys in the initial confusion of the assault, while they're distracted and uncertain what's happening."

"Pick them off? But you will not have a weapon. The Dragons will certainly disarm you when they take you inside."

"They're not going to have to disarm me. I'm approaching them unarmed. I want them to think I'm not a threat, just a clueless citizen, so their guard is down when I hit them from the inside. If I don't have a weapon, they'll feel fully in control. I know it sounds counterintuitive, but if I walk in there with a waving a gun around, I'll have no chance. I'll never survive."

"But my point is the same," Janousz said. "You will have no weapon with which to 'pick them off'."

"I'll find something to use as a weapon, or I'll use my hands. And as soon as I put the first Dragon down, I'll have that man's gun. I'll probably have more than one. At that point, we'll be off and running."

Janousz didn't respond. He gazed straight out the windshield, considering Jack's words. He'd been chewing gum when he got into the car, and now he snapped it a couple times, the "pop-pop" sound resembling miniature gunshots inside the otherwise silent car.

Then he said, "The way you explain it makes a certain amount of sense. But you are still taking a big chance, which means I am also taking a big chance. You may be disabled or even killed the moment the Dragons take you inside their facility. If that is the case, it is highly unlikely I will be able to complete the mission without being killed as well."

Jack nodded. "I won't deny that's a possibility. That's why I want you to feel free to adjust as necessary, even to the point of retreating, if we can't establish contact when you signal me. But put yourself in the Dragons' shoes for a moment. They're going to want to know why I was sneaking around their building. They're going to want to know what I know, and who I'm working for, and more importantly, how many people I'm working with."

Janousz nodded slowly.

Jack continued, "At the very least, they're going to question me. If I don't give them the answers they want, they'll probably torture me. One thing I think they're unlikely to do is kill me immediately."

"But even if you are alive, if you are being restrained you will not be able to participate in the assault and my problem will be the same."

"That's true," Jack acknowledged. "And that is why I tried to time your portion of the assault in such a way as to minimize the likelihood I will have been secured in any manner I can't escape."

"You are taking a lot for granted," the Eastern European hitter said.

"I agree. And this is primarily my battle, not yours. I trust you and I believe The Organization knew exactly what they were doing when they recruited you to back me up on this mission. I feel they couldn't have picked a better man. But with that said, if you begin the assault and it becomes clear I'm not able to participate and hold up my end, get the hell out in the rental car and fly back to Las Vegas and forget all about Lawrence, Massachusetts and the Eighth Street Dragons."

Jack glanced across the front seat to find Janousz staring at him, his face an unreadable mask. Then the man smiled. He said, "Did I mention you seem very different than the typical man or woman in our career field?"

Jack grinned. "Yes, you may have brought up the subject yesterday."

"I believe it is worth repeating."

"You're probably right about that."

22

Lowell Stevenson had never felt anything remotely similar to the buzz that was running through him. It was a literal buzz, like a low-voltage electrical charge thrumming inside every muscle and exploding out every nerve ending in his body.

It was a heady sensation, it made him feel vital and alive and invincible, and as he sat in the back of Marconi's parking lot he knew he'd made the right decision to move from an observer of the Dragons' rituals to a participant. It was a risky decision, to be sure, but not as risky as it might seem. If he were to be arrested *watching* someone be tortured, his career and his freedom—his entire life—would be over every bit as much as if he were arrested *participating* in that torture.

And, oh God, how he looked forward to participating.

* * *

He'd arrived at Marconi's early, because everything was riding on him getting the jump on McKenna. He parked in the back, as he'd said he would do, and then sat back and watched the clientele entering and leaving the restaurant from a distance of eighty to ninety feet. Business was steady, but Marconi's was not so crowded with diners that anyone besides Lowell would feel the need to use this section of the lot.

Lowell had reviewed the game plan multiple times in his head. It was simple and direct, and barring any unexpected developments—like a cop cruising through the lot at the wrong time or a customer deciding to park next to Lowell and McKenna—there was every reason to believe it would work.

By the time Chief McKenna's car wheeled into the lot, Lowell was primed and ready. His stomach was jumpy but in a good way, and he was shaking just a little, and as McKenna eased into the spot next to Lowell's car, Lowell climbed out of the front seat, right hand held inconspicuously—he hoped—behind his back.

McKenna parked. He killed his engine and then opened his door. "I don't think I can eat anything," he said miserably as he was exiting his car. Then turned and bumped into Lowell, who had moved right into McKenna's personal space while the man was talking.

"Jesus, give me some room," McKenna said, and then he froze as Lowell shoved the barrel of a Ruger Security-9 pistol into his ribs. Lowell wanted to be sure McKenna got the message, so he shoved hard. It seemed to take the chief's breath away.

"What the hell are you doi—"

"Shut up," Lowell said. "We're going to walk to my car together. You're going to get in the driver's side door and then slide across to the passenger side. Scream, or try to run, or do anything other than exactly what I say and I'll shoot you where you stand." In the back of his mind Lowell realized he was suddenly hard as a rock, and the butterflies fluttering around inside his stomach began moving a little faster, bouncing off his rib cage and each other.

McKenna's eyes were glazed, unfocused, like he didn't quite understand what Lowell was saying, and Lowell growled, "Move!" He kept his voice low, but punctuated his order by shoving the gun even harder against his friend's ribs, and although the chief's eyes didn't seem to gain much focus he began moving in a semi-shuffling gait around Lowell's car.

"I don't understand," McKenna said.

"You don't need to."

They reached the door and McKenna stopped, hands at his sides. Lowell didn't think the man was being uncooperative, he suspected that the stress the chief had been under for the last two months had combined with the trauma of a man he'd trusted shoving a gun into his ribs to reduce him to a near-vegetative state.

Good. It would make him easier to control.

Lowell snaked his hand around McKenna and yanked open the door while keeping his gun firmly pressed against his friend's spine. He doubted the chief was playing possum but had no intention of finding out the hard way that he was wrong.

"Get in," his hissed as he glanced quickly around the lot. They were still alone. Up in front of Marconi's, a couple was approaching the entrance, their backs turned to the drama playing out behind them.

McKenna hesitated and then dropped into the Buick's front seat and began sliding over as instructed. Lowell had left his beloved Jaguar at home tonight, knowing his forest-green Buick would be much less conspicuous, and also because he knew he would be forcing his victim to slide across the front seat to complete the kidnapping. A bench seat would make it a much easier task to accomplish than the Jag's bucket seats separated by a gearshift and a console.

The moment there was sufficient room, Lowell slipped into the car behind McKenna and pulled his door closed. A sense of elation washed over him as he punched the electric door locks. He was going to get away with it! This was the riskiest part of the whole plan, and now that he'd maneuvered McKenna into the car there was almost no way he could be caught, barring a car accident or a breakdown or something equally unlikely.

He kept the gun trained on his friend and took a deep breath, mostly to clear his head of the delicious visions of what he was going to do to Tim McKenna tonight. He was still rock hard and throbbing and knew he'd better get control of himself or he was going to lose it where he sat.

From next to him, McKenna said, "What exactly do you think you're doing?" He didn't seem afraid. The question sounded more like something a college professor might ask a roomful of unruly students.

"I'm doing exactly what I told you I would do. I'm bringing you to someone who can help you deal with your guilt issues."

"What kind of therapist sees patients at gunpoint?"

"You said I was taking you to see a therapist, not me. I just didn't correct you."

"So where are we going? It's obviously not someplace that will be good for me. And clearly dinner's out of the question."

"You said you couldn't eat anyway, so what difference does that make?"

"None, I guess. Where are we going, Lowell? Why did you feel the need to abduct me at gunpoint?"

"You'll find out soon enough."

"Why are you doing this?"

"Isn't it obvious? I couldn't allow you to spill your guts to Andrews. It's been clear to me for quite some time that's the direction you were headed, and there's just too much at stake for me to allow that to happen."

McKenna cleared his throat. He seemed to have recovered a bit from his initial sense of shock. "So you lied about us going to see the DA tomorrow."

Lowell blinked. For a second he wasn't sure he'd heard McKenna right. He looked across the front seat to see his friend staring at him with wide, injured eyes. "*That's* what you're having a problem with?" he said incredulously. "I'm threatening you with a loaded weapon, kidnapping you and taking you who knows where, and you're butt-hurt because you think I *lied* to you? What are you, a teenage girl?"

"So you admit you lied," McKenna persisted.

"As a matter of fact, I didn't lie," Lowell said. He was fed up with McKenna already and they'd only been in the car together for a couple of minutes. "I was perfectly truthful with you. If you're still unhappy with your situation after tonight, I will walk hand-in-hand into the district attorney's office with you tomorrow and give myself up."

"You're going to kill me."

"I'm sorry," Lowell said, although he really wasn't. He'd thought he would be, but he didn't feel any sense of remorse. He didn't feel anything at all besides excitement and anticipation.

"What the hell is wrong with you?" McKenna said. His tone was one of innocent wonder.

"I think you should shut up and sit quietly," Lowell suggested, "before I blow your head off right here and now." He turned the key and shifted into gear and began moving slowly across the parking lot. Marconi's Restaurant was located less than a ten-minute drive away from the Dragons' headquarters and he was anxious to arrive.

He assumed McKenna would ignore his threat and continue to badger him. It should have been obvious to any idiot—much less the fucking chief of police—that Lowell couldn't exactly shoot someone in the head inside his own car in the middle of downtown traffic before dark.

But McKenna surprised him by doing as he was told. He clamped his mouth shut and gazed out the windshield, every so often turning his head to look at Lowell in silent confusion.

They were less than half a block from the Dragons' headquarters building when the other shoe dropped with McKenna. "I'm going to disappear just like Greg Daly did, aren't I?"

"Shut up," Lowell said. A minute later he'd parked in an abandoned lot two buildings from the Dragons' headquarters.

He turned to McKenna and said, "Here's what's going to happen. We're going to get out together. You're going to walk two paces in front of me. You know where to go. If you take one step in the wrong direction or if you scream or do anything at all I don't like, you'll be dead before you know what hit you."

McKenna didn't answer.

"Get moving," Lowell said.

And McKenna did.

23

Jack circumnavigated Dragons' headquarters, beginning three blocks north of the old mill building and circling block by block until he and Janousz had had an opportunity to observe the surrounding area.

Most of the neighborhood was deserted. Empty shells of structures suffering from varying degrees of neglect shared space with the occasional triple-decker apartment building somehow defying the odds and still housing renters. Urban redevelopment had saved some of the mills a little farther away along the Merrimack River, but this section of Lawrence had escaped the contractors' touch and likely would continue to do so. There were only so many craft microbreweries, specialty clothing stores and custom furniture outlets to go around.

Eventually the inner-city driving tour reached a point where the rental car would be visible to anyone scanning the area from the roof. Jack drove past anyway. He wanted Janousz to get a reasonably close-up view of the building before darkness fell, and driving past in a car would be a lot less conspicuous than checking out the building on foot.

"Seen enough?" Jack asked as he wheeled the rental Focus around a corner and left the Dragons' building behind.

Janousz shrugged. "I guess so. It would be much more beneficial to see a diagram of the building's interior."

"I agree, but we don't have anything like that. This is the ultimate definition of a blind mission."

"Then I have seen enough."

Jack took a right and then another right, then eased into the parking spot he'd used the last time he was here. It was as close as he would be able to get to the Dragons' building and still remain out of sight. He killed the engine and turned to face Janousz.

"You remember how long I want you to wait?"

"I remember."

"Stay flexible. When you signal me, you can expect to get the return signal within sixty seconds. If that does not happen, you should assume I'm incapacitated, and react as we've already discussed. In the meantime, you'll have to cool your heels for a little while."

"Cool my heels? What is that?"

Jack chuckled. "It means you're going to have some time to kill before you have any work to do. It means you don't have to just sit here with your thumb up your ass. As long as you remain in the local area, you're welcome to do something else for a short time."

"Thank you," Janousz said. "I will be fine."

"Listen," Jack said after a moment's silence.

"Yes?"

"I know this is not the kind of mission you typically take on, so I appreciate your working with me on this."

"I want to show my employers back in Las Vegas I can handle anything they throw at me. Also, the kinds of missions I typically take on can be extremely...how do you say..."

"Boring?" Jack offered helpfully.

Janousz smiled. "Yes. Boring. This assignment is not boring. It is...interesting."

"Just remember what I told you before. If you get inside that building and it becomes clear I'm dead or incapacitated and can't participate in the mission, I want you to retreat out that back door, make your way to the car, and get the hell out of Dodge."

"Dodge? Where is Dodge? I do not understand."

Jack grinned. "Forget it, it's just an expression. If things are going bad, get out of Lawrence, drive to Logan Airport, and fly back to Vegas. Your employer out there can contact The Organization for reimbursement on the air fare."

"I am not worried about the air fare and do not expect to be flying back to Las Vegas until this mission has been completed successfully."

Jack reached across the front seat and offered his hand to Janousz. The Eastern European assassin took it and shook once, his grip strong and confident. "Good luck tonight, Janousz."

"And the same to you, Jack."

He pulled the key out of the ignition and passed it across the front seat. "If you decide to take a drive, remember to leave the ignition key under the left rear tire before you walk to the Dragons' building."

"I will not forget."

"Good man." Jack paused. "Things are going to be crazy the next time we see each other."

"I can handle it."

Jack studied his temporary partner's face. He liked what he saw. Janousz looked focused and intense, yet relaxed and competent. "I believe you," Jack said, and meant it.

He opened the driver's side door and stepped out of the vehicle, then began walking briskly away along the crumbling sidewalk toward a destination he knew he might never escape alive.

24

"I just can't believe you're doing this," Tim McKenna said as he stumbled over one of the many potholes littering the parking lot.

Lowell scoffed. "Bullshit."

"What do you mean?"

"Are you kidding me? What could you possibly not understand? You've admitted multiple times over the last few weeks you felt overwhelmed by this situation, and especially by the fact one of your officers was used as the subject of a Dragons' initiation ritual. When you told me you felt compelled to go to the district attorney's office, it was the last straw. You left me no choice, Tim. I'm sorry but I have to plug this leak."

"You're not sorry."

Lowell shrugged. "You're right."

"I thought you were my friend."

"I was. I am. Friendship has nothing to do with this."

"Obviously," McKenna said drily. "But we've known each other forever."

"Just about."

"And yet you have no problem threatening me with a gun and bringing me here where these reprobates will do...God knows what to me."

Lowell laughed. "If it makes you feel any better, it's not just the Dragon members who will be doing God knows what. I'll be participating as well."

"It shouldn't shock you to learn that doesn't make me feel better."

Lowell hardened his voice. "Then you shouldn't have threatened to bring everything crashing down on me."

They had nearly reached the fortified rear door of the old mill building, and McKenna's walking pace had slowed steadily until now he was barely moving.

"You know what your problem is?" Lowell said.

"I'm well aware of my current problem, yes."

"Not this. Think on a macro level, Tim."

McKenna sighed. "At the moment I'm a little too worried about what's going to happen to me tonight to manage a whole lot of introspection. So why don't you just fill me in: what's my problem, Lowell?"

"Your problem is you never grew a spine. For a lifelong law enforcement officer and the man in charge of a crime-ridden city's entire police force, you are a spineless fucking wimp."

"Thanks for that."

Lowell shoved McKenna in the back with his gun to remind him to keep walking. He was only half paying attention, though, as he ran his eyes over the damage that had been done to the building. He squinted in concentration. It looked like someone had pried away large chunks of the plywood that had been secured to the windows. The ruined pieces of wood littered the pavement, revealing the heavy iron bars de la Cruz had ordered installed way back when the Dragons were fighting two other gangs for control of the city.

"What the hell…" he muttered.

"Something wrong, Lowell?" McKenna said as he slowed almost to a halt once again. It was plainly obvious the chief had no desire to enter the Dragons' headquarters, believing—correctly—he would never leave the building alive.

"Shut up," Lowell snapped. He shoved McKenna in the back once more, and then decided to up the ante by pistol-whipping his old friend in the back of the head.

McKenna gasped and stumbled forward a couple of paces before falling to his knees. He placed a hand against the wound and it came away wet with blood.

"Get up and get moving," Lowell thundered. "And don't make me hit you again, because that was just a love tap compared to what you'll get next time."

McKenna shook his head tiredly. Whether it was out of disgust at Lowell's actions or an attempt to clear his scrambled brains Lowell didn't know, but in any event he staggered to his feet and continued toward the rear door.

Moments later they had arrived. McKenna stopped in front of the reinforced metal door and said, "Now what? Am I supposed to just walk in?"

"Shut up and wait."

Within seconds the door swung open and one of the Dragons—a man whose name Lowell didn't know but who'd been patting Lowell down since his first visit to the building—stepped aside to allow them entrance. He was olive skinned, as were most of the Dragons, with a shaved head and the muscular features of a dedicated bodybuilder.

And, of course, he had an intimidating black pistol strapped to his waist.

Lowell shoved McKenna thorough the door and then followed closely. They stepped forward a couple of paces to allow the sentry to close the door, and then Lowell said, "Stop."

McKenna stopped.

The door swung shut with a metallic clang that reminded Lowell of the sound a prison cell door might make rolling closed, an irony that was not lost on the judge. That sound had always made him question his decision to be here in the past, but this time it did no such thing.

There was no doubt left. Lowell knew he was exactly where he belonged.

The interior of the building—at least this portion of the interior—was cool and dark, like the inside of a cave. It wasn't pitch-black, but even though the sun had by now almost completely set, there was still more ambient light outside than in.

The sentry shoved McKenna face-first against the brick wall next to the door and began patting him down. He'd never been gentle with Lowell but was much more forceful with the chief. He pushed McKenna's face into the bricks and the police chief grunted in pain. Then the man ran his hands expertly over McKenna's body, beginning at his neck and chest and moving down, in as thorough a weapons check as any police officer had ever done.

Lowell almost felt sorry for his old friend.

That all changed when the thug dropped to his knees and used both hands to pat down McKenna's legs. He glanced up at Lowell with hooded eyes and lifted the cuffs of the chief's dress pants to reveal a small pistol resting inside a leather holster strapped to the chief's ankle.

Lowell felt his eyes widen and his blood run cold. Jesus Christ, it hadn't even occurred to him to check if his old friend was armed. Tim McKenna had at one time been a patrol officer, but that was decades ago and he'd been a bureaucratic grunt ever since. The possibility that he might be carrying a gun—and on his off hours—had never even crossed Lowell's mind.

The door sentry glared a moment longer at Lowell and then lifted the gun from the holster. He examined it for a moment and then said, "You are trying to get us killed?" His words were quiet and filled with menace, and he never took his eyes off Lowell as he spoke them.

"I-I didn't…I didn't think…" His voice trailed off and he swallowed heavily.

Finally the man tore his awful gaze off Lowell and returned his attention to McKenna. "Stand there," he commanded, pointing to a location on the other side of the closed door that put him beyond arm's reach.

McKenna looked from Lowell to the sentry and then moved slowly, doing as he was told.

"If you move from that spot," the man said, "I will shoot you with your own gun. I will not stop firing until the contents of your magazine have been emptied into your lifeless body. Every last round. Do you understand?"

"I understand," McKenna said. His voice sounded surprisingly calm and Lowell thought it was entirely possible that *he*— Lowell—was more frightened than McKenna at the moment. The sight of that gun had thrown him off his axis. *That son of a bitch had just been waiting for the right moment to pull his fucking gun out and blow me away!* He felt simultaneously numb from shock and furious at the knowledge a man he'd thought of as a friend could be so duplicitous.

He realized the sentry had said something and that he'd been so caught up in his shock and anger he had no idea what it was. But the man was looking right at him with those awful emotionless eyes again, so Lowell knew the words had been meant for him.

"I'm sorry," he said. "I missed that. What did you say?"

The man opened his mouth to speak but before he could, Tim McKenna spoke up. "He said it's your turn now."

"Against the wall and spread 'em," the sentry said. Then he turned to McKenna and said, "You keep your mouth shut."

Lowell had been thrown so far off his game by the sight of that damned gun that he'd forgotten he was still a guest and not a Dragons member, and was thus subject to the search McKenna had just suffered. He turned and placed his hands against the wall.

Tonight he would prove his toughness and his worthiness to de la Cruz. This would be the last time a Neanderthal like the sentry would put his hands on Judge Lowell Stevenson. Ever.

He closed his eyes and waited for the humiliation to be over.

25

Jack decided to circle the block and approach the Dragons building from the rear. He wanted to make it clear to the gang that
his actions were focused on them, but at the same time appear
unthreatening; like someone with more curiosity than brains.

It would be easier said than done, because he'd been an operative for more than two decades, and the lessons he'd learned both
from his military training and in the field were not easy to set
aside. He wasn't sure he'd be able to pull off looking clueless, but
he was going to try.

Once the old mill came into view, Jack slowed his pace. He
walked forward another few dozen feet and then stopped entirely.
He leaned against one of the ubiquitous abandoned buildings
and tried to make it obvious he was focusing his attention on the
Dragons headquarters.

He craned his neck and stared at the top of the building.

He leaned left and then right, examining the alleys running
along both sides of the building.

He moved forward a few feet and repeated his actions.

He doubted the sentry manning the rear entrance could see
him from this distance; the wire-reinforced slit in the door was too
narrow and the angle was wrong. But if the gang had placed a man
on the roof—and after the damage Jack had done the other night
to the plywood-covered windows, he suspected they had—his
stopping and starting and exaggerated movements should eventually draw that man's attention, even in the failing daylight.

Assuming, of course, the roof sentry was doing his job and not taking a nap.

Jack continued to move forward, inching along the sidewalk toward the building. After three or four tries at making himself visible to anyone on the roof, he decided it was time to change tactics. Further attempts would become too obvious and do nothing but make any observer suspicious.

He pushed off from the building and resumed a normal walking pace, moving in a direct line toward the gang's lair. In the distance Jack could hear ambient traffic sounds—the occasional honk of a horn, the muffled sound of a siren, a far-off train whistle sounding lonely and haunted—but this neighborhood appeared deserted. Every time Jack had been here this neighborhood appeared deserted. Undoubtedly the Dragons had made it clear to local residents that the immediate area surrounding their headquarters was off-limits.

Despite the lack of pedestrian or vehicular traffic, Jack got the distinct impression he was being watched. Maybe it was because he was *expecting* to be watched, but he didn't think it was that simple. He'd long-since learned to pay close attention to his instincts. A career in covert operations had convinced him the human brain can process much more information than whatever the eyes are feeding it, and oftentimes a *feeling* was simply the brain's way of passing along data from one of the other senses.

Jack rounded the corner of the building located directly behind the one the Dragons had repurposed into their headquarters— *urban renewal of the criminal kind,* Jack thought—and began circling it on the far side of the parking lot. His goal was again to make himself as visible as possible, accidentally on purpose.

It was unlikely the Dragons used a man to cover the rear door constantly. And even if they did, that man undoubtedly didn't spend all his time gazing out the little slit cut out of the metal. But if Jack had been successful in drawing the attention of the man on the roof, that sentry would certainly have notified someone downstairs, who would now be standing just inside the door, doing exactly that.

He crossed the parking lot and began edging toward the corner of the Dragons building. He thought he knew what was going to happen next, and he wanted to make it as simple as possible for the Dragons' sentry to take him. The less complicated things were, the more likely it was no one would get hurt.

Yet.

When he reached the corner of the building he snuck a quick glance along the rear wall.

The door remained closed.

He returned his attention to the alley running along the north side of the structure and then began moving slowly forward. If he'd played his part properly, things should start to get interesting.

The evening had passed dusk and was approaching full dark, and it was getting harder and harder to see. Jack crept forward, now barely able to make out the front corner of the building. He was halfway there and had just begun planning his next move in the event he wasn't intercepted by the time he turned the corner when he heard stealthy footsteps a few feet behind him and closing fast.

Finally. He smiled but continued to face forward, and a moment later was unsurprised to feel the cold steel of a gun barrel pressed to the back of his neck.

"Don't move," a nearly whispered voice commanded. "There is nowhere to run."

Jack didn't move. He had no desire to run. He was right where he wanted to be.

"What are you doing here?" the whispered voice asked.

"Could you speak up a bit? You sound like a little girl and I can hardly hear you."

The now-angry man behind Jack raised his voice slightly. "I said what are you doing here?"

"Isn't it obvious? I'm taking a walk. I feel people don't appreciate the importance of regular exercise. I mean, let's face it, none of us is getting any younger, am I right?"

"What the fuck are you talking about?"

"I'm trying to answer your question. And could you maybe point the gun somewhere else? I don't know if you've taken a fire-arms safety course recently, but experts recommend you minimize your time spent pointing a loaded weapon at other people."

"Is that what the experts recommend?"

"I'm pretty sure. Unless they've changed the recommendation. It's so hard to keep up, don't you agree?"

"You think you're pretty fucking funny, don't you?"

"Is that a no, you're not going to point your gun somewhere else? Because I can't help but notice you're still aiming it at me."

The gangbanger spit out a curse and said, "Why are you hanging around here?"

"Well, I couldn't help but notice this area's pretty much deserted all the time. I value my privacy."

"Fucking wiseass. Why are you sneaking around outside this building? And if you wise off to me again I'm going to put a bullet in your brain."

"Is that so?"

"Fucking A right that's so. Answer me."

"I'm sorry, what was the question again?" Jack knew it was about time to stop pushing this kid but he couldn't resist one last tweak. His goal was to piss the sentry off so badly the man hauled Jack inside Dragons' headquarters, but not so badly he executed Jack in the alley next to the building. It was a fine line to walk.

Instead of repeating his question, the kid said, "Did you pull the plywood off our windows?"

"Hmm." Jack cupped a hand under his chin as if trying to think. "Would those be the windows with the heavy iron bars installed in them? Because if so, then yes, that was me. I have to admit I'm a little curious as to why anyone would go to all the bother of boarding up windows that are so well secured to begin with."

"You talk too much, you know that?"

"Really? I thought we were bonding. You know, getting to know one another, establishing common ground, shooting the breeze, chewing the fa—"

The kid cursed again and pistol-whipped Jack in the back of the head. Jack's knees buckled and he dropped like a sack of potatoes, barely managing to avoid toppling onto his face on the pavement. *Yep. Definitely should have stopped pushing thirty seconds ago.*

"Shut up," the sentry growled as Jack began rising unsteadily to his feet.

"You could have mentioned the shutting up part *before* slugging me in the back of the head," he said. He felt blood tricking out from under his hairline and he resigned himself to suffering a pounding headache for the rest of the night.

Unless he got killed first.

Jack had worn a light windbreaker, and now the kid grabbed the back of it and yanked. He spun Jack around and pointed him in the direction from which they'd just come. Then he shoved him hard and said, "Get moving."

"Where to?"

"You're so curious about this building, dumb fuck, I'm going to show you what it's all about."

"You sound upset," Jack said. "Everything all right at home?"

"Shut the fuck up before I hit you again."

"And here I thought we were getting along so well."

"Shut up."

26

The sentry was even rougher with Lowell than usual in performing his pat down. He shoved his fingers into Lowell's gut hard enough to make him gasp and even semi-choked him, the second part coming without warning. Lowell assumed this was a primitive sort of payback for the sin of allowing McKenna into the building while in possession of a deadly weapon.

He supposed he could understand the man's testiness, but to Lowell it all seemed a bit unfair. After all, if not for Lowell's finely-tuned sense of perception and the initiative he'd shown in luring the Lawrence chief of police here tonight, Tim McKenna would at this very moment be preparing to visit the district attorney's office with information that would bring them all down.

Whatever. This lack of appreciation for priorities was what would keep Ricardo—or Enrique or Mateo or whatever the hell the sentry's name was—toiling in a subservient position in the Dragons' hierarchy forever. Hector de la Cruz would appreciate Lowell's contributions to the Dragons' efforts, and that was what would matter in the long run.

So Lowell put up with the unfairness of his rough treatment without complaint, thus proving his toughness to the idiot if the man had been paying the slightest attention, which he wasn't. The moment he was done with the assault masquerading as a pat down the guard ignored Lowell as if he'd suddenly somehow turned invisible.

Instead, the man faced McKenna and offered an evil smile.

"Nice of you to join us, *chief*," he said, putting emphasis on the last word as a way of showing his disdain. Lowell doubted this troglodyte would recognize Tim McKenna as the police chief on the best day he ever had, so apparently de la Cruz had spread the word that tonight's festivities would involve a local semi-celebrity and a man for which the Eighth Street Dragons should have no trouble generating the appropriate amount of hostility. "I hope you can stay awhile."

McKenna held the gang member's gaze and answered instantly. "Only long enough to send you straight to prison."

Lowell had to give the man credit: as shaky as his old friend had been, and as close as he'd seemed to be to cracking and spilling his guts, the police chief right now was acting solid, putting on a brave front. Not that it would matter. He was never going to leave this building alive, and when he was finally carried out, it would be in multiple pieces. The remains would be transported to Rodriguez Salvage Yard, where they would then be buried among other unfortunates within the dozens of acres of junk cars and trucks.

The gang member grinned at McKenna. It was a terrifying sight and one without the slightest pretense of good humor. "We will just see about that," he said. "I do not think you will be sending anyone to prison, ever again."

A doorway to Lowell's left opened onto a long hallway, and the Dragons' guard indicated it with a tilt of his head. "Get moving," he said to McKenna. The man was still ignoring Lowell, and after seeing the blood-chilling grin, Lowell decided he was happy to be forgotten, at least for the time being.

McKenna glanced from the gang member to Lowell and then back again. He shook his head in apparent disgust and began trudging through the door. Lowell knew the hallway led to the large, open area in which the Dragons held their initiation rituals, although he had never traversed it himself. He typically turned right upon entry and climbed a stairway that led to the second floor and his private viewing area.

Not tonight. Tonight the balcony would sit empty. Tonight he would be participating in the action, not merely watching it.

Apparently the Dragons' sentry hadn't forgotten about Lowell after all, because as McKenna exited the lobby into the hallway, the man turned and gestured at Lowell to follow. It was an impatient, *get moving* circular motion with his hands, and Lowell's immediate reaction was one of aggravation. Didn't this self-important little prick know who he was? Lowell Stevenson was probably the most accomplished man this little maggot would ever meet, a legal professional with sterling credentials and long history of success, and he was being treated like some small-time thug.

He forced back his anger and followed McKenna. The gang member fell in behind Lowell, and the strange group moved single-file down the hallway. "Where am I supposed to go?" McKenna said, his words sounding harsh and loud, echoing in the confined space of the hallway.

"All the way to the end," came the answer.

The lighting was dim and the corridor dingy, and at the end was a dented gray metal door. The door was closed, but McKenna pushed at the steel bar, stopping only long enough to shove the door open and walk through.

Lowell followed and the gang member came through last, and then they were all inside the initiation area. It was a wide-open rectangular room with a cement floor, empty but for three items. First was a heavy wooden chair placed directly in the center of the room. Next to the chair was a bucket, like something a housewife or janitor might use to mop a floor. Finally, a set of heavy-duty gardening shears lay on the floor next to the bucket.

The floor had been stained rust brown in a rough approximation of a circle surrounding the three items. The stain represented the blood of previous initiation victims. How many there had been Lowell wasn't certain, but it was obvious plenty of blood had been spilled here.

McKenna looked around semi-curiously, his face giving away nothing. If he recognized the significance of the brownish stain, he didn't acknowledge it.

Lowell guessed Hector de la Cruz was somewhere near, so he tried to play it cool, as if he'd participated in the torture and murder of an innocent man before, like it was no big deal, just another day in the life, but he couldn't help glancing up toward his viewing area. The perspective from here was so damned different from up there. He'd stared down into this killing room in rapt fascination so many times before, pretending he was one of the new Dragons removing the digits of their victims, hearing the screams of protest and of pain.

And now he was actually going to do it. And not just with any victim, with one of his oldest friends.

He realized he was getting hard just thinking about it, and he swallowed and forced his racing thoughts elsewhere. His face was flushed and his breathing ragged and even though no one was paying the slightest attention to him, he felt a little embarrassed, like the time his mother had walked in on him masturbating in his bedroom when he was twelve.

He sucked in a deep breath and blew it out forcefully, and realized Tim McKenna had said something. Both McKenna and the Dragons member were looking at him expectantly and Lowell realized whatever McKenna had said had been directed at him. "Excuse me?" he said, feeling silly now as well as embarrassed.

"I asked how you you're going to live with yourself after this." McKenna spoke slowly and softly and Lowell was dimly aware of the Dragons' kid smirking next to the police chief. He wondered whether it was due to the question or the fact the kid had noticed Lowell's situation below the belt.

He raised his chin in an effort to regain a little of his lost dignity and answered. "Don't worry about me, I'll be just fine. You would have been, too, if you had any kind of backbone and didn't suffer a fucking nervous breakdown."

"You can tell yourself that if you want, Lowell, but you're not going to be fine. Somewhere inside, you know what you're doing is wrong, and you're going to suffer. You'll suffer and it's not going to end well, you must know that."

"Shut up," Lowell said angrily, and realized the Dragons' guy had said the exact same thing at the exact same time.

"Everybody shut the fuck up," the kid said, "before I just shoot both of you in the head. Bang-bang and it is all over."

"But you can't—" Lowell spit the words out without thinking but stopped in mid-sentence when the kid lifted his big black pistol and aimed it in Lowell's direction. He'd always found the guy's weapon to be intimidating, but now, with its barrel looming in front of him, he literally could not breathe. His brain froze and he stopped talking and he damned near pissed himself.

"I can't what?" the kid said.

Lowell still couldn't speak, so he shook his head and hoped that would be sufficient.

"What happens now?" McKenna asked, and Lowell breathed a silent sigh of relief as the kid turned his attention away from him.

Instead of freaking out like he'd done with Lowell, the gang member said, "You'll find out soon enough. For now, just stand quietly and wait."

Then the kid smiled. This one was every bit as evil looking as the one he'd flashed back in the lobby. "Unless you'd rather sit." He gestured at the chair in the center of the room. "Feel free to take a load off."

McKenna held the man's gaze for a moment before dragging it away to glance at the chair and then back. "No, thanks. I'll stand."

"That's what I thought."

27

The gangbanger pushed Jack through the rear door and then slammed it closed behind them. Jack had been stumbling, one hand clapped to the back of his bleeding skull as the man shoved him forward out of the alley, but most of that was for show. He wanted to keep the guard convinced he was fully in charge.

Jack's head *was* pounding from where he'd been pistol-whipped, that part didn't need to be faked. But he'd suffered far worse injuries in the past and completed every mission successfully, so as long as he could see and hear and think, the head wound didn't particularly concern him.

The man locked the door. He said, "You wouldn't believe…" and then his voice trailed off as he realized the person he'd begun speaking to was absent.

"What wouldn't I believe?" Jack asked, although the words were plainly meant for someone else.

"I thought I told you to shut u—"

Jack spun and punched the gangbanger in the throat. The man had allowed his attention to wander for less than a second in his surprise at the lobby being empty, and his mistake would cost him. He fell with a strangled half-yelp, the sound of someone gargling and accidentally swallowing his mouthwash.

Jack was on him almost before he hit the floor. The banger's handgun dropped and skittered away, but Jack ignored the weapon for now. There was no way to know how long this room would remain empty and he needed to finish this before the Dragon who was supposed to be inside this lobby returned.

Jack dropped onto the Dragon, who was gagging and coughing and struggling to breathe. The gang member outweighed him by at least forty pounds, but was currently in no condition to put up much of a fight. Jack lifted the banger's head and pounded the back of his skull into the cement floor, and his eyes went blank and then he was gone.

The whole thing had taken less than five seconds.

Jack darted to his left and picked up the gun the Dragon had dropped. He glanced at it and then shoved it into the waistband of his jeans, already looking for a place to stash his victim. He hadn't struck the man's head on the floor hard enough to kill him and wasn't prepared to execute a helpless man, gang member or not.

A partially open door on the far side of the room led directly to a hallway. Jack assumed it would be a bad idea to pass through that door dragging the unconscious, bleeding body of an Eighth Street Dragon. There were only two other options: a door located directly behind Jack and a door off to his right. Both were closed.

He turned and yanked open the door behind him and saw a stairway leading just one direction—up. *Dammit.*

Jack had already begun adjusting his plan as he moved to the right side of the room and pulled open the only remaining door. Adjustment would not be necessary, however, as the lobby's weak yellow light revealed a mostly empty janitor's closet. This was as close to perfect as Jack guessed he was going to get, so he returned to the downed gang member.

The unconscious Dragon was bleeding heavily from the back of the head, so Jack flipped him onto his belly to avoid trailing a smear of blood across the dirty concrete floor. The man was bulky and heavy and not easy to move, like a two hundred fifty pound bag of dirt—an appropriate analogy, Jack thought—but Jack muscled him to the closet and then knelt next to his prone body.

The man had been wearing a flannel shirt unbuttoned over a dirty white t-shirt, and Jack worked it off his arms and over his head. He used his penknife to slice two strips of material off the bottom portion of the shirt. Then he bound the man's wrists and ankles with them. The rest he stuffed into the man's mouth before using the sleeves to tie the improvised gag tightly behind his head.

He stepped back and examined his handiwork. Not the most

secure job of immobilization he'd ever done, but under the circumstances it would have to suffice. Jack closed the door firmly but quietly and then hurried back to the spot just inside the rear entrance where he'd dropped the man. A four-inch wide splash of blood had puddled on the floor, and he used a greasy rag someone had tossed into the corner to soak up the blood as best he could.

He tossed the rag back into the corner and stood. The discoloration was still visible, but at least the fresh blood had been sopped up. Even the most casual of investigations would quickly reveal what had happened, but the rushed cleanup job would at least buy Jack a little time.

Hopefully.

Maybe.

In any event, he had to get moving. He could feel time running out; it was a nearly physical sensation. Jack was certain this lobby was not supposed to be empty, and that meant it would not remain so for very much longer.

He considered investigating the hallway with the partially open door, but of more interest—at least for now—was the other doorway, the one that opened onto to a set of stairs leading upward.

He double-timed to the rear entrance to unlock it. The plan had been for Janousz to slip up to the door from the side, out of sight of the sentry, and then make enough noise outside to draw the man's attention to the slit in the door. He would then jam his weapon into the sentry's face and force the man to unlock the door before putting him down.

But with the sentry now disabled, Jack could no longer be certain anyone would be manning this entryway when Janousz arrived. He didn't think it would be an issue. Janousz was a pro, he would be savvy enough to check the door if the original plan wasn't working. It was the first of what would likely be many adjustments to an already fluid plan.

He released the three deadbolts and then re-crossed the room and started up the stairs, remaining alert for the presence of gang members but encountering none. There were no voices; there was no movement. The place felt as silent and empty as a church at midnight, but Jack knew more people were here.

The stairway ended after just one flight, despite the fact the old mill building was four stories tall. It had been obvious from the moment Jack saw the stairway that it wasn't original to the building, and he began to suspect the Dragons themselves had either built it or commissioned its construction.

But for what purpose? Why go to the trouble and expense of adding stairs to an old factory building that must contain multiple stairways and likely a couple of ancient elevators as well?

The door at the top of the stairs was closed and windowless, so there was no way of knowing how many Dragons—if any—were on the other side, what they might be doing and how many weapons they might be brandishing. Jack breathed out slowly and then before inhaling, placed his ear against the door. He doubted he would hear anything and he did not.

But that didn't necessarily mean no one was there. The door appeared heavily reinforced, and if soundproofed properly, a party could be raging on the other side and Jack would never know it.

Until he opened it, of course.

In for a penny, in for a pound. Jack breathed deeply and then twisted the knob, cracking the door an inch or two, opening it just enough to get a glimpse of whatever might be on the other side. The sound of voices floated through the door, but they were muffled. Whoever the voices belonged to was definitely not standing on the other side of the door.

Now feeling a little more confident he wasn't about to be cut down in a hail of gunfire, Jack eased the door open further. On the other side was a small, empty room that resembled a theatre balcony.

He slipped through and eased the door closed behind him and examined the balcony curiously. It featured a few pieces of ratty furniture whose better days had come and gone decades ago, a tiny homemade bar and a boxy television with a DVD player. Ancient porn magazines littered a cheap wooden coffee table.

The "balcony" overlooked a large, open area that had at one time been part of a factory floor but was now devoid of equipment and furniture. And practically everything else. It was empty but for a single chair, a bucket and what looked like a large pair of gardening shears, all of which had been placed approximately in the center of the room.

The positioning of the chair reminded Jack of a stage that might have been prepared for a solo musician who wanted to be comfortable while he entertained his audience, although Jack had never attended any concert where the musicians needed a bucket and gardening shears as part of their show.

But he knew who might want a setup like the one on the floor below: a vicious street gang interested in torturing people like Officer Greg Daly to death.

The voices he'd heard a moment ago were coming from down there as well, and Jack edged forward, keeping his back to the side wall. He moved just far enough to observe an odd-looking group clustered a few feet away from the chair in the middle of the room.

There were three young men who were obviously Eighth Street Dragons. One of the men was Hector de la Cruz. The other two Jack did not recognize, but they were roughly the same age as de la Cruz and were also heavily muscled and tatted up.

What qualified the group as "odd-looking" were the other two men who comprised it. Both were older. Much older. Both were white men dressed in suits, unlike the Dragon members, who wore jeans and t-shirts similar to the outfit of the man Jack had disarmed a few moments ago.

The members of the group appeared extremely uncomfortable with each other. Their body language suggested the three Dragons would rather be in the company of almost anyone besides their two guests. Neither of the white men appeared comfortable either, but one in particular looked almost ill. He was pale and afraid, his fear obvious to Jack even from a distance. The man was trying to maintain a brave front but was failing miserably.

Jack watched for a moment, thinking. The picture seemed to be coming into focus, at least a little, and he was thankful he hadn't waited even one more day to execute his plan. It still remained to be seen whether he could do anything to end the infestation that was the Eighth Street Dragons, but he was sure as hell going to try.

28

Lowell was relieved when Hector de la Cruz entered the room. Standing around with these Dragon flunkies had been awkward and weird, not to mention dangerous. The guy with the big black gun hadn't pointed it in Lowell's direction again, but once was more than enough.

Now that de la Cruz was here, Lowell knew his treatment would improve. This initiation ritual was *his* idea, *he* was helping plug a leak that could have sunk the entire Dragons' enterprise, and he expected—hell, he *deserved*—to be treated with a little more respect than some lowly thug sticking a cannon in his face and threatening him with summary execution.

"When are we getting this show on the road?" Lowell asked. He raised his voice and spoke while de la Cruz was still crossing the room, wanting to prove to the punk with the gun that he was on par, status-wise, with the Dragons' head man.

"I told you to shut your mouth," the kid with the gun said. He began to raise his weapon in Lowell's direction and Lowell felt a spike of terror, but then de la Cruz raised a calming hand toward the kid. "It's all right, Diego."

Instantly the punk lowered his gun, and Lowell's fear turned to triumph. *See?* he shouted inside his head. *The leader respects me! If you know what's good for you, you'll do the same.* He wasn't quite comfortable enough to say the words out loud, though. Instead, he satisfied himself with a scornful glance in the kid's direction.

To his disappointment the look went unseen, at least by the punk with the gun. He was focused entirely on his boss.

"To answer your question," de la Cruz said to Lowell, "we can start any time. And the sooner, the better. I would like to get this over with."

"Where are the recruits?" Lowell asked. He looked around the room, expecting to see another gang member come through the door pushing two or three teenagers ahead of him. That was how the initiation ceremony had always worked in the past.

"Recruits?" The kid with the gun spoke scornfully. "What the hell are you talking about? This ain't the fucking army, man. *Recruits,*" he muttered again, shaking his head.

"Whatever you call them," Lowell said. "Recruits, initiates, whatever. Where are the kids who are going to take part in the initiation?"

De la Cruz smiled. The gesture was utterly lacking in warmth. "There are no kids to initiate tonight. This was your idea, and we are working on your timetable, so…"

The Dragons leader let his voice trail away as he gazed pointedly at Lowell, who swallowed heavily after a moment of confusion.

He was the initiate, or the recruit, or whatever. *He* would be expected to torture Tim McKenna to death. And while he'd fully expected to take part in the ritual—had been looking forward to it immensely, in fact—his plan had been to get his rocks off by chopping off a pinkie finger or something and then stepping aside.

He hadn't intended to dismember a man he'd known for decades and then watch him bleed to death.

"I-I-I'm expected to…" He had no idea what to say next, but it turned out he didn't have to say anything. De la Cruz nodded, still smiling, still without warmth, and said, "Yes. You are expected to."

"But you told me you had found a couple of kids you wanted to bring into the fold."

The man with the gun—Diego, de la Cruz had called him—snickered and Lowell ignored him. In his shock at the unexpected turn of events, he'd nearly forgotten all about the man *and* his gun.

"I lied," de la Cruz said simply, and then shrugged. "I am surprised you expected otherwise."

"But I—"

"What are you going to do to me, Lowell?" McKenna interrupted. He'd been watching the exchange with an almost clinical detachment.

Lowell didn't answer. He couldn't answer. He was too busy trying not to throw up all over his feet.

He realized de la Cruz was saying something else to him, and as he'd done earlier, he missed every word. There was a ringing noise in his ears and it was getting louder, and he was rapidly reaching the conclusion he'd made a big mistake.

Not in getting involved with the Dragons; they offered money and women and drugs and a sense of adventure Lowell had never before experienced. His mistake was in assuming he could get down and dirty with the animals that constituted the Dragons' "workforce."

His mistake was in assuming he could handle the messiness of gangland violence up close, the blood and the guts and the ugly realities of life on the wrong side of the law.

Lowell was about as far removed from a thug or a grunt as it was possible to get. He was a management person, a thinker, a planner, a big-picture type, much more suited for, say, Hector de la Cruz's role with the Dragons than for Diego's.

And it was time to speak up. Well past time, in fact. Time to let Hector de la Cruz in on the truth that had only now been revealed to Lowell Stevenson. So it didn't matter that Lowell didn't know what de la Cruz had just said to him. Lowell would do the talking now.

"I've made a decision," he said firmly.

"Is that so?" De la Cruz spoke calmly, and that damned smile was still plastered across his face. It was creepy. As a kid, Lowell had been terrified of circus clowns, and it occurred to him that Hector de la Cruz at this moment was the equal of any clown Lowell had dreamt about when he was little.

"Yes, it is so," Lowell said. "I've decided to take a seat in my usual spot upstairs and to observe as I normally do. You can take it from here, or have one of your men do it, whatever you feel most comfortable with."

Lowell sighed deeply, happy to be relieved of the burden of eliminating Tim McKenna and more than a little proud of himself for standing up to the leader of one of the most ruthless street gangs on the east coast. He had no doubt de la Cruz would recognize the guts it had taken to make his announcement and respect him even more for it than he already did.

He turned toward the door leading to the hallway that would take him upstairs to his personal observation balcony. He only realized de la Cruz hadn't answered him when the man took three steps to his left and blocked Lowell's path. Lowell had lowered his gaze to the floor while turning to leave, and now he raised his eyes to meet de la Cruz's.

"Where do you think you are going?" the Dragons leader said. His voice was quiet, barely more than a whisper, but it was filled with menace.

"I-I just told you. I've come to a decision, and I think—"

"Stop talking," de la Cruz said, and Lowell slammed his mouth closed. The Dragons' leader reached under the front of his shirt and pulled something out, holding it eye level in front of Lowell. The object was small, maybe two inches long, and slim, barely wider or thicker than one of Lowell's fingers. It had been hanging on a gold chain around de la Cruz's neck.

"What's that?" Lowell said. His voice shook and he hated that he was showing weakness in front of de la Cruz but he just couldn't help it.

"What does it look like?"

Lowell had only glanced at the object for a split-second, preferring to keep his eyes trained on de la Cruz. No matter what the man was holding in his hand, it couldn't possibly be more dangerous than de la Cruz himself. Now he forced himself to give it a closer examination.

"It's…" His mouth was dry and scratchy and the words stuck in his throat. He cleared it and tried again. "It looks like a computer memory stick."

"Precisely," de la Cruz said. "Would you like to know what this computer memory stick contains?"

"I very much doubt it," Lowell said.

The smile on de la Cruz's face widened, and for a moment his eyes showed actual amusement. Then the look was gone and the dead shark's stare returned. The smile stayed. "You are probably right about that. On this memory stick is a few minutes of video. Would you care to guess who is the star of this video footage?"

Lowell couldn't talk. He couldn't even breathe. He shook his head.

"It is you, my friend. You are the star of this little movie. You may not have noticed in your zeal to observe the torture that has taken place in this building, but one of the features of your observation area is a small surveillance-style video camera mounted into the ceiling. It is recessed, very difficult to see, but it is there, and has been since your very first appearance with us."

The world began to spin crazily and Lowell again thought he might be sick to his stomach. De la Cruz didn't seem to notice and in any event kept talking. "The footage shows your eyes glued to the action on the first floor. It shows you stimulating yourself to orgasm as people are dying in front of you, and by the most brutal methods imaginable."

Lowell swallowed heavily and wanted to sit. He needed to sit. But the only available place to sit was the killing chair in front of him. Somehow he managed to continue standing.

"I know what you're thinking," de la Cruz said.

"I doubt that."

"You are thinking," he continued, ignoring Lowell's words, "that the quality of the video taken by a camera small enough to escape your notice must be low, that no one watching it would be able to discern the identity of the disgusting pervert gaining sexual satisfaction by watching men get tortured to death. But trust me, my friend, the quality of the footage is outstanding. Every last inch of you is revealed in the highest cinematographic quality."

The thug with the gun snickered again and Lowell ignored him. Again.

De la Cruz continued. "The advances in miniaturization of video surveillance equipment really are quite impressive."

"Why are you doing this?" Lowell croaked.

"Because I want you to know that I own you. If I tell you to slice off this man's fingers one by one, that is exactly what you will do. If I tell you to stand on your head and piss into your own mouth, that is exactly what you will do. Because if you do not, this footage will be delivered to the FBI, anonymously, of course, within the hour."

De la Cruz's smirk widened and he said, "You will become a very popular person with all the heavy-hitting law enforcement agencies, Judge Stevenson."

"You have to know my immediate response to such an action would be to identify you and the rest of the Dragons to the authorities," Lowell answered. He tried to sound firm and resolute but managed only shaky and terrified.

De la Cruz's face darkened. "Of course I know that," he said. "But I have developed contingency plans for just such an occurrence. You would be dead before your words ever reached anyone who could do the Dragons any real harm."

"How could you—"

"If you believe we have influence only with local authorities, you are fooling yourself badly. I developed federal contacts before ever inviting you here, my friend. Those contacts would silence you long before you could implicate me or the Dragons in any serious manner."

"Why don't you just shoot me now, then?" Lowell said. The ringing in his ears had stopped for a few minutes but it was back. He didn't think it would disappear again any time soon.

"Because," de la Cruz answered. "This is arguably more effective than threatening your life. And it is unquestionably more fun."

29

Jack couldn't make out what was being said in the large room one floor below; the acoustics were poor and the men too far away. But the discussion between Hector de la Cruz and the more frightened of the two older white guys was an intense one. By the time it ended, the more-frightened white guy seemed *much* more frightened.

Terrified, even.

The other white guy looked on with interest.

The terrified man initially seemed to hold his own against de la Cruz—or at least didn't immediately crumble—but then the Dragons leader fished something out of his shirt and showed it to the older man and things tilted decidedly in de la Cruz's favor from that point on.

Jack didn't know what the object was, but it looked too small to be a gun or a knife, and what would be the point in de la Cruz threatening the guy with a weapon anyway, when one of the other Dragons had been waving a pistol around the whole time like he thought he was Joe Pesci in Goodfellas?

They conferred for a moment longer—de la Cruz doing most of the talking—and then the old guy tried to step around the Dragons' head man. The tattooed gang leader blocked his path, then blocked him again. De la Cruz forced the man back to his previous position next to the other white guy, and that was when the man visibly deflated.

It was obvious to Jack that that was the reaction de la Cruz had been going for. He'd intentionally pushed the man until forcing him into submission. Once accomplished, de la Cruz disregarded the man. He turned and spoke to one of his lieutenants, the gang-banger who'd been waving the gun around.

The lieutenant nodded once and then hurried across the large room, disappearing from view into the hallway that Jack knew led to the building's rear entrance and lobby.

Where another Dragon was supposed to be guarding the door.

Where Jack had knocked that man unconscious and then trussed him up and tossed him into a closet.

That man would likely soon be discovered, and when he was, things would get very interesting very quickly.

Even if the Dragons somehow missed finding their compadre, they certainly wouldn't miss noticing he had disappeared, and that would be almost as bad. They would know something was wrong, and while they might not immediately realize what that something was, Jack's only advantage—surprise—would be well on its way to vanishing.

He slipped into the shadows.

Retraced his steps down the stairway.

Prepared to move on to the next stage of his mission.

30

"Now get to work," de la Cruz said.

"I...uh...wh-what?" Lowell was having trouble concentrating. Everything he'd done with the Eighth Street Dragons to this point had been of his own free will. He'd been happy to take advantage of the drugs and the women his association with the gang provided, and the torture he observed during their initiation rituals had opened his eyes to a world that had previously existed only in his most fevered fantasies. The sexual thrill those previous Dragons initiations gave him had been the most satisfying experience of his life, sexual or otherwise.

But the pair of gut punches he received in the last few minutes had rocked him, coming completely out of left field and rendering him virtually unable to breathe, much less to think logically and figure a way out of this mess. Finding out he alone would slice off Tim McKenna's fingers and then he alone would watch the man bleed out and die had been bad enough, but learning of the existence of Hector de la Cruz's blackmail video was the straw that broke this particular camel's back.

Lowell's sense of free will had been nothing more than a mirage. His association with the Dragons had been exciting and rewarding when he'd thought he could walk away if the relationship became too dangerous. But now, knowing he was at the mercy of an amoral sociopath, it was all he could do to avoid crumpling to the floor and curling into the fetal position.

If that happened, he knew he would die. De la Cruz would simply shoot him where he lay. He would have to—

"HEY!"

Lowell jumped. His nerves were shot and he literally jumped into the air at de la Cruz's shout. He stumbled when he landed and nearly fell on his ass.

"Pay attention," the man said.

"What do you want?" Lowell tried to speak firmly and confidently, but the words came out mumbled and hard to understand.

"I told you to get to work, and you ignored me like I was not even here. Now, unless you wish to become an instant movie star, I suggest you get busy securing your police chief friend to the chair. Maybe you have all night, but I have things to do, matters that are much more pressing than this."

Lowell blinked and squinted as he looked up at de la Cruz. God, it was so hard to think. "Where are the rest of the Dragons?"

Hector shrugged. "There are a few of us in the building."

"But isn't everyone usually here for these ceremonies?"

De la Cruz snorted. "Ceremonies? Do not kid yourself, Judge. This is no initiation. You are not an Eighth Street Dragon and you never will be."

"Then what is…" Lowell gestured at McKenna and the chair and the bucket in the middle of the floor. "…all this?"

"You told me we had a problem we needed to deal with immediately. This is how we are dealing with it."

McKenna had remained mostly silent, but now he turned to face Lowell. He coughed out a humorless laugh, and when he spoke, his eyes were steely. "That's all I was? A problem for you?" He shook his head and when he continued speaking, it was in a voice dripping with contempt. "You make me sick, Lowell. I mean it. Physically ill. I've made mistakes, obviously, and I've regretted getting involved with this gang of thugs and murderers almost from the very beginning. Now that association will cost me my life. But no matter how badly I may suffer tonight, I wouldn't trade places with you for all the riches in the world."

A little of the old self-assurance began to rise inside Lowell as McKenna spoke. Who the hell was *he* to question Lowell's choices? And he might not want to trade places now, but once the cutting started, Lowell was pretty sure he would change his mind on that score, and quickly.

Lowell was about to tell him to shut the hell up, but he realized McKenna had already stopped talking. He'd apparently said his peace and lapsed back into the stoic silence he'd exhibited for most of his time inside the Dragons headquarters.

De la Cruz grinned as he watched the exchange between the two old friends, but now he focused his attention once again solely on Lowell. "Get him in that chair," he said quietly.

Lowell turned to McKenna. "You heard him. Move."

He expected the police chief to resist and if that happened he didn't know what he was going to do. Tim McKenna was in better shape than Lowell and as a career cop, undoubtedly more accustomed to physical confrontation, even though it had been decades since he'd patrolled the streets.

To his surprise, though, McKenna didn't resist. He walked to the chair and sat. His face was pale but composed, a look of quiet expectation on it.

Lowell followed, and as he got closer to the chair he realized a roll of duct tape had been thrown in the bottom of the bucket. He was obviously expected to use the tape to secure McKenna. He thought back to the last initiation ritual he'd watched and recalled seeing Officer Greg Daly's forearms, wrists and ankles all heavily covered with duct tape, which had been wrapped around the chair's sturdy wooden arms and legs.

This was what de la Cruz was waiting for him to do.

Lowell bent and retrieved the tape. He turned toward McKenna, and as he did, a couple of things happened at virtually the same time: a man's voice shouted in surprise and alarm from the rear of the building, and a series of firecrackers exploded immediately afterward, POP-POP-POP.

Lowell froze. Why in the hell would anyone be setting off firecrackers inside the Dragons' headquarters? It was confusing as hell and he had no idea what to do, so he did nothing. He stood motionless, his head turned toward the rear of the building, where the firecracker explosions seemed to be occurring.

De la Cruz didn't freeze, though, and neither did Tim McKenna. The Dragons leader cursed in Spanish, an angry, guttural sound, and then he began to bolt across the room, his destination the hallway leading to the rear of the building.

At the same time, McKenna sprang from his death chair like a circus performer being shot out of a cannon. He darted past Lowell and moved straight for the Dragon who'd escorted them here. The man was preoccupied, staring in concern in the direction of the chaos, clearly confident neither Lowell nor McKenna was a threat.

But he was wrong. Before the man could defend himself—before he could react at all, other than to make a weak, futile attempt at ducking the blow—the Lawrence police chief hammered him in the face with a roundhouse right.

The Dragon was younger than McKenna by decades, muscular where McKenna was flabby, and toughened by life on the streets where McKenna was soft from time spent behind a desk, but he dropped to the floor like a felled steer and lay still.

De la Cruz skidded to a stop and turned at the dead-weight sound of the body hitting the floor. His eyes widened and he took one step back toward Lowell and McKenna, pulling a gun and pointing it in their direction.

Lowell knew he was about to die.

But he didn't die. More firecrackers began exploding from the other side of the building, and de la Cruz cursed again and resumed his headlong dash toward the hallway.

Lowell still hadn't moved. Things were moving much too fast, and he was much too afraid, and he felt more dim-witted than he ever had in his entire life. He didn't know what was going on here but was coming to the realization it wasn't firecrackers at all he had heard. He turned toward Tim McKenna—who was most certainly *not* confused and dim-witted—and as he did, his fear turned to icy dread.

Because McKenna had dropped to his knees next to the unconscious Dragon and grabbed the man's gun off the floor.

And in about half a second, Hector de la Cruz would disappear down the hallway and then McKenna and Lowell and the unconscious Dragon would be alone in the room.

For the second time in seconds, Lowell knew he was about to die.

31

Jack had just reentered the rear lobby from the balcony, when one of the Eighth Street Dragons—a man he hadn't seen before—appeared through the door on the opposite side of the room. He wasn't quite running but he was moving quickly, a man on a mission.

And he didn't see Jack.

Yet.

The man was saying something in Spanish that included the name Ricardo.

Jack now knew the name of the man he'd left trussed up in the janitor's closet. Ricardo.

He slipped back into the stairwell and out of sight. Unless the Dragon's destination was this specific doorway, he should be safe for the moment. He lifted his weapon and trained it on the doorway, prepared to send the Dragon to hell should he step through it.

He didn't step through it.

After a ten count Jack eased to the door and risked a glance around the corner. The Dragon was looking around the lobby, muttering something half under his breath. He turned a full three hundred sixty degrees as if Ricardo might suddenly materialize out of thin air. Then he walked two-thirds of the way to the rear entrance before stopping in his tracks and focusing his attention directly on the janitor's closet.

Had Ricardo regained consciousness and kicked at the door or drawn the man's attention in some other way? Jack hadn't heard anything, but he was farther from the closet than the Dragon, and it seemed the only possibility that made any sense, unless the thug possessed mystical powers of divination.

Jack doubted that was the case. The man looked like dimwitted and slow, like divining the time would be a stretch.

In any event, the Dragons thug stood motionless for maybe two seconds, staring at the closed closet door. He cocked his head like a puppy hearing an unusual sound. Then he began sidling in the direction of the janitor's closet.

Jack had been holding his weapon at his side, but now he raised it as the Dragon reached the closet door. The man grasped the doorknob with his left hand, gun held in his right. He held the knob uncertainly, then yanked the door open in one sudden, violent motion.

The Dragon stared into the closet in shocked surprise for a heartbeat. Then he shouted something in Spanish and dropped into a crouch, sweeping his weapon left to right around the lobby.

Jack had stepped partially clear of the doorframe the moment the Dragon opened the janitor's closet. The game was about to be up and he needed to get off a kill shot.

The thug's instincts had been good in dropping to a crouch and sweeping the room, but his execution was poor. In his adrenaline-fueled excitement he moved too quickly, swinging his gun past Jack before he could get off a shot even after he'd spotted the intruder. He reversed motion and fired, but the shots were wild, missing their intended target by three feet and spraying the wall to Jack's right.

Jack returned fire, squeezing off three rounds in rapid succession. All three caught the Dragon in the chest. He staggered backward, a look of disbelief on his face that faded to slackness before his body hit the floor. He sprawled onto his side and lay still as his gun skittered away across the concrete.

Things had gotten out of hand, and much sooner than Jack had expected. His presence was no longer a secret. It was time to shift this mission into high gear.

And he would have to hurry. The firefight would undoubtedly have drawn the attention of Hector de la Cruz and the rest of the Dragons, and while they would know better than to charge headlong into the lobby where they could be cut down in a hail of gunfire, they might even now be beginning the process of surrounding him.

Jack knew he should check the pulse of the Dragon he'd shot, but the man was still motionless on the floor and was clearly no longer a threat. He was either dead or nearly so. Instead of wasting time he did not have, Jack stepped over the downed man and picked up his gun. He shoved it into the waistband of his jeans at the small of his back, exactly as he had done with the first thug's weapon, which was now in his hands.

Then he turned to the janitor's closet. The gangbanger he'd trussed up inside it had indeed awakened, and now he stared up at Jack with a look of abject terror. He knew he was about to die and knew also there was not a damned thing he could do about it.

Jack should finish the man off. There was no longer any reason not to bury two slugs in the guy's skull. Jack's cover had been blown with the previous gunfight and the whole point of coming here had been to decimate the Dragons.

But he couldn't do it. He simply couldn't bring himself to discharge a weapon point-blank into the body of a helpless man, no matter that thug's complicity in the crimes the Eighth Street Dragons had committed over the last several years.

The man who'd assassinated more evil people than he could count in a career spanning nearly two decades didn't have the stomach for this kill.

He trained his gun on the Dragon, who was now whimpering through his gag. Said, "Shut up," and the man immediately stopped whimpering. "I want total silence out of you, or I'll come back and empty this magazine into your brain, do you understand me?"

The man nodded, blood still running sluggishly from his skull and down in his neck, disappearing under his shirt, which had soaked through.

Jack stepped back and eased the door closed once again. What he'd just done was unquestionably foolish. He had allowed an enemy combatant to live when he could have ended the man, and he'd wasted far too much time in doing so. He was outnumbered and outgunned, and this kind of poor judgment was the sort of thing that caused operatives to die.

But he'd made his decision and he wasn't going to change it.

He put the wall at his back and considered his options. There weren't many, and what few he had were all risky.

He could take the hallway leading to the big room where Hector de la Cruz had intimidated the two older white guys, but that would presumably lead him straight into de la Cruz's arms. There was no way the Dragons' leader wasn't coming to investigate the sound of gunfire in the lobby.

He could race up the stairs to the balcony, but while it was a tempting option—establishing the high ground was always desirable—there was one problem, and it was a big one: the balcony was accessible from only the one door. He would be trapped once the Dragons realized he'd taken cover up there.

That left two choices: a door to his right and another to his left. He had no idea where either entrance led, and no clue whether a Dragons foot soldier might be standing behind either or both, ready to blow him away the moment he stepped through the door.

One thing he did know was that he couldn't stay here.

He chose the door his left for the simple reason it was closer. Walked to it keeping his gun trained on the hallway entrance, staying prepared should Hector de la Cruz show the extreme stupidity of charging through it.

When he reached the door, Jack grabbed the knob and eased it open a couple of inches. He swiveled his weapon away from the hallway behind him to the door in front of him and gazed through the narrow opening.

It was another hallway.

And it appeared empty.

This was the best chance he was going to get.

He breathed deeply and moved through the door.

32

Lowell was astonished when De la Cruz bolted through the door and disappeared down the hallway. Apparently he had made the split-second decision that it was more important to investigate the sound of gunshots coming from the rear of the building than to put a bullet in Lowell's forehead.

But there was still the matter of Tim McKenna. The police chief now had a loaded gun in his hands and a look of steely determination in his eyes and no longer seemed like such a lily-livered pussy to Lowell Stevenson.

And Lowell had no idea what to do.

Literally.

None.

There was nowhere to hide and nowhere to run, and even if there had been, Lowell was carrying a good forty pounds of excess weight on his frame and hadn't run anywhere but to the liquor cabinet in thirty-plus years.

So he froze.

For one brief, shining, optimistic moment Lowell thought his old friend had forgotten he was here. The chief's attention was on the door de la Cruz had gone through. Whether that was because he thought the Dragons' leader might come back or because he was just as befuddled about what the hell was happening as Lowell was anyone's guess.

But McKenna wasn't pointing the gun at Lowell—yet—and the judge considered that a positive development in a situation that still appeared as close to hopeless as he'd ever seen.

Then the positive development vanished. McKenna turned and faced Lowell head-on. He pushed himself to his feet, the gun aimed halfway between Lowell and the floor.

He began walking slowly toward Lowell, and after a second's hesitation Lowell began backing away just as slowly. There was still nowhere to run, of course, but Lowell was damned if he would just stand there and let an armed man—and undoubtedly an angry one, at that—place a gun against his temple and blow his brains all over the room.

For a moment the distance between the two men remained constant. One step forward by McKenna, one step back by Lowell.

One step forward.

One step back.

One step forward.

One step back.

Not only could Lowell not think, he could barely breathe. His ass banged into the wall and he could retreat no further. He was trapped.

In his flustered state he considered making a play for McKenna's weapon, ripping it from the cop's hands and saving himself by gunning the man down. He would shoot his friend in the head and then charge out of the building, taking out anyone who got in his way, including—and especially—that two-faced asshole, Hector de la Cruz.

He tensed, preparing to leap at McKenna and claw the gun out of his hands or die trying, when he realized the cop had stopped coming. McKenna man turned and eased into the sturdy wooden chair that until just moments ago had been intended to hold him against his will as Lowell Stevenson methodically chopped off his fingers and tortured him to death.

The police chief sat quietly, examining the handgun as if he hadn't become intimately familiar with dozens of pistols just like it over the course of his career. He ran a finger along the barrel and lifted his head, gazing in the direction of the door de la Cruz had just run through.

Lowell continued sidling along the wall, edging away from McKenna, praying the motion didn't catch the chief's attention and cause him to turn and begin firing. To say Lowell was confused would be an understatement. He had expected to be bleeding out on the floor by now.

Maybe McKenna's brain had short-circuited from the stress. Maybe even now he was melting down into a catatonic state; Lowell didn't know and didn't much care. He'd gotten an unexpected reprieve and he intended to make the most of it. There was a long way to go before he could consider himself safe, but at least he was still breathing. That was an unexpected step in the right direction.

McKenna mumbled something and then lifted his head and locked eyes with Lowell, who stopped moving immediately. The gun was still pointed away from him for now, but that could change at any moment. The two men stared at each other, McKenna with an expectant look on his face, and after a moment Lowell realized why: the thing he had mumbled was meant for Lowell's ears and he was awaiting a response.

"Uh…I missed that, Tim, what did you say?"

"I said I'm tired. I'm so fucking tired, Lowell."

He could have said he'd discovered the gateway to the lost city of Atlantis and Lowell would not have been more surprised. Tired? Now? What the hell was that even supposed to mean?

But much more importantly, how should Lowell answer? The wrong response would likely get him killed, but for the life of him, Lowell couldn't imagine what any *right* response might sound like.

He opened his mouth with no idea what he was going to say, when McKenna saved him the trouble by continuing to speak. "There's no way out of this. You know that, right?"

Warning flags. Alarm bells. Lowell wondered if he would feel the bullets enter his brain or if everything would just go black. "Don't think that way, we can alw—"

"My life is over, my career gone. I've shamed my family. My wife will leave me and my kids will never speak to me again. I'll die in prison, and sooner rather than later. It's over."

"Everybody makes mistakes." It sounded monumentally stupid even as he was saying the words, but Lowell had no idea what else to say. What he *did* know was that if McKenna was talking to him he wasn't shooting him, so it was very much to Lowell's benefit to keep the lines of communication open until he could figure a way out of this shitstorm.

Apparently Lowell's response was irrelevant, because McKenna continued speaking as though he hadn't heard a word. "Everything's come crashing down. It's all over and there's not a goddamned thing I can do about it."

McKenna had been running his finger back and forth along the gun barrel as he talked, his touch soft like a lover's, and the action was making Lowell increasingly uneasy. The police chief had definitely lost it, and his line of reasoning was chilling. Lowell resumed shuffling along the wall toward the door. The action might make him a target, but at this point it was a risk he was willing to take because it was obvious McKenna was about to gun him down anyway.

It took a moment for McKenna to notice, but when he did he lifted the weapon and pointed it directly at Lowell. "Stop right there."

Lowell stopped. So did his heart.

"I want you to see this," the cop said.

"I don't understand, Tim. I…I need to see something?"

"That's right."

He shook his head in confusion, wishing the lunatic would aim the fucking gun in a different direction. "What…what do I need to see?"

McKenna hesitated for a moment, and Lowell thought maybe he'd decided not to answer. Then he said, "This."

He opened his mouth widely and placed the gun barrel inside it.

Then he pulled the trigger.

His eyes never left Lowell's.

33

Jack crept along the hallway. It was dimly lit and narrow, claustro-phobic. It was like being stuck inside a giant MRI machine.

It hadn't taken long for him to realize that with the exception of the large open room he'd seen from the second-floor observa-tion post, the remainder of the ancient mill building consisted of a warren of corridors and small machinery rooms. He wondered what the hell product might have been manufactured here a century ago, and then kicked himself mentally for allowing his attention to wander.

It was the kind of mistake that would get him killed.

He tensed at the sound of footsteps from above, coming from the direction of the rear lobby. Someone was approaching, and quickly. Three or four quick steps were followed by a heavy thud, and then the cycle was repeated, and Jack knew he'd made the right move in abandoning his previous position. He would have been a sitting duck had he stayed put. A man was charging halfway down a set of stairs and then leaping onto a landing, before repeating his action on the next set of stairs.

Stealth didn't seem to be part of the man's plan of attack.

Jack squinted in concentration. The mill building was only four stories tall, so even if this Dragon were approaching from the farthest distance away—the roof—he would soon run out of stairs to thunder down, and reach the first floor. It was critical he learn whether the man was approaching or moving away.

The footsteps were getting louder.

The man was definitely moving closer.

Given the maze-like nature of this structure's interior, it was entirely possible the man would choose a different route to take to investigate the gunshots. The mill would have been an urban combat nightmare for a team of men to attack, never mind just one. Jack would eventually have backup, of course, but assuming Janousz was following their agreed-upon plan of attack, he hadn't even breached the building yet.

The sound of hurried footsteps reverberating down metal stairs continued to increase in volume before coming to an abrupt end. The man had obviously reached the first floor and would now be rushing...somewhere. If he were headed in Jack's direction he would round the corner at the end of the hallway—close to twenty feet away—at any moment.

Jack flattened himself against the side wall. He wished he could move to one of the closed doors and step behind it, get some kind of cover, but the nearest door was dozens of feet away and he doubted he had time to reach it. He didn't want the man to appear at the end of the hallway while he was running, and have to try a shot while on the move. The distance was too great and he would almost certainly miss.

Better to hunker down here and be prepared.

He slid into a shooter's crouch, concentrating on the near end of the corridor, where the gang member would—or would not—appear. He worked on slowing his breathing, aware of the adrenaline racing through his system. Aimed the weapon straight down the hallway, prepared to adjust as necessary when—if—the Eighth Street Dragon came into view.

A rustle of clothing from behind him was followed by a thud as a man rounded the corner too fast and rammed his shoulder into the wall. Jack heard a muffled curse in Spanish, and knew his worst fear had been realized. He'd been approached by an enemy at his six while defending against the possibility of one at his twelve.

He was facing the wrong way.

He jammed his heels against the wall and dived forward onto the filthy floor, rolling onto his back as a shot from behind echoed down the hallway. His upper left arm began to burn and he knew he'd been hit but had no idea of the extent of the damage.

And no time to worry about it now.

He squeezed off a shot from his back, just as the Dragon fired again.

Both men missed.

Jack got a look at his assailant as he fired a second shot. It was Hector de la Cruz. The Dragons' leader cursed again and flinched, before disappearing back in the direction of the lobby.

Now Jack had no choice but to move. If de la Cruz returned at the far end of the corridor and the man whose footfalls he'd heard rounded the other corner, lead would rain down on Jack. Survival would be impossible.

He pushed to his feet and ran down the hallway in a crouch. His upper left arm burned and he wanted to press his right hand to the bullet wound but had to keep his weapon trained straight ahead in case an assailant appeared. He waited with every step for the sound of gunshots from behind him and for slugs entering his back that would knock him face-first to the floor.

None came.

Five seconds to run fifty feet, his left arm throbbing.

His internal stopwatch told him if the roof sentry were going to appear in the hallway he should have arrived by now, but he knew he had no real reason to think that. The man would be moving cautiously if he had any operational sense, and that was especially true now that shots had been fired in this section of the building.

Jack slowed as he approached the end of the corridor. Maybe he'd hit de la Cruz and injured him and that was why the man had retreated instead of pressing his advantage. Or maybe he was even now approaching from a different direction.

There was no way to know.

As he moved, Jack shook out his injured arm. It burned and throbbed, but he was able to lift it and control his hand, so whatever damage the slug had done was not structural. If Jack was going to die tonight, it would not be from this wound.

He pushed the injury from his mind and by the time he reached the corner he'd once again dropped into a low crouch and moved against the wall. His heart was pounding and the blood rushing in his ears sounded like Niagara Falls. He breathed slowly through his mouth and listened for anything that might indicate the presence of another human being waiting around the corner.

Nothing.

One deep breath, in and slowly out.

Then Jack placed his right foot at the ninety-degree angle where the two hallways intersected. He pushed off with his left and spun around the corner, leading with his weapon, ready to fire.

Nothing. The cross corridor was empty.

He crept forward, staying low, now focusing his attention on the end of this hallway, knowing the roof sentry could be lurking behind any of the half-dozen or so closed doors running down each side. He made it three duck-walking steps before a man's upper body poked warily around the corner at the far end, a pistol pointed in Jack's direction. The man flinched at the sight of Jack and pulled his trigger reflexively.

The slug whistled harmlessly into the ceiling.

Jack squeezed his own trigger just as the man was retreating behind the corner. What would have been an easy shot under most circumstances was complicated by the burning in Jack's injured arm and his inability to prevent his left hand from shaking.

But the slug struck its target. A grunt of surprise and pain was followed by a thud as the man hit the floor, and that was followed by the heavy metallic sound of his weapon clattering out of his grasp.

And Jack moved. He stood and sprinted the distance of the hallway. The man's bullet wound might well be no worse than Jack's, and he could even now be gathering his wits—and his weapon—for another attack. It was time to take one more Dragon off the board.

Jack slowed as he approached the corner. He crouched again and gripped his weapon with two hands, less concerned about his unreliable left hand at close range than he'd been from a distance. One quick deep breath and then he turned the corner exactly as he had the last one.

The gangbanger was crawling toward his gun, which had skittered maybe eight feet away when he fell. He was bleeding heavily from the shoulder/neck, crimson arterial flow soaking through his t-shirt in the few seconds it had taken Jack to approach. He was a goner, bleeding out, but either he didn't understand that fact or wanted to make his last act a deadly one, because he was gasping and struggling but had almost reached his weapon.

Jack squeezed off two quick shots that echoed off the century-old walls and made his ears ring even worse than they'd already been doing.

The man fell still. He crumpled face-first to the floor, his outstretched hand eighteen inches from its goal. Jack stepped over the body and kicked the gun farther down the hallway, a conditioned act based entirely on his training even though it seemed obvious the Dragon was no longer a threat.

He knelt and placed two fingers behind the man's ear, checking for a pulse that was never going to come. His fingers came away coated in blood and Jack swiped them clean on his jeans before moving to the gun and picking it up. He checked the magazine. He now had a second backup.

With this immediate threat neutralized and no other Dragons showing themselves, Jack took a moment to examine his left arm. It was a risk he needed to take at some point, because he had to learn how badly he'd been injured by Hector de la Cruz's bullet.

He shrugged his windbreaker down and used the main body of his shirt to sop up blood from the upper arm. When he'd done so he smiled. A narrow furrow ran along the outside of the arm where the slug had dug out a chunk of skin before continuing on into the corridor wall or wherever it had eventually come to rest.

The injury was bloody and painful but definitely not life threatening, and that was all Jack needed to know. He put it out of his mind and slipped the windbreaker back over his shoulders.

He remained in a crouch, sweeping his gun right to left, grateful no Dragons had come along during the fifteen seconds it had taken to check the severity of his wound. As he did so his cell phone vibrated. It was the agreed-upon signal from Janousz, and it meant it was time for Jack to begin making his way back to the rear lobby.

He slipped his phone out of a rear pocket and texted the acknowledgment that Janousz would be waiting for.

Then he rose out of his crouch and kept moving.

34

The gun roared and McKenna's body lifted off the chair in a death spasm as blood, bone and gore splattered out the back of his head.

Lowell couldn't see the cavity the gunshot had blasted through McKenna's skull, the angle was wrong, and for that he was grateful because it must have been massive. The amount of blood and tissue was shocking. He only realized he'd begun screaming when he had to stop to puke. He bent at the waist and splattered the floor with yellowish bile, getting some on his six hundred dollar Salvatore Ferragamo dress shoes and not caring.

He dropped to one knee, smearing his trousers in the puke. Wiped a long string of drool off his mouth with his sleeve and tried to will the sight of Tim McKenna's head deflating like a popped balloon out of his consciousness. It didn't work. It was never going to work.

He moaned and panted and then moaned some more. None of Lowell Stevenson's erotic fantasies of torture and mutilation had included anything remotely similar to the sight he'd just witnessed. He'd fully expected to see Tim McKenna die tonight, but this was not what he'd envisioned. This was just…messy and ugly and horrifying.

By the time he lifted his head and glanced back across the room at McKenna, the man's body had slipped off the chair. He lay crumpled on the floor, the torture chair on its side next to him, a small pool of blood spreading around his shattered head like a grotesque crimson halo.

For a moment Lowell thought he might get sick again but didn't, and after choking back more bile he staggered to his feet. He was shaking uncontrollably and running through his body was a sensation that felt exactly like someone had attached an electrical wire to his nervous system and was running a low-wattage charge through it.

He was in shock, he knew that, and why wouldn't he be? He'd just seen one of his oldest friends blow his own head off with a gun. The fact that Lowell had planned this man's death was irrelevant. It was supposed to happen in a much different manner, a manner that would have been, if not cleaner, at least less...shocking and disgusting.

And then there was the matter of the single gunshot McKenna had blasted into his brain. Lowell had never actually seen a handgun fired before, and the sheer power and destructive capability of such a small machine was breathtaking. It was a revelation.

Because despite the fact he was in shock and had been emotionally traumatized in a manner from which he might never recover, now that he'd had a chance to breathe and a moment to think Lowell realized the handgun with which his friend had ended his life might just provide the means for Lowell to save his own.

The weapon lay on the floor next to the dead man, just waiting to be picked up and used again. Say, by a circuit court judge who'd gotten in over his head with a group of bloodthirsty thugs, a man who needed something powerful and deadly to provide protection as said judge tried to escape.

Maybe Tim McKenna had felt death was the only way out, but Lowell Stevenson sure didn't.

Everyone seemed to have forgotten all about Lowell and McKenna in the chaos, and that was just fine with Lowell. He'd heard the occasional staccato bark of gunfire at random moments since de la Cruz had run out of the room. The sounds had come from various locations within the big building, and Lowell hoped that whatever was happening would continue happening long enough for him to slip out unnoticed.

The original shots had come from the rear of the building, where the armed guard had patted Lowell down so unnecessarily roughly, and he had no intention of trying to escape that way.

Whether an Eighth Street Dragon with a gun was stationed at the front entrance or not he had no way of knowing, but if a man was there, Lowell liked his chances of escaping as long as he could catch the man by surprise.

But he needed that gun.

And that meant stepping over or around a still-bleeding corpse.

Lowell began moving toward the toppled chair and McKenna's ruined body. He knew he had to hurry but his body would not cooperate with his brain. He simply could not force himself to move toward the disgusting corpse any faster than he was currently doing.

He slipped in his own vomit and regained his balance and continued shuffling across the floor. He felt his gorge rising again and swallowed heavily. There was no way he was going to be able to step over McKenna—he pictured the man coming back to life and grabbing him by the ankle and pulling him down to the floor where he would hold Lowell in a bear hug in the blood and the brains and the gore until de la Cruz returned and put a bullet in Lowell's skull—so he began circling the police chief in a wide arc.

Finally he reached the gun. He bent and picked it up off the floor and immediately backed away from McKenna's body. Once again he nearly puked. The weapon was coated in slime, the inevitable result of being thrust deep inside a man's open mouth and then fired.

Lowell wiped it on his trousers and then again on his shirt for good measure. He realized he was whimpering but could no more stop himself than he could turn back time and avoid ever becoming involved with Hector de la Cruz and the Eighth Street Dragons in the first place.

When he'd finished cleaning the gore off the weapon it was still sticky and nasty but at least Lowell could hold it without throwing up. He didn't know how many bullets this handgun held because he'd never had the slightest interest in them, his own pistol notwithstanding. He thought old revolvers held six but knew modern guns like the ones the Dragons used held more.

In any event, McKenna had only lived long enough to pull the trigger once, and Lowell was betting it had been fully loaded before. Whether that meant the gun still held five shots or many more would be irrelevant, because if Lowell couldn't escape within five shots, he knew he wouldn't be escaping at all.

He held the gun in two hands like he'd seen in the movies, his finger resting on the trigger, ready to blow away anyone who might cross his path. The big room remained silent and still. From a distance he heard a panicked scream that ended abruptly. It was so abrupt Lowell couldn't tell from which direction it had come.

He began moving toward a closed metal door he hoped would bring him in the direction of the front entrance. The door was located directly across the room from the hallway leading to the rear entrance, so it struck Lowell as the most likely possibility.

As he approached the door, Lowell reached for the knob with his left hand, clutching the gun tightly in his badly shaking right.

And his finger was still on the trigger.

And the gun went off.

Fire belched from the barrel with a deafening roar, and in an instant a slug blasted a crater in the wall nearly the size of a baby's fist.

Lowell screamed and almost dropped the gun. He juggled it and damned near pulled the trigger again. He realized he was crying and had no idea when he'd started.

He yanked open the door with no pretense of stealth and stepped into an empty hallway.

Began walking toward what he hoped would be the front entrance.

Tried to force himself to stop shaking and could not.

He half expected to be ambushed and shot dead at any moment, baby-fist-size holes riddling his body, but somehow that moment never came. No one appeared in front of or behind him. Lowell thanked the gods of chance that de la Cruz had limited tonight's festivities to only a trusted few upper-level Dragon members. Had the entire gang been present, he would never have survived.

The corridor was long and mostly straight, with a slight jog to the right at the far end. It was similar to the setup at the rear entrance, and Lowell knew he'd chosen the correct hallway even before he'd turned the corner far enough to see the front lobby.

He realized he was nearly panting with anticipation. He could hardly believe his good luck. Somehow he was going to escape what had just a few minutes ago seemed like certain death. He was still crying but smiled widely in anticipation of sweet freedom.

Lowell hurried into the lobby and caught a blur of movement out of the corner of his right eye. He sensed it as much as saw it, and screamed in surprise and terror, bracing for impact just before colliding with a heavily muscled and tattooed Dragon member rushing into the room from a different corridor.

The impact knocked both men to the floor, and as Lowell fell he gripped his gun so tightly it discharged again, and then he dropped the gun in a panic and screamed for the second time in two seconds. Or maybe he simply continued his initial scream; he had no way of knowing because everything was a blur.

Inside his head he cursed the sudden change in his fortunes. He'd come so goddamned close to escape, but it was going to be for naught. He squeezed his eyes shut and waited for the gang member's bullet to enter his brain. This night had been a wretched failure, as had his whole association with the Eighth Street Dragons, and now he was going to die, and he still had so much yet to achieve, and—

Wait a second.

He was still alive.

Why hadn't the Dragon killed him yet?

Lowell forced his eyes open, certain he would be staring straight down the barrel of the Dragon's gun, certain the man was fucking with him and would put a bullet between his eyes the moment Lowell opened them.

But he wasn't staring straight down a gun barrel, and the man wasn't fucking with him.

He wasn't doing anything, in fact, except bleeding out onto the floor.

Lowell's accidental gunshot had struck the Dragon in the head and he was lying perfectly still, his gun clutched in his unmoving hand.

Lowell hadn't stopped crying, and now he swiped his sleeve across his eyes to clear his vision, not quite able to believe what he was seeing. He looked again and when he did, the gang member was still bleeding and still not moving, and Lowell took that as a clear sign that he needed to get the hell out of the old mill building while he—somehow—still could.

He pushed to his feet, and even in the midst of his panic and terror was proud of himself for having the presence of mind to retrieve the gun he'd dropped. The police would be investigating this horror show, and Lowell's prints would be all over a weapon that had just killed a man.

He picked up the gun and pushed through the door to the outside and began skirting the front of the building, holding the weapon down by his leg in case any pedestrians happened to see him, but nobody seemed to be around. He made it safely to the mill's northwest corner and turned left.

He jogged down a trash-littered alley and continued past the rear of the building to the lot where he'd left his car. Christ, it seemed like he'd parked the damned thing years ago, rather than less than an hour.

His hands were shaking so badly it took three tries to unlock the door with his key fob, but finally he managed it and dropped into the front seat, sweating and shaking and feeling like he might puke. Again.

Breathe, Lowell. He took a moment to gather his wits and marvel at the fact he was still alive. Then he pressed the button to start his car—thankful he didn't have to stick the key in the ignition, because it would have taken at least another three tries—and pulled away from the curb. He would cross the Merrimack River on his way home and while doing so would toss the handgun over the side of the bridge.

The river was wide and deep in this area.

The gun would never be seen again.

Then he would continue straight home. He promised himself he would fall into bed and sleep for the next three days.

35

Janousz Bejko received the acknowledgment text from Sheridan's burner phone and then waited in position a block south of the target building. He still didn't fully understand or agree with his temporary partner's operational plan, but Sheridan was the one shouldering most of the additional risk from doing things his way, so who was Janousz to argue?

Besides, at least here in Massachusetts he was finally doing what he'd been recruited to do when he agreed to leave Eastern Europe and fly to the states to join Tony Mercadante's crew. Mercadante was paying him handsomely for his experience as a hitter, but he didn't seem to have a clue how to use his new man now that Janousz was here. Big Tony had stuck Janousz behind a reception desk to answer telephones for his marginally lawful import/export business while local Vegas clowns with a tenth of Janousz's experience—and absolutely no finesse whatsoever—executed hit jobs Janousz could have handled without breaking a sweat.

This was better.

This was far better.

This was why he'd traveled halfway around the world.

He might disagree with certain specifics of Jack Sheridan's plan, but Janousz could tell the man was a true professional, confident without being cocky and as competent an operator as anyone Janousz had ever worked with. A bit too human and empathetic for his own good, maybe, but he was a man with whom Janousz would happily work again, given the opportunity.

After Sheridan had handed him the key and climbed out of the rental car, Janousz had taken a short, cautious walk in order to study as much of the exterior of the mill building as he could. It was time not particularly well spent.

After a while, Janousz tired of staring at the crumbling red brick façade. He returned to the car and drove around Lawrence for a while, no destination in mind, cruising the city streets as the anticipation and adrenaline started to build. He thought about ordering takeout from a fast-food place, but Janousz never felt hungry before working and doubted he could have eaten a meal to win a bet.

Once the job was over he would be starving, but eating before an assignment made him feel logy and slow.

Eventually, as the agreed-upon time approached, Janousz returned to the abandoned neighborhood surrounding the Eighth Street Dragons' home base. Janousz wondered about the name, since the gang's lair was not located on a street named "Eighth," and, in fact, he hadn't seen a street by that name in his travels through Lawrence.

He shrugged. There were a lot of things he didn't understand about life in his new country, he supposed this was one more item to add to the list.

Sheridan had told him the gang had effectively cleared out a one-block-plus no-go zone in all directions, with the building at the epicenter. The effect was to create a kind of modern-day moat, where anyone approaching from any direction would be visible to the gang from a long distance away unless that person was very stealthy.

Janousz planned to be very stealthy.

He parked the car just outside the Dragons' ring of exclusion, approaching the building from the rear. Activity this close to the danger zone was minimal, but the occasional pedestrian walked the streets and every once in a while a car would cruise past.

Janousz climbed out of the car and popped the trunk. He lifted the rig containing the gear Sheridan had obtained from his Organization contact and shrugged into its shoulder harness. It felt lighter than Janousz had expected, well balanced, leaving him relatively maneuverable. He hadn't expected that, given the contents of the dual tanks.

He slammed the trunk lid and began moving in the direction of the Dragons' stronghold, melting into the shadows next to empty buildings and keeping to narrow alleyways. He avoided the sidewalk altogether. If Sheridan had done his job, the roof sentry would be long gone by now, but Janousz couldn't think of a single reason to take unnecessary chances, and lots of very convincing ones not to.

Like staying alive.

He kept the wall of another abandoned factory building between himself and the Dragons' fortress for as long as possible. Soon he reached the open space directly behind their building, where he would no longer have the benefit of cover once he continued on. As he slowed and peered across the lot he was surprised to see movement on the far side of the structure, along the exterior.

It was a man. He was older and overweight, completely out of place in this setting. He wore a suit, and even from a distance Janousz could tell it was an expensive one, if currently rumpled and bloodstained. The man was in a big hurry, half-running, half-shambling, and in his hands he held a pistol that bounced around as he moved.

Janousz eased back into the shadows as he kept his eyes trained on the man, worried at first that he'd somehow been spotted. He had no doubt he could take the overweight stranger out, armed or not, but a confrontation in this place and at this moment was something he could ill afford.

The man continued moving, the entirety of his attention focused straight ahead, and Janousz realized he could have sprinted into the middle of the empty parking lot and begun singing Polish folk songs at the top of his voice and the man likely would not have noticed. He was fleeing something, probably Sheridan's activities inside the Dragons' home base, and he wasn't thinking about a single thing besides getting away. The term "Situational awareness" was not in this man's vocabulary.

The stranger disappeared behind a building, and for a moment Janousz considered either following him to neutralize him, or at the very least, waiting to be sure he didn't return. Then he decided the man could safely be eliminated from consideration as a threat based on his obvious terror. There was no way he would be returning under any circumstances. Not tonight, and probably not ever.

Janousz returned his attention to the Dragons' building. He decided that if the strange-acting overweight man had crossed the parking lot without drawing the attention of anyone inside, he should be able to as well. So he settled the harness into place and double-timed to the rear door, which was located exactly where Sheridan had said it would be.

He put his back to the wall and lifted his weapon as the tanks clanked against the brick surface. He banged on the door several times and then swiveled on his heel and placed his gun barrel directly against the metal screen covering the small slit in the otherwise impenetrable door. The moment an Eighth Street Dragon showed his face to challenge the intruder, Janousz would force the man into an easy decision: open the door or have the entire front of his skull blown off.

Once the door was unlocked, Janousz would blow the man's face off anyway.

He waited a moment but saw and heard nothing.

Banged on the door again and waited again. Still nothing.

Obviously, Sheridan had gotten the Dragons' attention so effectively the door guard had either abandoned his post or was already dead. Janousz reached for the doorknob. He would give it a try and when he found it locked, as he knew he would, he would circle the building to the front entrance and try the same ruse there.

But the knob turned. It was oversized, larger than a typical doorknob, and made of heavy-gauge steel, clearly designed for use in tandem with a heavily reinforced door. But with the knob unlocked, the door would be no more effective at preventing entry than a big piece of cardboard, no matter how reinforced it was.

Janousz shoved it open. He entered the building gun-first and immediately smelled the stench of gunpowder. Weapons had been discharged here, and recently. He was unsurprised.

He'd entered a small lobby and the first thing he noticed was the dead man lying in front of an open door. The second thing was the trussed-up guy inside the janitor's closet just beyond the dead man. Clearly Sheridan had overpowered the dead man and taken his weapon, but why he hadn't used it on the second Dragon—who was still clearly alive—was a mystery to Janousz.

But how to resolve that situation was no mystery. Janousz crossed the room, covering the other entryways as he walked. When he reached the janitor's closet he stepped over the dead man and placed his gun against the side of the gang member's head. The man was conscious and had been gagged, but despite the fact his words were unintelligible, their meaning was quite clear.

He was begging for his life.

It meant nothing to Janousz.

The man met his gaze. He was shaking his head, quick little convulsive movements, as tears poured down his face, and none of that meant anything to Janousz, either.

He squeezed the trigger twice, an economical but effective double-tap, and the man's head jerked sideways as his upper body slumped to the floor. His legs spasmed twice and then fell still.

Janousz was turning to contemplate his next move before the man had stopped kicking.

36

The corridors Jack had seen all featured rooms of varying shapes and sizes off each side. He assumed they'd been manufacturing stations a hundred years ago when the mill was built, but now they sat silent and mostly empty, their doors closed.

Those doors featured blocky windows covered with thick glass, and Jack had tried to glance through the ancient windows and inside as many of the rooms as possible while hunting down Dragons in this ghostly building. Given everything else happening it had been a hit-or-miss proposition, but he'd tried to do it anyway, for two reasons: he *needed* to ensure no one was inside any of them waiting to ambush him, and he *wanted* to check the rooms out for evidence of drugs, weapons, or other gang materials that could be used to kill civilians.

Those kinds of materials had to be here somewhere; the Eighth Street Dragons had gone to a lot of trouble to quarantine the area surrounding their fortress and Jack knew they hadn't done so just for kicks.

They'd been protecting deadly assets.

He continued to do check the rooms as he moved toward the rear lobby to meet up with Janousz. He'd seen nothing inside any of them until reaching the corridor where he'd shot the latest Dragon.

But along here he struck pay dirt. Knockoff AR-15-style rifles were stacked inside one room, along with handguns and knives and other weaponry. The room was a good-sized space, but there were so many different types of weapons crammed inside, many still packed in shipping crates, it was nearly stuffed nearly to overflowing.

The next room he passed contained a makeshift drug lab. He was moving too quickly to get much more than a general idea of the room's contents, but he was certain there was fentanyl/heroin in there, as well as cocaine, methamphetamine and doubtless many other potentially lethal illegal pharmaceuticals.

He was getting close to the rear lobby, and he thought he knew what he would find behind the next closed door. He approached slowly and flattened himself against the wall. Eased one eye up to the window and discovered his suspicion was on target. He'd found Hector de la Cruz.

This room was an office of sorts, and the leader of the Eighth Street Dragons was inside it, standing behind a desk, facing the door but looking down as he spoke frantically into a cell phone. He was calling in reinforcements, Jack knew, instructing the Dragon on the other end of the call to round up as many gang members as possible and storm their headquarters in an attempt to regain control of the building.

If Jack and Janousz were still here when that happened, they would never escape with their lives.

They needed to finish this mission now.

Jack backed away from the window and tried the knob. He expected it to be locked and it was.

He had to move fast but recklessness could be fatal, so despite the gravity of the situation he took a moment to consider his options. Kicking in the door would give de la Cruz too much time to react, and besides, if this one were reinforced as much as some of the others he had seen, he might very well discover he couldn't access it anyway.

But there might be another way. The glass in the window looked thick but old and delicate, reinforced with wire mesh but definitely not bulletproof. It was probably original to the building.

That clinched it. He had his plan. He stepped in front of the door and fired three shots in rapid succession through the window.

The glass spider-webbed and then broke apart, not quite shattering thanks to the wire mesh, but Jack didn't care about that. He didn't need it to shatter. He jammed his gun through the opening and squeezed the trigger again as de la Cruz was lifting his own weapon to return fire.

In his surprise and panic the Dragons' leader began backing away from the desk instead of dropping behind it and using it for cover.

It was an understandable mistake but it would cost him his life. Jack's first shot buzzed wide, but by the time he fired again, he'd honed in on de la Cruz.

The man squeezed off a wild return shot and then realized his error. He launched himself at the desk in a desperate bid to put it between himself and his attacker.

He was far too late. Jack wouldn't miss again. His second shot knocked de la Cruz sideways to the floor and his third stopped the man cold.

The Dragon's gun had flown out of his hand and halfway across the room when the first slug struck him. Jack felt he could risk stepping back from the window and attempting to kick in the door, exactly as he wasn't willing to do when the man represented a legitimate threat.

He smashed the door at the handle and it gave way with a loud *crack* but didn't quite open. A second kick did the trick, though, and the door rocketed inward and smashed off the back wall.

Jack stopped it on the rebound with his left boot, and then advanced on de la Cruz, his gun trained center-mass on the man the entire way. If the prone gangbanger was playing possum he was doing it very effectively, but Jack was taking no chances. The Dragons' leader had proven himself brutal and resourceful in bringing the city of Lawrence to its knees, and if anyone could make that old trick work, it was Hector de la Cruz.

Jack knelt and felt for a pulse. Found none. His second and third shots had both struck de la Cruz in the chest and stopped his heart so immediately there was very little blood.

He wasn't playing possum.

He wasn't playing anything.

De la Cruz had hit the ground so violently something had been jarred out of his t-shirt. The item was hanging around his neck on a gold chain, and Jack at first assumed it was simply a cross or a gang sign or some other item of jewelry. It lay on the floor next to the dead man and as Jack took a closer look he realized it wasn't a piece of jewelry at all.

It was white plastic, rectangular in shape, roughly the dimensions of his pointer finger. On top was a beige slide handle.

Jack picked it up and pushed on the slide and a USB connector extended from the far end. He was about as far from a computer expert as it was possible to be in the year 2018, but even Jack Sheridan knew what this item was: a computer thumb drive.

Jack's forehead furrowed in concentration. The question was obvious: what information could be so important to the leader of the Eighth Street Dragons that he carried it around his neck at all times?

He couldn't imagine what the answer to that question might be, but the fact that the drive had been important to de la Cruz made it important to Jack. He pulled it clear of the dead man's body by its chain. He didn't bother lifting de la Cruz's head as he did so. De la Cruz wouldn't feel any pain from the chain scraping across his skin. De la Cruz would never feel anything again.

Jack stuffed the thumb drive into his pocket and stood. He stepped over the body and moved to where de la Cruz's gun had come to rest six feet away. Another gun would do him no good, so he kicked it out of sight under the desk.

Janousz was on his way, which meant this would be over soon, so the danger inherent in leaving a loaded gun lying around was minimal. Jack doubted there were many more Dragons left alive inside the building at this point, but if there were, nobody would have time to scour this office, find the gun, and then use it on Jack or Janousz. Not with what he had planned next.

Jack took one last quick look around the office. It was bare bones and sterile, with just the metal desk, a well-used chair, and another similar chair that had been banished to the far corner of the room. There was nothing the least bit interesting about any of it.

He hurried to the desk and tried the drawers.

All locked.

He knew he could access them given a little time, but time was a luxury he didn't have. Jack stepped over the body of Hector de la Cruz one last time and then moved to the office door.

He scanned the corridor in both directions and saw nothing. Then he left the office and continued toward the rear lobby.

37

Janousz turned away from the dead Dragon and found himself face to face with Jack Sheridan. The man had seemed to materialize out of nowhere, and Janousz was reminded why Sheridan came so highly regarded.

Janousz didn't miss a beat. "What now?" he said.

"Follow me." Sheridan turned and strode through one of the doors leading out of the lobby. He had his gun out but didn't seem particularly concerned about the possibility of ambush.

"Anyone left alive?" Janousz asked.

"I don't think so, but if there are any rats still scurrying around this sinking ship, they'll show themselves soon."

Sheridan moved purposefully along the dimly lit corridor, opening doors along each side as he went. In the distance, not quite where the hallway terminated in a cross-corridor, Janousz could see the prone body of an Eighth Street Dragon. The man was unmoving. He thought they were going to walk right past the dead man, but before they made it that far Sheridan veered left, turning into a room with an open door.

Janousz followed and his eyes widened at the sight of an armory that would be the envy of any medium-sized-city's police force. Military-style semi-automatic rifles, some undoubtedly converted to full auto, were stacked in neat piles. Other rifles were stacked nearby, as were an impressive array of handguns, knives and ammunition. The sheer number of weapons was staggering.

"Roast them," Sheridan said.

"What about explosives?" Janousz said, staring at the crates stacked next to the weaponry. "There must be ammunition in those boxes. Possibly grenades. Who knows what else?"

"This building looks decrepit, but these walls are constructed of solid brick and thicker than you've probably ever seen. As long as we're not inside this room when the fireworks start, we should be fine."

"*Should* be fine," Janousz repeated.

Sheridan grinned. His face was filthy and flecked with blood and he was bleeding from his left upper arm. "No guarantees in this world, my friend."

Janousz hesitated, unsure how to respond, and Sheridan's grin widened. "Come on, brother, where's your sense of adventure?"

Then he turned serious. "Really, though, we're running out of time. We need to finish this." He pointed at the weaponry stacked against the far wall and said, "Do your thing."

Janousz waited for Sheridan to step behind him and then lifted the hose attached to the dual tanks strapped on his back. He twisted a thumbscrew on the handle and pointed the hose at the far wall. Then he engaged the trigger.

The hose sputtered for a half-second and Janousz thought they had been given faulty equipment. Then a stream of liquid fire burst from the end of the hose. It flew across the room and splattered into the weaponry and the wall and instantly the room was ablaze, flaming fluid dripping down the wall like molten lava, fire climbing greedily toward the ceiling.

Janousz played the hose side to side and then released his grip on the trigger and instantly the fire stopped belching from the end of the hose. The flamethrower was one of the most devastatingly effective weapons of war ever invented, but its tanks were limited and they had more work to do.

Sheridan tugged on Janousz's arm urgently and he turned and exited as Sheridan pulled the door firmly closed behind them. "We need to get away from the door," he said. "It's the room's weak link. The walls are thick but the door is not. You don't want to be standing in front of it when those explosives ignite."

As if on cue, a sound similar to the popping of popcorn began inside the room. It rose quickly in volume and intensity as the super-heated chemical fire began igniting more of the explosives until with a roar, the closed door was blasted off its frame and into the hallway. It shot across the corridor and smashed into pieces against the far wall.

"See what I mean?" Sheridan said. "That damned door would have taken our heads off, but the wall is holding strong."

Janousz placed his hand against the brick wall and felt a slight vibration but nothing more. He looked at the ruins of the door and shook his head. If Sheridan hadn't pulled him away when he did…

"Let's go," Sheridan said. "We've got more to do and before long everything inside this building but the bricks is going to be burning like a crematorium."

They double-timed back down the corridor in the direction of the rear lobby, passing a couple of empty rooms before ducking into another one. This one was a drug lab. It was even bigger than the armory and filled with measuring equipment, baggies, beakers and other packaging, measuring and mixing materials. There were ovens and freezers. Janousz hadn't spent much time in school, but the setup resembled what he imagined a well-funded university's chemistry lab would look like.

He didn't bother waiting for Sheridan's instructions this time. Instead he gestured his tour guide behind him and then unleashed liquid destruction on the room. In seconds it was a roaring inferno, exactly like the armory down the hall, where the explosions were lessening but hadn't yet faded away.

With the experience of the explosive ammunition uppermost in his mind, Janousz blasted the room and then quickly exited, closing the door and moving hurriedly down the hallway. As far as he could tell no ammunition was being stored inside the lab, but there was a good probability that most of its chemicals were highly flammable and some even explosive.

Sure enough, a new round of popping and blasting began, accentuated by the sounds of smashing glass and toppling equipment. The explosions were muted compared to the sounds coming from the armory, and the door stayed on its hinges, but Janousz was taking no chances.

He said, "Let us continue. Where to next?" He realized Sheridan had opened the doors to the empty rooms lining the hallway for a specific purpose: to accelerate the burning process. Sheridan wanted this entire gang fortress to be nothing more than a smoking ruin when he was finished with it, and his choice of equipment to achieve that outcome was inspired. Janousz had never seen flames burn with anything close to the kind of intensity a few seconds of flamethrower magic could achieve.

A makeshift office was next, and this time Sheridan didn't even bother entering. He indicated the room with a nod of his head and then stood aside to allow Janousz access.

Janousz stepped inside and wasted no time igniting the room. Lying next to a desk in a pool of his own blood was another gang member, and Janousz glanced at the man stoically as he sprayed the room. The sight of another corpse meant nothing. The body was simply a sign the job was one step closer to completion.

In seconds the room was ablaze, and as Janousz backed through the door he saw that the fire had worked its way outside the first room they'd attacked: the armory. The explosions had died away and the thick walls had held, exactly as Sheridan predicted, but the flames were moving methodically—and rapidly—along the corridor in both directions as well as into the empty room directly across the hall.

"We've got to move!" Sheridan had to shout to be heard over the guttural roar of the fast-moving fire. "The way this thing is spreading, it could get behind us in seconds and if that happens, we're toast. Literally."

The pair hustled back along the hallway and burst into the rear lobby mere yards ahead of the advancing blaze. It was feeding on itself, picking up speed at an alarming rate. Janousz glanced back along the hallway and could see only a wall of fire roaring toward him like a freight train.

They burst into the rear lobby and Janousz hurried to the exterior door. As he reached to open it, Sheridan stopped him. "Turn around and spray whatever's left in the tanks into the lobby. Every little bit helps. Once the tanks are dry, we'll get the hell out of here."

Hell is right, Janousz thought. Sweat was soaking through his shirt and even though it couldn't have been more than five minutes since he'd started dousing the building in fire, he was as thirsty as he could ever recall being. The fire was roaring and the building was groaning and anyone stuck inside it as the flames worked their way up to the second floor and beyond would soon wish they'd been shot dead instead.

He turned and squeezed the trigger one last time, and one last time the liquid fire burst from the nozzle. It splattered the far wall, joining forces with the flames advancing into the lobby from the hallway. The hose sputtered and shook, and then with almost no warning the flamethrower was empty.

"That's good, let's go!" Sheridan said.

Janousz couldn't have been happier if the man had told him he was paying him a million-dollar bonus for a job well done. The ferocity of the fire was terrifying and the sooner he could get the hell away from it, the better. He would rather face a dozen armed men than this inferno, and it wasn't even a tossup.

He turned and pushed open the exterior door and the flames exploded in intensity. Oxygen was sucked in through the door and then a backdraft of superheated air chased the two men out of the building as they bolted into the parking lot.

Janousz muttered, "Cholera jasna". He was panting and shaking and thrilled to finally be outside the building and away from those damned flames.

"I didn't catch that," Sheridan said. "What did you say?"

"I said 'holy shit' in Polish."

Sheridan grinned. "I couldn't have put it better myself. Now let's get the hell out of here. This place is going to get very popular, very soon."

38

Jack felt reasonably confident no one had seen him during the assault on the Dragons home base. At least, no one still left alive.

Additionally, he'd scouted the area surrounding the old mill for security cameras prior to the assault and found none, and while it was always possible he'd missed one or more—the technology was so good now, almost anyone could install a miniature video camera in a location where it would not be seen—he didn't think that was the case. The area was deserted and run-down, and outside of the Dragons' fortress, there was nothing of any value anyone would want to protect. Since the Dragons hadn't bothered to install cameras on their own building, Jack couldn't imagine they would have placed any on the surrounding buildings.

But there was never a reason to take unnecessary chances, and in that spirit he had worn a battered old jacket he picked up for a few bucks at the Goodwill store that was two sizes too big for him, as well as a Tampa Bay baseball cap that was so old it said "Devil Rays" instead of "Rays."

He'd insisted Janousz wear a similar outfit, and once inside their rental car he gathered up the clothing and stuffed it into a trash bag, which would then be deposited into a random Dumpster somewhere between Lawrence, Massachusetts and Londonderry, New Hampshire. He'd bled all over his jacket after getting shot in the arm, but there was nothing he could do about that.

Mr. Stanton had assured him years ago that there was no record of his DNA or his fingerprints anywhere in the system, and that was good enough for Jack. He'd seen enough of the Organization's operations to know that if they wanted to keep that kind of information—or any kind of information—out of local and federal databases, they absolutely had the capability of doing so.

But he would make sure the jacket was never found, anyway.

They had traveled less than three city blocks on their way to the interstate when a string of fire/rescue vehicles raced past them, sirens blaring, in the direction of the blaze. Jack wanted to tell them to slow down and take their time, that they would be doing nothing more than cleaning up the empty shell of a brick exterior, but they would discover that on their own soon enough.

He steered the rental onto I-495 toward I-93, and as they approached the exit to turn toward New Hampshire, Janousz said, "Logan Airport is south of here, is it not?"

Jack cast a puzzled glance at his temporary partner. "Yes, it is. But Manchester is north, and that's where your hotel is located."

Janousz shrugged. "I no longer need any hotel. I would prefer to get back to Las Vegas as soon as possible."

Jack flicked off his turn signal and continued under the interstate to the southbound on-ramp. "It's getting late and we worked our asses off back there. Aren't you tired?"

Another shrug. "Sure. But I can sleep on the plane and as long as my work is done, I would like to get home if possible."

"That's definitely possible," Jack said. "You didn't leave anything back at your hotel?"

"Nope." Janousz grinned. "Everything I have is in one bag and it is right here." He pointed into the back seat.

"Fair enough. I actually have to talk to Mr. Stanton anyway, to make plans to get his flamethrower back to him. I was going to do that tomorrow, but maybe he can meet me in Boston and I can make the exchange tonight."

He accelerated onto the interstate and then punched the numbers for Mr. Stanton's private encrypted cell, wondering how many flights to Vegas were still scheduled out of Boston at this time of night. If there were even one, he knew Mr. Stanton would get Janousz a ticket in the thirty minutes it would take to reach Logan, likely a first-class ticket at that.

The Organization's head man answered on the first ring and Jack explained what he needed.

"Give me five," Mr. Stanton said, and disconnected the line without waiting for an answer.

They drove for a while in silence, and then Janousz said, "I almost forgot. There is something you should know."

"Okay. Hit me."

"As I was approaching the Dragons building this evening I saw a man walking the other direction. He looked out of place and extremely fearful."

"Out of place how?"

"He was not young and in shape like the gang members. I also do not believe he was Hispanic, although I admit it was difficult to gauge the man's complexion in the dark."

"Did he come out of the Dragons' building?"

Janousz shook his head. "I cannot be sure. I know he did not exit the rear door, but he may have come out the front. When I saw him, he was hurrying along the alley next to the building."

"And you don't think he was a gang member?"

"Most definitely not. He was heavy, out of shape. And he was terrified. That much was obvious."

"Interesting. Thanks for letting me know."

"Do you think—"

Jack's phone began trilling and he glanced at his watch. Four minutes and forty-five seconds since Mr. Stanton had told him to expect a call back within five minutes. He shook his head and smiled. The man was nothing if not punctual. "Go ahead," he said after accepting the call.

"Our friend is booked on National Airlines Flight 317 out of Logan in one hour exactly. I assume that timing won't be a problem?"

"None," Jack said. "We're already on our way."

"Excellent. And as far as our equipment transfer is concerned, an Organization driver will meet you in the parking lot at Antonio's Restaurant in the North End in ninety minutes. He'll be driving a New Bedford Fish Market van and has been instructed to assist you in any way possible."

"All he has to do is open the rear van doors and let me toss it in."

"You won't even have to do that. Park next to the van and offer a friendly little salute and he'll do all the heavy lifting. You'll be in and out of there in about a minute and a half."

"Good, because I'm tired. I'm getting too old for this career."

"Not at all," Mr. Stanton answered. Jack pictured him waving away the comment with a flick of his wrist. "Experience, my friend. Experience counts for a lot."

"Retirement counts for something, too."

Mr. Stanton laughed heartily and said, "You tried that and it didn't suit you, remember? I consider this an outstanding start to the second half of your career." He paused briefly and then said, "Speaking of experience, how was yours with Mr. Bejko? Satisfactory, I hope?"

"More than satisfactory. I would work again with him in a heartbeat."

"Glad to hear it," Mr. Stanton said. "I'll pass along a good word to Mr. Mercadante in Vegas."

"Speaking of that," Jack said.

"Yes?"

"I don't know how much you paid for Janousz's services and I don't need to know. But I hope the scales tilt a little more in favor of the man who actually put his life on the line to help me, and a little less in favor of some mob jabronie sitting on his ass in the desert."

There was the hint of a smile in Mr. Stanton's voice when he answered. "Put the phone on speaker, please, so Mr. Bejko can hear, since this concerns him."

Jack pulled the phone from his ear and thumbed the button on the screen. The he adjusted the volume upward and held the phone above the steering wheel. "Go ahead," he said.

"I've already made a direct deposit into Mr. Bejko's private checking account, the one the Mercadante crew knows nothing about."

Jack glanced across the seat to see Janousz's eyes widen comically. The man said, "I…I had…uh, I…no one knows about that account."

"Don't worry, Mr. Bejko," Mr. Stanton said soothingly. "Nobody besides me is aware of the existence of that account. Your employers in Las Vegas are none the wiser. What you choose to do with the payment is entirely up to you, of course. But rest assured, your employer has already been paid handsomely for allowing us to work with you. What he doesn't know won't hurt him. And he'll never learn of your extra payment from us, I promise."

Janousz looked utterly bewildered. He glanced from the phone to Jack's face and then back to the phone. "How…how did you…?"

Mr. Stanton ignored the question. "Is there anything else I can do for you gentlemen this evening?"

Janousz wasn't about to answer; he looked like he'd swallowed his tongue. Jack said, "No that'll do it. Thanks for your help."

"Think nothing of it. You'll be hearing from me soon, Mr. Sheridan. I'm so pleased we'll once again be working together. Enjoy the rest of your evening." And then he was gone.

Jack dropped the phone into his pocket and turned toward Janousz. The man still appeared nonplussed. It was the look of a guy who'd just seen a ghost.

Jack smiled. He decided to take pity on the man. "The Organization is everywhere, and they have contacts like you would not believe."

"So I see," Janousz said. "I would have been willing to bet my life that no one in the world knew about that bank account, much less could access it to make an electronic deposit."

"That's The Organization," he said. "You get used to the surprises after awhile. And for what it's worth, your account is completely safe. If your bosses in Vegas ever find out about it, that's when you'll need to worry, but I can vouch for Mr. Stanton's guarantee: they won't learn of its existence from him."

"I wonder if I should now close the account and open another somewhere else."

Jack shrugged. "Sure, if it will make you feel better. But you don't need to worry about The Organization. I don't care how much money you have stashed away in your account, they are playing for stakes that are much, much higher. They don't want your money, and they especially don't want their operators to know they can't be trusted knowing about your money. Because if they know about yours, they know about mine and everyone else's they decide they're interested in."

Janousz looked unconvinced.

"Besides," Jack added. "If they found this account they'll find the next one you open, and the one after that, if they're so inclined. I've learned I sleep much better at night not worrying about things I can't control."

Janousz swallowed heavily. He still looked shaken up, and Jack felt a little sorry for him. On the other hand, Mr. Stanton had just admitted to paying Janousz a handsome fee for participating in the same job Jack had done for free. It was hard to work up too much sympathy.

The rest of the drive to Logan took place mostly in silence.

* * *

Jack dropped Janousz at the National Airlines curb in the departure terminal. Janousz had already called up the flight reservation on his phone, and as he was traveling with just one small carry-on bag, he would have ample time to get cleaned up in a terminal rest room before boarding the plane. And that was a good thing, because between the heat and the smoke, he looked like he'd just finished servicing one of the engines on the Boeing 757 that would be taking him to Vegas.

Jack shook his hand and said a quick goodbye, and then he pulled away from the curb and exited Logan in the direction of Boston's North End. Traffic was relatively light at this time of night, so barring anything unusual—you could never rule out a car accident or nighttime road construction in this city—he would arrive at Antonio's long before Mr. Stanton's ninety minutes had passed.

But he didn't care. Maybe the organization driver would arrive early. Jack wanted nothing more than to make the transfer of the flamethrower and be back on I-93 northbound to New Hampshire as soon as possible. He hadn't been kidding when he told Mr. Stanton he was tired. He was also achy and dehydrated and his back hurt.

It sucks to get old, he thought.

*   *   *

It turned out that the Organization driver was early. So early, in fact, that Jack spotted the van already in position at the rear of the lot when he drove in. He wasn't particularly surprised. The poor bastard behind the wheel was probably every bit as anxious as Jack to get this over with and get home.

He eased across the lot and backed into the empty space next to the van. Mr. Stanton's choice of locations in which to make the transfer was perfect, exactly as Jack had known it would be. There was enough customer activity at the restaurant/tavern that neither of the vehicles would look out of place, and that was especially true since the logo on the side of the van was that of a fish market. Anyone paying attention—not that it appeared anyone was—would assume the van driver had decided to take a break or grab a bite to eat after making his last delivery of the night.

Jack lifted his hand to his forehead in a two-finger salute, exactly as Mr. Stanton had said to do. Following directions to the letter was important for both parties if the two operators were unknown to each other and thought of getting shot didn't appeal to either man.

The driver returned the salute and Jack opened his door as the other man was opening his. "It's in the trunk," he said, and popped the lid. This portion of the lot was quiet and relatively private, and the exchange would only take a moment.

"I got it," the other man said, and waved Jack back inside his car as he walked to the trunk.

"Sounds good," Jack answered. "Thanks."

He remained outside the vehicle, though, facing the rear. It was one thing to trust The Organization, it was another issue entirely to turn his back on a man he'd never worked with or even seen before. That was especially true since he knew that other man would be armed to the teeth.

In less than a minute, the flamethrower's tanks, hose and harness had been placed in the back of the van. Even from his position on the other side of his rental car, Jack could smell a strong fishy odor the moment the driver opened his door. It smelled like low tide at Hampton Beach.

The driver slammed the doors and climbed back into his vehicle without another word. He fired up the engine and the van rumbled out of the lot, turning toward downtown Boston and—presumably—wherever The Organization's armory was located.

Jack continued standing, watching the New Bedford Fish Market truck until it disappeared from sight. Only then did he drop into the front seat of his rental car.

He still had to return the car and walk the half-mile to where he'd parked his truck. He guessed he could do that and be home within ninety minutes or so. If that were the case, he would be asleep within two hours.

The countdown was on.

He couldn't wait.

39

Edie's car was parked at the end of Jack's driveway.

What the hell? He checked his watch, a reflexive response since he already knew the time: it was a little after midnight. Edie Tolliver had a seven year old daughter who needed to get up for summer camp tomorrow, not to mention a job running the Three Squares Diner that required her to get to work immediately after dropping her little girl off.

Being awake past ten p.m. was a foreign concept to her.

Being out of her house at midnight was practically unheard of.

Jack tensed. Something had to be wrong. He pulled his truck to the side of the driveway and killed the engine. He stepped out of the cab, but before his feet hit the gravel, the driver's side door on Edie's car flew open and she was charging across the driveway toward Jack.

She launched herself into his arms and he staggered backward. She was tiny and barely weighed a hundred pounds after eating a big meal but had been running at full speed before leaping into his embrace. She wrapped her arms around his shoulders and her legs around his waist and buried her face in his neck.

"Oh, thank God," she whispered. Her breath was warm and moist.

"What is it, Edie? What's wrong? Is Janie okay?"

She lifted her face from his neck and Jack felt wetness on his skin. She was crying and he had no idea why.

"Tell me what's wrong," he said again.

"Nothing. Nothing's wrong," she said. "In fact, it's just the opposite. Everything is right."

"Then…what…I don't understand, Edie. What's going on? Why were you parked in my driveway crying in your car at twelve-fifteen in the morning? Help me out here."

"Can we go into your house?"

"Of course. I don't know why you're here, but once you decided to come you should have been inside anyway, not sitting out in the driveway." Jack placed Edie gently on the ground and turned toward the front door.

She grabbed his elbow and stayed right next to him as they walked. Her hip was brushing his outer thigh and she seemed to crave closeness. He unlocked the door and shoved it open and they walked inside. Moved to the kitchen table and sat.

Before he could speak, Edie said, "I know you're not much of a wine drinker, but I brought a bottle a few weeks ago and I happen to know it's still in your fridge. Would you join me in a small drink?"

"Edie, what's going on?"

"Just one small glass of wine. Please?"

Without another word, Jack rose from the table and crossed the kitchen to the fridge. He pulled out the bottle and grabbed two small water glasses and then brought everything back to the table.

After pouring two drinks and retaking his seat, he said, "Okay. I did what you asked and we're having a drink. Now, spill it. What's going on? If everything's okay, why are you crying outside my house in the middle of the night?"

Edie took a sip of her drink and followed it up with a deep breath. Then she said, "I was worried about you."

"Worried about me? Why?"

She flashed him an incredulous look and then lowered her gaze to the table. "Why would I be worried about you? Well, let's see. You're taking on a ruthless gang of thugs, a gang that's brought an entire city to its knees. You're doing it alone. Oh, and you're doing it because I told you to."

"Edie, we've been over th—"

"And filthy dirty and your arm is bleeding, which means you

nearly got killed tonight. You could be retired, sitting in front of your TV watching sports like a normal guy, and instead you're…"

She'd started crying again. Jack reached across the table and grabbed her hand and she held it with the unyielding grip of a drowning woman grasping her life preserver. He started to speak and she lifted a finger to stop him, still refusing to meet his gaze.

"You're risking your life and it's all my fault." She spit out the words and then sobbed.

"Are you all done? Can I talk now?"

She nodded and he reached across the table with his free hand. Placed two fingers under her chin and lifted until she was looking him in the eyes.

"First of all," he said gently, "I'm not bleeding." He glanced at his upper left shirtsleeve, now crusted with dried blood and matted against his skin. He wrinkled his nose. "Not much, anyway."

She started to speak and he stopped her. "It's my turn, remember?"

Reluctantly she closed her mouth and he continued. "Secondly, we've been over this. You are not responsible for my actions. I'm a big boy and I make my own decisions. No matter what had happened down in Lawrence, even if things had gone horribly wrong, even if I had been hurt or killed, none of it would have been your fault. This is my chosen career, Edie. It's what I do."

"But you had ret—"

"There are no buts. No ifs and definitely no ands. Whatever happened in Lawrence, and whatever happens moving forward, it's all on me. Do you understand? Me. Nobody else."

"Happened?" Her eyes were moist as they searched his face. "I'm sorry? I don't understand."

"You said, 'happened.' You said 'Whatever happened in Lawrence.'"

"Yeah? So? I'm not following you."

"Past tense," she said. "Like it's all over."

The shoe finally dropped. "Ohhhhh," he said. "Yes, it's all over. Mission accomplished. You don't need to worry about me, Edie."

"You avenged that poor man's son?"

"The best I could, yes. But it's not going to bring him back. His children are still without a father and his wife is still a widow, and

Larry Daly is still a heartbroken old man. But yes, it's done. It will take a long time for the Eighth Street Dragons to rebuild their operation, if they ever do."

"It won't bring him back, but maybe your work will give his family a measure of peace."

Jack had been doing his job well over two decades and he'd learned a long time ago that there was no such thing as closure, no such thing as peace. The pain of losing Greg Daly would linger for his family, and with luck, eventually that pain might fade into acceptance.

It might not, too, and even if it did, it would take far more time than anyone involved could imagine.

But that knowledge would do Edie Tolliver no good; it would only bring her more anguish, and Jack had already brought this woman enough anguish for ten lifetimes.

So he simply nodded. "I hope so," he said, his voice a whisper.

She delicately wiped her eyes with a napkin and took a small sip of wine, and Jack said, "I still don't understand why you were crying in my driveway tonight."

"I told you, I was worried about you and was drowning in guilt."

"But you didn't know I was planning to take down the Dragons tonight, specifically."

"I didn't have to. I know *you*."

"Meaning?"

"Meaning, once you set your mind to something, you don't waste any time getting it done. It was almost a lock that you would be doing something dangerous tonight, and I just couldn't stay away. I was too worried."

"But what about Janie? What about work?"

She smiled. It transformed her face from tear-stained and anguished to radiant and heart stopping. Edie Tolliver's smile was the first thing he'd noticed about her during his initial visit to the Three Squares Diner after moving to New Hampshire. Her smile was the thing that had drawn him to her.

It raised his spirits but also broke his heart, because she'd once been his and now was not.

"Janie is spending the night at my mom's," she said, "and she'll get Janie off to camp in the morning. And I've told Mark Goetz that he's in charge tomorrow. I'm taking the day off work."

Jack blinked in surprise. "Really? You never take days off work. The only time I know of was…"

"When Janie was missing."

"Yes. So what's the deal? Even if you were worried about me, that all seems a little…I don't know…extreme."

She looked down at the table again and traced a scar in the wood with her finger. Then she glanced shyly back up at Jack. This circumspection was unusual for a woman Jack had learned long ago was as direct as they came. There was no deception about Edie Tolliver.

"What is it?" he said.

A shaky sigh. "I was hoping I could spend the night here…you know, with you."

"Are you saying…?"

"Yes. I'm saying."

"Oh my God, are you kidding? Of course you can stay the night. I've told you before you were always welcome here. But are you sure you want to…? I mean, you made it clear you couldn't deal with the way I'd deceived you about my career choices. You said—"

It was her turn to raise a finger to his lips.

"I know what I said," she whispered. "And I meant every word of it."

"Then, why…?"

"I love you," she said. "I've loved you from the moment we met, and I can't be apart from you. You're the finest, most honorable man I've ever known, and the best role model for Janie I could ever ask for. And I want to be with you, if you'll still have me."

Jack swiped the back of one blood-splattered hand across his eyes, which had suddenly become unreliable and leaky. "Yes, I'll still have you," he whispered. "Of course I will."

"Then I think we need to celebrate."

"Hence the wine."

Edie smiled. "Exactly! But I think our celebration should include something a little more…physical."

Jack blinked his eyes clear. "I couldn't agree more, but I need to get the stench of Eighth Street Dragons off me. Give me twenty minutes in the shower, okay?"

"You also need to clean that arm up." She reached for the bloody mess of his shirt, crusted around his upper arm, but stopped short of touching it."

"It's not as bad as it looks," Jack said. "I promise."

"I think it needs a woman's touch. How big is your shower again?"

Jack felt his eyes widen but couldn't help it. He grinned. "I think we can make it work."

"Let's go." Edie stood and waited for Jack to lead the way.

He recalled how tired he'd felt just a few minutes ago. Suddenly that exhaustion was just a memory.

40

Edie was still snoring softly when Jack slipped out of bed. They hadn't fallen asleep until nearly three a.m., and since the time was now barely seven-thirty, Jack guessed he wouldn't be seeing her downstairs for at least a couple more hours. But he rarely slept more than five hours at a time, and he'd been awake for a good thirty minutes already.

Sleep wouldn't be returning anytime soon. Coffee was in order.

He padded across the room and closed the door quietly behind him. Walked into the kitchen and started the coffee brewing. Then he moved to a living room cabinet and retrieved the thumb drive he'd taken off the body of Hector de la Cruz last night.

Its storage over the last few hours had been less than secure, but since nobody knew he had it, it seemed safe to assume no one would come here looking for it, no matter what sort of information it contained. And his theory was that it must contain something explosive. A computer thumb drive wasn't the sort of fashion accessory anyone would typically associate with a ruthless gang leader.

And while Jack Sheridan was no kind of computer expert, he guessed even he could plug a thumb drive into his desktop's USB port and access the drive's contents, and that was what he intended to do.

Maybe he wouldn't find anything of value.

But maybe he would.

* * *

He was staring at the computer monitor, watching the video it contained for the fourth time, when his bedroom door opened. He'd been focused intently on the screen, but that came to an abrupt end when he looked up to see his once and—fingers crossed, maybe—current girlfriend exit his bedroom and turn toward the living room.

She was breathtaking. Her blonde hair was tousled from sleeping on Jack's lumpy pillows, and she squinted as she tried to blink the sleep from her eyes. She'd brought pajamas and a change of clothes but had foregone the pjs in favor of one of Jack's button-down dress shirts.

He doubted either the shirt or the young woman inside it had ever looked so good.

She stumbled down the hallway stifling a yawn and smiled when she saw him watching her. She covered her face with her hands. "Don't look," she said in mock horror. "I'm a mess!"

"Are you kidding?" he said. "Heidi Klum should be so attractive. Giselle Bundchen should be so radiant. I would go on but I've exhausted my supermodel knowledge. I'm sure you get the idea."

"Stop," she said, smiling. "I glanced in the mirror before venturing out of the bedroom, so I've seen the damage. Heidi and Giselle would dive back under the covers in shame before they walked around looking like this."

"Then they're damned fools," Jack said. "You look terrific." He stood and gathered her into his arms. Then he leaned down to kiss her but she pulled away.

"I haven't brushed my teeth yet," she protested.

"I don't care," he said, and after a moment's hesitation she lifted onto her tiptoes and met him in a kiss.

They pulled apart much too soon as far as Jack was concerned, but given the way he felt right now, an hour would have been too soon.

"I need coffee," Edie breathed, her wide eyes zeroing in on Jack's empty mug.

He grinned and walked into the kitchen. As he poured her

coffee, he called back into the living room, "I don't know how non-coffee-drinkers jump-start their hearts in the morning with only juice or milk."

"Neither do I," she agreed. "And I have no intention of ever finding out."

He returned with coffee for Edie and a refill for himself and found her seated in front of his computer. He'd paused the video when she exited the bedroom and now her mouth was hanging open, her forehead wrinkled, as she stared at the image frozen onto the monitor.

"What the hell are you watching?" she said as she accepted her coffee.

"Just a little light entertainment, why do you ask?"

She flashed him a look that was part amusement, part revulsion. "I'm not buying that for a second, Mister. What is this, really?"

She scooted over on the chair as he moved to sit. There wasn't enough room for both of them, though, so Jack began to stand again.

Edie pulled him by the arm. "Sit," she said, and rose to her feet next to the chair.

"No way. I'm not going to take the only seat and make you stand. I'll slide another chair over and we can both—"

"I've got a better idea," she said firmly. "Sit."

Jack shrugged. "Yes ma'am," he said with a smile.

"And don't call me 'ma'am.' I hate that. It sounds like you're referring to my grandmother. 'Boss' will do just fine."

She waited for him to sit and then eased down onto his lap. "See? Isn't this better than you pulling a muscle dragging a heavy chair across the floor? You can't be too careful at your age," she added with a giggle.

"I'm sorry, Boss," he said. "What were we talking about? I've suddenly found it impossible to maintain my concentration."

She wriggled on his lap. "Good. And I'm not surprised. The mind is one of the first things to go."

"May I remind you I'm only a little older than you?"

"A little? Hah! Apparently your definition of the word is a *little* different than mine."

They sipped their coffee and then Edie nodded at the computer monitor. "But seriously, what in the world is this?"

"Work stuff," he said.

"Work, meaning it's related to the situation with Mr. Daly's missing son? The situation you said last night had been taken care of?"

"The very same," Jack said. "And I don't think you need—or want—to know the messy details. What you see when the situation down in Lawrence hits the news will be bad enough."

"Okay," she said. "I'm sure you're right. But what is this video, specifically? It looks…I don't know…pornographic."

And she was right. The video was paused on the scene of an older, overweight white male sitting in a chair, gazing at something happening off-screen. On his face was the hungry look a predator might display just before tearing apart its prey. His trousers had been lowered to his knees and his right hand was wrapped around his erect penis.

Jack chuckled. "I told you that you didn't want to know the details, but you wouldn't listen."

"What does…this…" she wrinkled her nose in disgust, "have to do with gang kidnappings and murders taking place down the road in Massachusetts? I don't know much about criminal activity, but that guy sure doesn't look like a bloodthirsty thug."

"Looks can sometimes be deceiving," Jack said. "But I agree, he doesn't look anything like the rest of the Eighth Street Dragons, at least not the ones I got up-close and personal with last night. I'm trying to figure out how he ties in with them."

Edie squinted and leaned forward to take a closer look. "The guy looks…kind of familiar, like maybe I've seen him before, but I'm not sure where or when."

Jack grinned. "He looks familiar? Above or below the waist?"

Edie turned on Jack's lap and punched him in the arm. "Very funny, Jimmy Kimmel. Where did you get this footage, anyway?"

"The Eighth Street Dragons leader gave it to me."

"Voluntarily?"

Jack shrugged. "Let's just say he wasn't in any position to argue about it."

Edie shuddered. To Jack she felt small and insubstantial in his lap. Delicate. She spun around and hugged him tightly and whispered, "I'm so glad you're safe."

"I'm fine," he said. "Good as new, I promise."

She held him for another few seconds and then said, "Play the footage."

"I don't think you want to see—"

"If you can take it, I can take it. Play it."

He tilted his head and looked at her curiously. "Random Casablanca reference?"

She smiled. "What can I say? It's one of my favorite movies. You get bonus points for recognizing it."

"Is that so? What can I buy with my points, and when do I get to cash them in?"

"You can buy anything you want, big boy. And to answer the second part of your question, Janie's at camp until four, and I don't work today. You do the math."

"I always hated math. Suddenly I love it."

She snuggled into him and then said, "I haven't forgotten about that video. Click 'Play' or I will."

He shook his head. "You are relentless, aren't you?"

"It's one of the things you love about me."

He couldn't argue the point.

*   *   *

To call the video disturbing would be an understatement. It had appeared slightly grainy with the image frozen on Jack's computer monitor, but once it resumed playing, the resolution was clear and crisp.

The man on the screen stared in rapt attention at activities happening off-screen. He was stroking himself slowly and breathing heavily, as a series of faraway voices, mostly garbled, came through Jack's speakers.

"There's sound?" Edie said. "What kind of video surveillance includes sound?"

"The expensive kind," Jack said. "It's illegal in a lot of situations to monitor sound as well as video, but obviously that wouldn't have stopped the Dragons. The question is why would they bother to install such a sophisticated surveillance system inside their own headquarters? And why in this location? Why are they keeping tabs on this guy when he's clearly there with their knowledge and permission?"

"How do you know it was even taken at their headquarters?"

"Because I recognize this spot from last night. I stood right where that guy is sitting. It's a jerry-rigged balcony of sorts, overlooking a large room one story below, which I believe they used as their torture/murder room. It looks like the Dragons constructed the balcony themselves, maybe just for this guy or others like him."

"So he could…watch the torture and get off on it?"

"It looks that way. Are you sure you want to keep watching? It gets worse."

Edie nodded grimly.

On the monitor the man continued to stroke himself idly. The voices fell silent off screen, but only for a moment. Then a man's anguished shriek filled the speakers. He screamed long and loud, lapsed into grunts and sobs for maybe ninety seconds, and then screamed again.

The overweight man in the chair began stroking himself faster as the screams continued, until he finished what he was doing and collapsed back in his chair. Off camera the agonized screeches continued for several long minutes.

When the man in the chair began to get hard again, Edie said, "That's enough. I can't watch any more."

Jack stopped the video and hugged her tightly. "I'm sorry," he said.

"The voice in the video, the man screaming. That was Mr. Daly's son, wasn't it?"

"Yes. Or one of their other victims."

"Mr. Daly could probably identify the voice as his son's."

"Probably."

"But? You sound unsure, so I know there's a 'but' in there."

"But Mr. Daly is never going to see or hear this video."

"He might have to, in order to prosecute this man, if he can be identified."

"If he's identified, prosecution will be the least of his worries. Trust me."

She shuddered again, and again he said, "I'm sorry. I wish you hadn't seen this."

"I'm glad I did. It's going to take me a long time to come to terms with your job, if I ever can. But seeing something like this makes it a lot easier to understand why you do what you do."

He hugged her tightly and she said, "And Jack…"

"Yes?"

"I think I might know who he is, God help me."

41

Jack loosened his grip on Edie and she pushed off his lap. Then she turned to face him, her eyes troubled.

Jack sipped his coffee, taking his time formulating his question. "How in the world would you know this man's identity?"

"I...I'm not positive this is the right man. I don't want to accuse someone of...of...*this,*" she nodded at Jack's computer monitor, "if I'm not one hundred percent certain I'm right."

Jack studied the woman he'd fallen so deeply in love with. This was the woman with whom, until less than twenty-four hours ago, he'd been certain he would never again have a romantic relationship. Now it appeared she was planting the seed of a second chance, and the last thing he wanted was to jeopardize that seed before it had even begun to grow.

He sipped his coffee again and reached for her hand. "You were a pretty good student in school, weren't you?" he said.

She blinked in surprise. "Actually, yes. I earned straight A's. Almost. I never could figure out Pre-Calculus. But what does that have to do with anything?"

"You must have taken hundreds of quizzes and exams, right?"

"Thousands, probably." She laughed. "Or at least that's what it felt like."

"And out of all those tests, a lot of them must have included multiple choice questions, right?"

She shrugged. "Sure. The majority of them, probably. Again, what are you getting at?"

"Some of your teachers must have given you advice about how to take those kinds of tests. I wasn't anywhere near the student you were, but even I remember what I was told about answering multiple-choice test questions."

She smiled. "They said that if you've studied the material, you should always trust your first instinct when picking an answer. Never second-guess yourself and change it."

"Exactly."

"I understand what you're getting at," she said. "But if my first instinct was wrong while taking a tenth-grade geography exam, I might get a B or a C on a test. Not the end of the world. If my first instinct is wrong here, the consequences to an innocent man's life could be catastrophic. Besides, this isn't material I've studied. This is a memory, and memories can be extremely untrustworthy."

"Lay the memory out for me," he said. "Let's examine it together and see where it leads, if anywhere. That can't hurt, right?"

"I suppose not."

Jack squeezed her hand tightly and led her to the couch. Placed her coffee on the end table and then settled in next to her. "No pressure," he said. "Just take your time and tell me what you remember."

She sighed miserably. "I don't know if I want to be right or wrong about this."

"You want to be right," Jack said instantly. "This guy was getting off to the torture and murder of an innocent man. He was complicit. He's every bit as guilty as the ones committing the crime. He needs to pay."

She nodded. "Okay. A while ago, maybe six months or so, I saw a news report on one of the Boston TV stations about a Massachusetts District Court judge."

"The judge was the focus of their report?"

"That's right. Apparently this guy had a history of being very tough on certain crimes, like drugs, prostitution, that sort of thing."

"They did a whole news feature on a guy just because he's tough on crime?"

"Not exactly," she said. "The point of the story was that he'd historically *been* tough on crime—maximum sentences, denial of bail to accused offenders, that sort of thing—but that he'd suddenly done a complete reversal. The reporter went over all the cases this guy had adjudicated over the last year or more, and discovered that in many recent cases he'd given minimum sentences to violent offenders, and had let others off entirely after bench trials despite convincing evidence of their guilt."

"He was on the take."

"The reporter never came right out and said it in so many words, but that was clearly the inference. I was furious that nothing could be done to an obviously crooked judge who was putting the community at risk with his sentencing policies. That's why I remember the report so clearly."

"And they showed the judge in this report."

"Yes. He wouldn't talk to them on camera, but they had plenty of footage of him entering and leaving the courthouse, and some more of him inside his courtroom."

"I'm assuming you don't remember his name?"

She shook her head. "Like I said, I'm not even sure it's the same man."

"You don't have to be sure. I'll take responsibility for being sure."

"How are you going to do that?"

"Through the miracle of modern electronics."

Edie smiled. "Of course. You're going to look him up online."

"Damn right," Jack said. "Do you recall which district in Massachusetts this judge served in? That would simplify things, but if you don't it's not a deal-breaker, we'll just have to dig a little deeper."

She squinted in concentration and then said, "I seem to recall it was..." her eyes widened. "It was the Lawrence courthouse. I remember being angry that it's not that far away from here, and I had to worry about some crooked judge letting violent felons off who might then endanger Janie."

"Okay, that's where we'll start." He didn't mention the obvious connection between a Lawrence judge and the video of the overweight man sitting inside the Eighth Street Dragons' headquarters getting off to a scene of torture and murder, but he didn't have to. Edie wasn't stupid.

He crossed the living room to his computer and brought up

his Internet search engine. Typed "Lawrence District Court" into the text box, and roughly half a second later a series of links filled his monitor, each claiming to offer information on the portion of the Massachusetts judicial system dedicated to serving the city of Lawrence and three surrounding communities.

One of the links read, "Lawrence District Court Judges," and Jack muttered, "Bingo." He clicked the link and waited a moment and a site popped up featuring a single name: Lowell C. Stevenson. The name was a clickable link as well, and when Jack followed the link a page appeared that offered a brief biography of the judge and a summary of the his judicial qualifications.

But the bio was unaccompanied by a photograph.

"Dammit," Jack muttered.

"It doesn't matter that there's nothing here," Edie answered. "It's not possible that a man could rise to the position of district court justice without leaving a long trail to follow online. Google his name and let's see if I'm right."

She was. Hundreds of links appeared, each dedicated to information regarding the Honorable—or, if Edie's memory was correct, the despicable—Lowell C. Stevenson. Jack scrolled down slowly, looking for one link in particular.

He didn't have to go far. He'd barely gone a third of the way down the screen when the news report Edie had referenced rolled up to his cursor.

That was the one he clicked on.

An archived copy of the video report popped up. It had run on Boston's Channel Seven News last winter. Jack clicked the arrow at the lower left portion of the video to launch the report.

The tape began rolling and the first face to fill the camera was that of the reporter, a middle-aged blonde woman named Amanda Cooper, who identified herself as the "Seven News Court Reporter." With the Lawrence District Courthouse as a backdrop, she began by detailing Judge Stevenson's career, and as she highlighted the abrupt shift in his sentencing patterns, Cooper's image disappeared, replaced by footage of the judge.

Unless Judge Lowell Stevenson had a twin or a doppelganger, it was the same man.

The resemblance was impossible to miss. It was apparent

within three seconds of viewing the footage, particularly given the crystal-clear quality of the Dragons' surveillance video.

"Wow," Jack said. "You should have been a detective. You have an amazing memory."

"Not really," Edie answered. "I only remember because the story made my blood boil. I'm getting angry all over again watching it now."

"Don't waste your energy getting upset about this slimeball. He's about to discover his life is going to get extremely complicated."

"How are you going to get at a man as high-profile as a district court judge? Won't that be a little…I don't know…risky?"

"Anything worthwhile is worth a little risk," Jack said. "But in this case, I don't think I'm going to need to get within twenty miles of Stevenson to accomplish my goal."

"I don't understand," Edie said.

Jack didn't answer. He winked at her and drained his coffee. "I need to make a phone call," he said.

42

Jack doubted he would have much trouble setting up another face-to-face with Mr. Stanton, and once he explained what he needed, The Organization's head man agreed to the impromptu meeting without hesitation. Jack wasn't even a little surprised to learn Mr. Stanton had the connections necessary to place Judge Lowell Stevenson's head squarely on the chopping block.

"I've got to run out for a couple of hours," Jack told Edie after hanging up with Mr. Stanton. "But I'll be back long before Janie gets out of camp. Maybe when I return, we can go out to lunch?"

"Why don't I just go with you, and we can stop for lunch after you finish with whatever you have to do?"

"I would love that," Jack said, "but this is work stuff and I would put you at risk unnecessarily by bringing you along. I love that we're back together...ish..but—"

"There's no 'ish' about it," Edie interrupted. "As far as I'm concerned, we're back together. I love you, and I've come to realize I always will."

"That makes two of us," Jack said quietly. "But that's all the more reason you need to sit this one out. I will not put you or Janie in danger."

"Another thing I've learned is that we're all in danger, all the time."

"That's true, but my goal is to minimize that danger to the ones I love."

"I understand," Edie said. "But you'd better drive that cute butt straight back here the minute you're finished." She pinched his ass and he jumped in surprise.

"You can count on it," he said.

*　*　*

The rendezvous took place, as so many others had over the course of Jack's career with The Organization, at Logan International Airport in East Boston. The terminals were typically crowded and noisy, which made for a relatively safe environment in which to carry on a conversation, and while no destination in or around Boston could be considered easily accessible by car, Jack had long ago learned many different routes into and out of Logan in order to minimize the likelihood of hours spent sitting in bumper-to-bumper traffic.

Unlike previous Logan meetings, where the two men had sat in terminal restaurants and shared a meal, no food was involved. Mr. Stanton was clearly preoccupied and anxious to conclude their business in order to get on with the rest of his day, and Jack felt exactly the same. For most of his career the only thing waiting for him at home was an empty house, but now that house held Edie Tolliver.

And that was where he wanted to be.

Mr. Stanton flashed a wry smile as he appeared as if by magic off Jack's left side while strolling through Terminal B. "Your hand-iwork in Lawrence is the talk of the news, as I'm sure you've seen."

"I rarely watch the news," Jack said, "unless I'm looking for something specific."

"Then you should watch tonight."

Jack passed Mr. Stanton a sealed envelope containing the thumb drive that would bring down Judge Lowell Stevenson. "I'll be sure to do that. Which Boston channel should I tune in to?"

"Whichever you prefer. The soon-to-be disgraced judge will be the lead story on all of them, if this video clip is even half as illuminating as you say. By tomorrow morning, the national networks will undoubtedly be carrying the story as well. This footage is far too salacious for them to pass up."

Jack knew the answer to his next question before he asked, but he couldn't stop himself. "You know people at all the Boston TV stations?"

"In this case, I wouldn't need to know anyone, I would simply have to outline what the video contains. But to answer your question, yes. I'm a little hurt you even felt the need to ask."

Jack laughed. "Sorry about that."

"If there's nothing else," Mr. Stanton said, "I really must conclude our little meeting. A busy day awaits."

"Likewise," Jack said. "And thank you for the help today, and with this entire mission."

Mr. Stanton winked. "It's not a problem, my friend. Always good to have a man of your skills in my debt." He then spun on his heel and disappeared into the throngs of tourists and businesspeople hurrying to meet their flights.

The comment hammered home to Jack what Mr. Stanton had orchestrated from the beginning by sending Larry Daly to his front door. Returning to The Organization was now as good as a lock, and for Jack, it wasn't the worst outcome in the world. He was good at his job and was doing important work, work most people had neither the stomach nor the skills to handle.

But still, the knowledge he'd come so close to escaping the only career he'd ever known was bittersweet.

That was an issue for another time, however. Edie was waiting for him in New Hampshire, and already his thoughts had shifted back to the beautiful blonde.

He'd barely been gone an hour and he couldn't wait to get home.

43

Lowell Stevenson could not stop pacing. Back and forth. Back and forth. He felt like a human metronome but he just could not force himself to sit still.

Surprisingly, he'd slept like a baby after driving home from the debacle at the Dragons' headquarters last night; or maybe it wasn't all that surprising. He'd been exhausted. Physically, mentally, psychologically, and any other way exhaustion was possible.

But this morning, instead of feeling better about things, he felt much worse. He felt cornered, like a wild animal being tracked by a relentless hunter. Certain the police were going to come knocking at his door at any moment, he'd begun making preparations for dealing with that eventuality.

Preparations that had taken maybe twenty seconds.

Then Lowell had called in sick to work.

Then he'd begun pacing.

He had of course turned the television on. He was a news junkie and always watched at least thirty minutes of coverage in the morning before leaving for work. But given all that had happened last night, it was especially important today that he stay informed.

And the news reports were eye-popping. Somehow, after he'd escaped the Dragons building with his life, the old mill had caught fire, burning with an intensity that was shocking to observe. Channel Seven devoted nearly all their coverage to the fire in Lawrence, two hours worth, including video footage shot from their news copter showing flames breaking through the roof and leaping thirty-plus feet skyward. Firefighters were forced to battle the blaze from a distance thanks to the extreme heat.

Lowell watched, spellbound, even as he continued to pace. His mind was working overtime, processing the ongoing story coming out of Lawrence and its potential consequences to him.

Because given the intensity of that fire, there might just be a way out of this. Maybe, just maybe, the police *wouldn't* come knocking at his door at any moment.

Lowell had no doubt he'd left his fingerprints and his DNA all over the Dragons building. It was indisputable. He'd touched things, he'd cried, he had shot a man, for Christ's sake. *Police Chief Tim McKenna had killed himself inside that building.* It had been a bloodbath. A nightmare.

But the fire, that beautiful, cleansing fire, was burning with such savage ferocity that there was no possible way any fingerprints or DNA evidence could survive. Hell, it would probably take days or even weeks just to identify the victims lying inside the building, and even after identification had been completed, Lowell doubted whether the cause of any of their deaths could be reliably determined.

He continued to pace, but his unreasoning terror began to abate. It didn't disappear entirely, not yet, but it slowly started to recede, like the waves of the Atlantic at low tide.

He might just survive this.

As the morning wore on, every minute that passed without the police banging on his front door added to his hopefulness. His wife had left him years ago and they'd never had children, so Lowell wasn't forced to try to conceal his anxiety from anyone.

It was a good goddamned thing. Such a feat would have been impossible.

Noontime came and went, and with it, more live reporting on the Channel Seven News from the scene of the massive blaze. Firefighters had been called in from surrounding communities, and it was clear they were making progress. It was also clear the devastation left behind would be virtually complete.

And still no visit from the police.

The afternoon felt interminable, but in a good way. Lowell

had been convinced when he got up this morning that he would no longer be a free man by this time of day, so he wasn't about to complain. He marveled at his unlikely good fortune and even began planning for the future he now felt reasonably certain he was going to have.

It seemed that, against all odds, he was going to get away scot-free.

At a quarter to four, Lowell finally persuaded himself to stop pacing. He was exhausted but happy, like a man who'd been training for the Boston Marathon his entire life and then finally gotten the chance to run the race. He poured himself a generous helping of Jameson's and dropped onto his living room couch to watch Channel Seven's four o'clock news. He had no doubt the Lawrence story would again lead the reporting.

The teaser leading into the newscast was intriguing, to say the least. In typical muckraking media fashion, BOMBSHELL EVIDENCE IN LAWRENCE MILL FIRE was splashed across the screen in large white letters set against a blue banner with the fire blazing away in the background, while off-camera the anchor read the exact same words. He finished with, "Stay tuned for Channel Seven News, coming up next!"

Lowell raised his eyebrows in surprise. Bombshell evidence? What possible evidence could already have been gathered? The damned fire wasn't even out yet, which meant it would be at least tomorrow before investigators could even access the remains of the building. If the mill was deemed structurally unsound, which it probably would be, the time frame might be much longer.

He sipped his drink and shook his head. It was probably all bullshit, anyway. *Bombshell evidence, my ass. Just television's version of clickbait.*

Then the broadcast started.

And Lowell Stevenson's world fell apart.

"According to anonymous sources," the grave-faced anchor read, "Massachusetts Circuit Court Judge Lowell Stevenson has been inextricably linked to violent gang activities, as well as to dozens of felonies taking place at the abandoned mill building currently ablaze in Lawrence. These crimes include torture and murder. Be advised, the video we are about to show you is graphic. We encourage sensitive viewers to leave the room."

A moment later the TV screen was filled with the image of Lowell sitting at his balcony in the Dragons' headquarters building, his pants around his knees. He languidly stroked himself to the accompaniment of Officer Greg Daly's death screams, which mercifully took place off-camera. His hand and his junk was blurred out, but to anyone over the age of ten—and probably to many of those younger than that—there was no absolutely mystery what he was doing.

The identity of the man in the video was also absolutely no mystery. The footage was as clear as if it had been shot on a Hollywood soundstage. This was obviously the video on the thumb drive Hector de la Cruz had threatened Lowell with just before all hell broke loose last night, the video Lowell had assumed was burned beyond recoverability in the fire.

Somehow that video had survived. De la Cruz must have escaped the building and decided to burn Lowell down for his part in the travesty that had burned his criminal enterprise to the ground.

The report continued, the anchor stressing the fact that the video had just come into Channel Seven's possession within the past hour. He continued speaking but it all became background noise, an unimportant blur, a piling-on of words that were utterly irrelevant to Lowell Stevenson.

Because it was all over.

Everything.

Lowell's escape from consequences had been nothing more than wishful thinking. Hector de la Cruz blamed him for the collapse of the Eighth Street Dragons empire, and this was his revenge.

Lowell finished his drink in one gulp.

Then he rose from the couch, fire burning in his gullet and tears streaming from his eyes. He tried to convince himself they were from the whiskey but couldn't quite manage it. His arms and legs were shaking uncontrollably as he climbed the stairs to his bedroom.

He didn't know if he would have the courage to do what needed to be done when the time came, but he didn't have to wait long to find out. Ten minutes after the start of the newscast came a loud banging on his front door, along with angry cop voices demanding he open up. Lowell walked to the window and saw what appeared to be dozens of police cruisers outside, parked up and down the street in a crazy quilt of black and white sedans and SUVs.

All their light bars were flashing.

Lowell had originally intended to dump the gun he'd used to kill the Dragons member in the Merrimack River on his way home last night. But then he'd had second thoughts about that plan. Keeping the weapon at first glance seemed foolish in the extreme, but the more he thought about it, the more Lowell realized it didn't really matter.

If the police came for the gun, the game would be up anyway.

And in that scenario, having a pistol might come in handy.

He opened his mouth wide and placed the barrel inside, just as the cops breached the front door with a loud *crash!* The gunmetal tasted oily and heavy. Deadly. He thought about Tim McKenna and the incredible amount of blood and bone and gore that had exploded from his skull last night.

Lowell's hands were shaking so badly the gun clattered against his teeth and the thought crossed his mind that if he didn't hurry up and finish this, he might just knock them all out.

The police were shouting his name and telling him to show himself, and to come out with his hands in the air. He could hear at least some of them ascending the stairs.

He still didn't know whether he could actually pull the trigger.

Then he discovered he could.

44

Jack sat in front of the TV, munching on pizza and sipping a beer. He rarely turned the damned thing on, and at one point had even considered taking it out of his house and leaving it on the side of the road somewhere. But he never did, because some of his Organization assignments involved dealing with public and semi-public figures, and in those cases the television occasionally came in handy as a vehicle for tracking them.

Tonight was one of those times.

His injured arm throbbed and changing the bandage every day until it healed would be a major pain in the ass, but the arm and hand remained fully functional. Had de la Cruz's shot struck him in the shoulder, or had it struck bone, things might have been totally different. He flexed it and grimaced, never taking his eyes off the television.

Edie had left a couple of hours ago to pick up Janie and bring her home from camp, and while Jack missed her already he decided her absence was probably for the best. He would call her tomorrow and hopefully they could get together again within the next couple of days, but she had much more valuable things to do tonight—like spend time with her little girl—than watch the horrifying and depressing events unfolding in Lawrence.

The minute Jack passed the thumb drive to Mr. Stanton earlier today, he'd known The Organization's head man would make good on his promise to get a copy of the video it contained on the air on every local news channel.

That being the case, he'd known as well that only one of two outcomes were possible: either the newscast would broadcast live footage of the disgraced judge being led to a squad car in handcuffs, or it would show the judge's corpse being wheeled into an ambulance inside a body bag.

There was no other way the story could end.

Jack had a pretty good idea which outcome would prevail. Guys like Lowell Stevenson were bullies, and bullies were cowards. They loved to push people around when they held the upper hand, but turn the tables on them and their spines instantly became jelly.

Jack couldn't imagine Stevenson having the intestinal fortitude to do the perp walk in front of TV cameras, much less withstand a very public, high-profile criminal trial.

He would choose the coward's way out.

Less than one minute into the broadcast of the six o-clock news, Jack learned his guess was right on target. Stevenson was dead of a single self-inflicted gunshot wound suffered inside the bedroom of his million-dollar home as police closed in this afternoon.

It was over. The Eighth Street Dragons were decimated and would likely never regroup. An amoral officer of the court would no longer stain the earth with his presence. And no more innocents would die gruesome deaths, at least not from this particular band of sociopaths.

Jack had called Larry Daly earlier and told him to keep an eye on the news, but it hadn't really been necessary. He knew the man would be watching anyway. His sole purpose in life was to achieve some small measure of justice for his son, and he'd told Jack he spent hours scouring news reports on every channel he could find for information in an effort to advance that goal.

Daly had sounded relieved the nightmare was over, but mostly he sounded exhausted. Hollow. Jack wondered how the man would find the strength to continue moving forward now that the driving force of his life was gone.

He would either find a way or he would not.

Jack ate his pizza and he sipped his beer. He knew he should feel satisfaction but he didn't, not really. A job had needed doing, so he'd done it. No more and no less.

Another gang would fill the vacuum in the Lawrence drug

trade, and weapons trade, and prostitution trade, and it would happen sooner rather than later. Maybe the gang that took over wouldn't kill innocent cops but they would ruin lives just the same.

Jack had long felt that eliminating evil was like playing Whac-A-Mole, only the moles were firing semi-automatic weapons at you when they popped out of their holes. And you might win one round, but there were always more moles popping out of more holes. It was a never-ending battle.

He drained his beer and thumbed the remote to shut off the TV.

Sat in the shadows thinking.

He wondered when he would get to see Edie and Janie again, and hoped it was soon.

Eventually he padded down the hallway to his bedroom and slipped under the covers.

Jack Sheridan will return soon in his fourth pulp thriller. To be the first to learn about new releases, and for the opportunity to win free ebooks, signed copies of print books, and other swag, take a moment to sign up for Allan Leverone's email newsletter at AllanLeverone.com.

Reader reviews are hugely important to authors looking to set their work apart from the competition. If you have a moment to spare, please consider taking a moment to leave a brief, honest review of *Death Perception* at your point of purchase, at Goodreads, or at your favorite review site, and thank you.

About the author

Allan Leverone is the *New York Times* and *USA Today* bestselling author of twenty novels, as well as a 2012 Derringer Award winner for excellence in short mystery fiction and a 2011 Pushcart Prize nominee. He lives in Londonderry, New Hampshire with his wife Sue, and has three grown children and two (soon to be three) beautiful grandchildren. He loves to hear from readers and other authors; connect on Facebook, Twitter @AllanLeverone, and at AllanLeverone.com.

Also from Allan Leverone

Thrillers

Parallax View: A Tracie Tanner Thriller
All Enemies: A Tracie Tanner Thriller
The Omega Connection: A Tracie Tanner Thriller
The Hitler Deception: A Tracie Tanner Thriller
The Kremlyov Infection: A Tracie Tanner Thriller
The Bashkir Extraction: A Tracie Tanner Thriller
The Lonely Mile
Final Vector
The Organization: A Jack Sheridan Pulp Thriller
Trigger Warning: A Jack Sheridan Pulp Thriller

Dark Fiction

Mr. Midnight
After Midnight
The Lupin Project
Paskagankee
Revenant
Wellspring
Grimoire
Covenant
Linger: Mark of the Beast (Co-written with Edward Fallon)

Novellas

The Becoming
Flight 12: A Kristin Cunningham Thriller

Story Collections

Postcards from the Apocalypse
Letters from the Asylum
Uncle Brick and the Four Novelettes
The Tracie Tanner Collection: Three Complete Thriller Novels